Home Again

Julie Parker

This is a work of fiction. Names, characters, places, and incidents are products of the author's imagination or are used fictitiously and are not to be construed as real. Any resemblance to actual events, locations, organizations, or persons, living or dead, is entirely coincidental.

World Castle Publishing, LLC
Pensacola, Florida
Copyright © 2025 Julie Parker
Hardback ISBN: 9798288180705
Paperback ISBN: 9798891264175
eBook ISBN: 9798891264182
First Edition World Castle Publishing, LLC, June 30, 2025
http://www.worldcastlepublishing.com
Licensing Notes
Cover: Cover Designs by Karen
Editor: Karen Fuller

For Cam & Steph.
May your love be the light that always guides you home.

Chapter 1

The letter in my hands shook. Or my hands were doing the shaking, no doubt due to the contents of the letter I'd just read.

"Thea? Are you okay?" Jehrel asked me.

Not yet trusting myself to speak, I passed him the letter instead, which he took after a bit of gentle prying. Many emotions crossed his face as he read. I knew each by heart — surprise, shock, intrigue, then concern. He lifted his gaze to seek mine.

"Um, wow," he said, taking great care to refold the missive and place it on the coffee shop table between us.

"I know, right?"

"So, what are you going to do?" He kept his voice low. Not that the other three customers appeared remotely interested in our drama.

Or that my life had just been turned upside down.

No one more than Jehrel, my best friend for the past four years, would understand the ramifications of what I now faced.

"You only just started up your business."

Not that I needed the reminder of how the timing of this whole thing was rotten. Granted, my business hadn't *just* started up. It'd been running quite smoothly for almost a year now. And the beauty of owning your own retro-reno-design company was that you could literally take the show on the road. But Hadleigh was almost four hours away.

The way Jehrel's gaze searched mine, I knew what was going unsaid.

Rory Macintyre. AKA Heartbreaker. A resident of Hadleigh and the main reason I'd avoided that town as much as possible. Jehrel knew all about him after the '*Had one drink too many and cried for hours*' breakdowns I was prone to when we'd first met.

"Couldn't you get someone else to handle things for you there? You don't need to go yourself considering—"

"That I couldn't be bothered to go to the funeral, you mean? And no, you know there's no one else."

Jehrel reached out to put his hand on mine. "Honey, I just meant there's nothing there for you anymore. And about the funeral, no one blames you for that."

His gentle tone almost made me tear up when I remembered how devastated I'd been.

"You nearly died!"

I smiled at his dramatics. "My appendix almost burst, but it didn't."

He reached for his coffee and lifted it to his lips before saying, "But it could have."

"Okay," I relented with an eye roll.

"What about your dad?" His cheeks puffed out with the giant sip he took, a habit which always made me smirk. He set down his cup, added another packet of sugar, and stirred.

"He's off with his newest girlfriend on a Mediterranean cruise," I reminded him.

He sipped again. "Oh yes! I would love to take a cruise for our honeymoon, but Alan wants to tour Europe—if we can ever get our wedding plans off the ground. And if we can save enough money. So, what do you think you'll do?"

When I'd received the official correspondence in the mail, I suspected it had to do with my aunt's death. I'd called Jehel and had him meet with me here straightaway. I'd known that once the solicitor had tracked me down—no easy feat considering I'd moved three times in the past six months — I'd have to face things finally.

The last time I'd seen Aunt Agnes was at Christmas time. She'd been slowly failing health-wise since my Uncle Jimmy passed away three years ago.

At least I'd made it to his funeral.

And despite Rory being there as well, I'd neatly avoided any interaction with him.

Then, on a blustery day the first week of January, Alicia Gains, my aunt's acquaintance, had called and left a message on my cell, breaking the news about her passing. I'd been all set to make the drive to Hadleigh. I'd packed a bag, gassed up my car, and headed out. The pain in my right side had started about an hour into the drive. Another hour later, I'd been forced to pull over and call 911. An ambulance arrived and rushed me to the nearest hospital. When I'd dug through my purse for my cell to call Jehrel and tell him what had happened, it was then I noticed I didn't have it. I'd either lost it in the mad shuffle to the hospital or left it in my car at the side of the road.

The hospital staff had been kind enough to arrange for my car to be towed to a garage close to the hospital. Not that I'd be able to drive for a while. Unfortunately, when the truck arrived to hitch up my car, they'd discovered it'd been ransacked. The doors were pried open, and everything of value — material and even sentimental — was gone. I'd used the hospital phone to call Jehrel a few hours after my emergency operation. He and Alan had dropped everything and sped over to see me. A mere seven hours after my procedure, I'd been released. My friends had picked up my car, even paid for the tow, and arrived to get me. Jehrel drove me back in my car while Alan drove theirs home. I'd stayed with them for a week only to finally make it back to my apartment and discover a Notice to Vacate stuck to the door.

With more help from the guys, I'd packed up my stuff and

moved to a tiny apartment a few blocks over from my old one. With all that going on, by the time I'd had a moment to lament over missing my aunt's funeral, I wasn't sure what to do. There hadn't been anyone to call and express condolences to. My mom had passed away when I was nine. Aunt Agnes had been her only living family member besides me, and Agnes and Uncle Jimmy didn't have any kids. I could have called Alicia Gains to let her know what had happened to me and why I didn't make the funeral, but I didn't even have her phone number since it'd been on my lost cell. Anyway, it all seemed kind of pointless. If she'd called me out of genuine concern, I would have made the effort to track her down, but I knew that woman as the town gossip and didn't feel the need to supply her with my excuses. And despite entertaining the idea for a moment or two, I didn't attempt to get a hold of Rory either (I knew his number by heart) and explain my absence. No doubt he'd made it to the funeral.

"I can't believe she left you the resort. Like...wow. So generous," Jehrel said, snapping my focus back to the present.

"Yeah, though the wording was kind of strange. All that legal jargon is hard to understand. I think I get the house, but I'll have to meet with Mr. Bailey to go over the details."

I'd always known I would inherit the resort, so it wasn't really a big shock to me. And the resort was beautiful, but totally impractical with my life now. Especially being so far away. It was a huge deal to have to go down there and organize everything just to get it sold. I didn't see any other option. As much as I loved the place, I couldn't handle the upkeep from here. And getting someone to oversee the care of the main house and the rental cabins would be too expensive at this time. Moving there was not an option.

"Meet with him in Hadleigh," Jehrel clarified. "You can't get the lowdown over the phone, I guess?"

I avoided that knowing look, I knew he was wearing. "No,

stuff to sign and all that."

"I would go with you if I could, you know that, right?"

The tears threatened again, so I just nodded and took a sip of my strong black coffee.

"What time is the showing?" Jehrel asked, neatly changing the subject.

I set my mug down and checked my watch. "At three. I guess I better head over there and make sure everything's ready." It would give me almost two hours, which should be plenty of time to prepare.

It was reveal day, and we were doing a taping. Not that I had a TV show yet. But soon, hopefully. This would be the first whole house reno I had completed. I'd done single rooms before, but it was hard to find someone willing to plunge right in. I'd made some short videos with my cell phone of me doing the renos and even shopping for some items as well. Professionally taping the reveal had only occurred to me once I had finished the work. I planned on posting the video on social media sites, and wherever else I was able to. I hoped to link some of the pre-reveal stuff in the comments, which I felt would give it that personal touch. I could always get the crew to film some of the pre-reveal stuff on jobs in the future. The many jobs I hoped to gain if this went well.

When I got to the house, my key got stuck in the older-fashioned door as I tried to let myself in. *Of course.* Just when I thought I'd have to get in the back way, it finally worked. Inside, I played around with the lock, spraying a bit of WD40 — which I kept in my oversized purse for just such emergencies — and poked the key in and out about a zillion times until I was satisfied. It wouldn't do at all to have the owners arrive and be forced to boot their own door in. Especially since this would be on camera.

Touring the house, making tiny adjustments as I went, I deemed it worthy when I went to stand out front to await the film crew. The guys I'd hired pulled up in a blue van with the logo *Caught on Camera* splashed across the side of it. They were cheap but came highly recommended. At least they were on time.

Jake, the guy I'd met to give the deposit, address, and particulars to, jumped out of the driver's side of the van and gave me a wave.

I smiled as he walked over to me. "Ready for today?" I asked.

"Yeah, sure. Though Joe is sick, food poisoning, he thinks, so I brought my brother with me."

Joe had been the tall, blond, silent one who'd smiled at me while I completed my business with Jake. I don't think he'd spoken the entire time I'd been in their little shop.

"Oh no, that's too bad. I hope he's okay," I said politely, eyeing the little brother who was now struggling to get equipment from the back of the van. Something clattered to the ground, making Jake cringe.

"Jeesh, Cory, come on, man! Take it easy," Jake said, hurrying over to give him a hand.

"Relax, it's all good," Cory insisted.

While the guys set up under my direction, I kept an eye on the steadily darkening sky. It wouldn't dare rain in the next ten minutes when the Comptons were due to arrive.

As Ted and Jillian Compton pulled up into their driveway, cameras rolling, big hopeful smiles all around, the first dollops of rain began to fall. Thankfully, the big reveal would be filmed mainly inside of the house. The exterior had been left the same, only a slight refreshing of the garden — bleeding hearts, a must-have — and a bit of paint on the metal shutters. A trellis with roses had also been installed between two of the bedroom windows. The house, being brick, had remained pretty much the same over the years. At least according to the pictures Jillian had provided me with.

Jake, afraid of his equipment getting wet, took a few pictures and got Cory to help him gather up their stuff and go around the house to the back door. The rain began picking up in earnest, so I made a grand gesture toward the front door, urging the Comptons in that direction. Ted held out his hand for the key, which I passed over before he presented it to Jillian, who looked about ready to burst. The key worked — *thank God* — and the pair stepped inside with me following.

The entryway was a small landing area, as the house was a raised bungalow. Before us were two sets of stairs going in both directions. Jake and Cory had taken up positions at each level to catch every angle. The space was open, allowing a good view of the upstairs living room on the right and the kitchen straight ahead. Jillian moved slowly up the stairs, taking in the changes I'd made. The look on her face said it all — *nailed it!* Then, she promptly burst into tears.

"Oh no, oh Jill, honey, please don't cry," Ted begged, digging around in his pocket for a Kleenex. I handed him a box of tissues I'd strategically placed near the front door. I couldn't deny those tears brought me great satisfaction. Looking around at the hard work I'd done, I could see through Jillian's eyes the years melting away. The house was a perfect rendition of her childhood home — complete with seventies and eighties décor. It'd been almost impossible to replicate the wallpaper, curtains, and the furniture, not to mention the corded dial telephone and stereo cabinet. But I had. The basement bedroom and rec room had been made over with wood paneling, paint by number pictures, and thick wall to wall carpeting. For the kitchen, I'd even found a classic chrome dinette set the exact same color as Jillian's photograph. The appliances were vintage, but they worked. The three main floor bedrooms and den — which had been Jillian's brother's room — had all been remodeled as well.

This being her childhood home, her indulgent husband had

been completely on board with the idea of not only buying it when she happened to notice the For Sale sign during a drive-by one day but also to restoring it the way Jillian remembered. Watching her face, I could almost imagine the memories bombarding her right now. Apparently, she and her family of six — mom and dad and four kids — had lived here until Jillian's younger brother, the baby of the family, had turned eighteen. There was a lifetime of birthdays, Christmases, Easter egg hunts, hide-and-seek games, laughter, and tears in this home. Now, she could reimagine them at her leisure and reminisce with her family when they visited.

As we ventured down the hall, she exclaimed over the old wooden doors with glass doorknobs — so difficult to find. Outside her bedroom, I heard her suck in her breath. I checked to make sure the guys were getting this shot, especially.

"Oh, Ted," she had to swallow over the obvious lump in her throat.

Ted, who'd taken in the décor like a champ, now couldn't suppress a chuckle. "Shag carpet!"

"White… just as I had… growing up," she said between gulps of air.

I'd even hung up a poster of Rick Springfield — a real pain in the butt to find — and Duran Duran. Jillian entered the room, crossing the shag carpet to touch them, laughing through her tears when she noticed the poster with the row of kittens I'd found.

"It's the same," Jillian said, turning around in a slow circle. "Although everything seems so much smaller than I remember. I guess because I'm grown."

"I'm feeling a little nervous," Ted admitted, taking an exaggerated look around the room. "Your dad could come barging in any minute and demand to know what I'm doing in his daughter's bedroom."

We all laughed over that.

The couple moved through the house, exclaiming in awe and delight over their discoveries. The smallest details I'd added were observed. At the end of the tour, Jillian took my hands and stared into my eyes.

"Thank you," she said with such emotion that I felt myself tearing up as well. "I cannot tell you what this… means… to me." Over her shoulder, Ted was beaming and even gave me a thumbs up.

I nodded and smiled at Jillian, trying to keep my composure. Moments like this were the reason I'd started my company.

Outside, the rain had mercifully stopped, and the sun began to peek out from behind the clouds. Jake took a final wrap-up line from me I'd been practicing before the mirror last night.

"I hope you enjoyed the big reveal," I said, smiling brightly for the camera. "And remember… I'm Thea James and… You Can Go Home Again." It was the name of my company. With any luck, and probably a million dollars that I didn't have, it would one day be mainstream.

I packed my odds and ends into my car, leaving the happy couple to enjoy their showpiece. The great satisfaction of this job made me almost forget about the lawyer's letter I'd received. Almost being the keyword. I'd soon be bombarded by my own memories once I went to Hadleigh and claimed my inheritance. The reality of my aunt and uncle being gone forever suddenly washed over me, threatening to drown me in sadness.

"That was awesome," Jake said, startling me out of my doldrums.

"Yes. It really was. Can't wait to see the finished project."

He nodded. "Give me a few days to put it together, and I'll get it to you."

"I'm heading out of town this weekend. Do you think I can have a copy by then?" It was only Tuesday, so it should give him more than enough time.

"Yeah, for sure. I can't wait to see what you do next. Keep us in mind for future projects." He began walking away, then turned and waved. "See you around." Having finished packing up all his equipment, he climbed into his van, and as he drove away, Cory waved at me.

The wind blew, giving me a slight chill despite it being late June. I hurried to get into my car, suddenly feeling very alone. Even with the great success of today's reveal, I couldn't help but feel a ripple of foreboding. There would be a reckoning once I got into Hadleigh. And I knew the man I'd been avoiding all these years would be the one to deliver it.

Chapter 2

Rory wound up and tossed the softball underhand to the young boy standing ready. Gavin, legs apart, knees slightly bent, glove in position, reached and snatched the ball out of the air.

"That's the way!" Rory cheered, feeling no small amount of pride.

Gavin ducked his head to hide his smile, but Rory had seen it. That smile was the first since picking up the youngster from school. Checking his watch, Rory noted it was after four. Their visit had gone by all too quickly. Waverly wanted their charges returned before dinner. Gavin noticed him checking the time, and Rory heard him sigh. Despite wanting to offer reassurance it wouldn't be for much longer, he refrained. Instead, he reached out to ruffle the boy's brown curls with affection.

Waverly, Hadleigh's home for children, was a huge old house about a ten-minute walk from the riverside park. In the past, it operated as an orphanage Rory had attended in his youth, but it was no longer referred to as that. Now, it mainly housed children in need of mental health services while they learned coping skills. The home also offered care to children whose parents struggled with mental health issues, addiction, physical limitations, and other various conditions. It also served as a temporary home for children who had no one to take care of them. Most of the children in that situation went into foster care, but Gavin, finding himself without a guardian, had been placed in the home since all the nearby foster homes were full.

Rory went over to the bench and picked up Gavin's backpack. Gavin joined him, and put his glove inside, and grabbed his water bottle.

"Ready, sport?" Rory asked.

Gavin nodded, passed over the bottle, and waited while Rory secured it in the netted side pocket of the bag. Together, they walked across the park toward the sidewalk.

"How're classes going?" Rory asked. He knew from the pointed look Gavin's teacher gave him today that he continued to struggle. It wasn't the lessons that troubled Gavin in the grade one class. It was fitting in with his peers. Since he'd had to leave his aging Grandmother's home several months ago and been placed at Waverly, Gavin had struggled. When she had died suddenly, things had gotten worse. Rory knew all too well the emotional struggles kids could face. Building new relationships during an upheaval in life was hard.

Gavin shrugged in answer to Rory's question.

"Hey, I think there's time to grab a cookie at Genie's if you like?"

"Okay," Gavin said, earning Rory his second smile that afternoon.

Within a few minutes, they entered the bookstore café and went to place their order.

"Can I do the ladder?" Gavin asked the woman wearing an apron behind the counter.

"You bet," Genie said, giving him a wink.

Rory watched him charge across the floor and smiled. "You indulge him way too much," he chastised.

"Says the guy buying him cookies," Genie retorted.

Rory shook his head. "Touché. Just give us a couple of the double chocolate chip, please." While he waited for his order, he watched Gavin race up the spiral staircase only to rush down the short walkway on the balcony, turn around, race back, and barrel back down the stairs.

"Slow down, sport. They won't look kindly on me bringing you back with bumps and bruises."

Gavin hurried over to the counter as Genie passed the bag into Rory's hands. "I won't fall," he insisted.

"Boys," Genie said, rolling her eyes.

"Yeah, yeah," Rory replied. He put a couple of bills on the counter and gave Genie a nod in thanks. Opening the door, Gavin rushed past him, throwing a "Thank you" over his shoulder at Genie. As the door swung shut, Rory heard her call out, "You're welcome."

They strolled down the sidewalk. Rory passed Gavin a cookie to munch on and stuffed the other one for later into the boy's backpack he had swung over his shoulder.

"Hey, it's Friday. Isn't pizza on the menu tonight?" Rory asked.

Gavin shrugged.

"I thought you loved pizza?"

He looked up at Rory. "Yeah, when you and me eat it. Can't we go out for dinner?"

Rory frowned. "Sorry, buddy. I have to get you back."

"I know," Gavin said with a sigh.

Once more, Rory refrained from offering false hope to the boy. He slowed his pace when Gavin slowed his, knowing neither of them were in a hurry to part company.

Not much longer, Rory vowed silently.

~

"Sure you're not missing something?" Jehrel asked, sitting on the edge of my bed while I finished packing. It wasn't my luggage he inquired about.

"No." I'd called Mr. Bailey a few times through the week. The first time, after I was still on a high from the reveal taping. The second time was this morning. I'd told him during the first conversation that I did receive his letter, and I planned to head to Hadleigh unless it was at all possible to put things off. He told me it was up to me, but the details of the inheritance weren't cut and dry, and it would be in my best interest to meet with him in person. What those details were, however, he would not elaborate on. At least not over the phone. Not even via video chat. When I called him again, hoping for a change of heart, he explained I needed to see the resort in person. Why I had to drive over four hours to see a place I knew better than the back of my hand, I had no idea. Something to do with right-of-ways and access roads, and meeting with a land surveyor and discussing boundary lines, he said. Whatever all that meant.

When I mentioned this to Jehrel upon his arrival, he'd immediately begun speculating on the possibilities. Now, he was growing thoughtful again.

"What if she left one of the cabins to someone? That would explain the need for all those things your lawyer mentioned."

"He's not my lawyer. Well, not technically."

He rolled his eyes, and then they bulged. "Oh! What if she left a cabin to…"

Halfway through zipping my suitcase, I paused to drill him with the death stare to stall that sentence. "Don't even think it. Alicia Gains was just an acquaintance of Aunt Agnes's. Not even close to being someone she'd leave property to."

"That wasn't who…"

Again, I stared hard at him. "Don't," I warned, not daring to allow my thoughts to even venture in that direction.

"It makes perfect sense. About her leaving a cabin to someone. Or maybe a neighbor is disputing the boundary?"

Jehrel knew the resort, having been up there with me a bunch of times. It was where he proposed to Alan. Whenever I went there, which wasn't usually more than three or four times a year, I tried to bring him, or both of them, with me. Even as I tried to avoid the place because of Rory, I still wanted to visit with Aunt Agnes. And Jehrel was the stealthiest person I knew. One time, we'd even pulled off the road nearly a mile past the resort when we spotted a truck that looked like Rory's parked on the roadway nearby. We'd detoured around and doubled back through the forest on foot. It wouldn't have been so bad, except it'd been May, and the blackflies were horrible. We'd spied on the place until the truck pulled away. After all that, it hadn't even been Rory. That had been a miserably itchy visit with my aunt.

The resort was situated on Talan Lake, about fifteen miles from the town of Hadleigh. Being surrounded by acres and acres of forest, it was quite exclusive. It was also quite popular. Only a small number of cottages were on it, and crown land occupied much of the waterfront, so properties were at a premium. I didn't think I'd have any trouble listing it and making a quick sale. The thought of letting go of the resort distressed me, yet I knew I had no place or time for it in my life. Running a resort was a huge deal. Of course, running your own retro-reno-design business was as well. But I knew running both of them was out of the question.

"I haven't been there in a while," I said. "Maybe something's changed? Like some property being sold off by the Crown? It's been known to happen. Especially if the price is right."

Jehrel appeared to give this some thought. "If the Crown did sell off a few acres, and someone bought it, that could explain all the stuff your lawyer talked about."

"He's not my... Oh, forget it. It may be something like that. But I guess I'm not going to know until I get there."

Jehrel got up, opened my drawer, and stuffed another few pairs of socks and panties into my case. When I raised an eyebrow, he shrugged. "It's a minimum four-hour drive. You may decide to spend a few extra days before coming home. It is the season, and you're long overdue for a vacation."

"I think I can wrap everything up by Monday, Tuesday

at the latest." I was taking the weekend to drive up and settle in before meeting with Mr. Bailey on Monday. After all, I needed to look around and do an inventory of everything so that when I posted the listing, it would be as detailed as possible. The resort consisted of the main house and five furnished cabins. I figured I would have to sell the property with contents included. My apartment was only one bedroom, and I couldn't possibly store stuff. I did plan to bring home any sentimental items I couldn't bear to part with. And if it came down to it, I could possibly get a storage rental unit here in town to keep stuff until I had more space. I wasn't planning to live in my tiny apartment forever, but I'd added that to my Some Day list.

After a weepy goodbye with Jehrel — his tears, not mine — I was on the road. Remembering the last time I attempted this trip, I double-checked my cell phone's location in my purse, which sat within reach on the front passenger seat.

Following obscene traffic, one planned and one unplanned pitstop, I arrived in Hadleigh just an hour and a half over schedule. The clock on my dash said it was almost eight-thirty pm, and my stomach growled its displeasure since I'd not bothered to eat anything on those pitstops.

Hunger was a good sign, I decided, as I pulled up in front of the main house of the resort. The knot in my gut for most of the ride had made putting anything into my belly other than the two Cokes I'd downed seem like a bad idea. But now, as I turned off the engine and my car gave a sigh of relief, I felt a weight lift off my shoulders I hadn't known was there.

Staring at the house that had been a second home to me caused emotions to gallop forth. Despite the expected feeling of loss over my aunt's passing, there was something else I hadn't anticipated. Contentment. Like the feeling I'd get when I was little and made the long trek here with my dad. Usually, I would fall asleep, and he'd have to carry me inside. Of course, I always woke a bit, being jostled around and no longer swayed by the movement of the car. But then I'd peek open my eyes and see the familiar surroundings, smell the familiar scents, and then feel the familiar bed beneath me as Dad would lie me down and pull the familiar quilt up over me. He'd kiss me on the head, and I knew he wouldn't stay until the morning. He'd be gone, but I'd have my aunt and uncle to fuss over me. Love me. Make me feel welcome. Like I was the most important person in the world for a whole summer.

This time, my aunt would not be here to greet me. Yet, despite her being truly gone, I'd somehow never felt so close to her. My uncle, as well. As though they were embracing me fully, even more than the warm, tight hugs they'd given me over the years. Like their spirits immersed with mine, welcoming me here in this place we loved so much.

After grabbing my purse, I used my key to get in. When I went back for my suitcase, I felt the first spattering of rain. The sky was darkening faster than it should, and overhead, I saw black clouds moving in. From the past, I knew how quickly a storm could whip up. Inside, I set down my case and went directly to the kitchen to check for flashlights and candles, also aware the power tended to cut out in such storms.

Armed with a flashlight, I went into the utility room on the main floor and pushed up the power bar on the electrical panel. Thankfully, I could hear the hum of the pump of the septic as it turned on, and when I tried the light in the room, it gave off a bright glow. The air had a musty scent to it, which seemed out of place since I'd never associated it here. I felt a sudden pang in my belly, which could have sprung from hunger or loss. Ignoring it, I went to work opening some of the windows on the first level consisting of a full bathroom, kitchen, utility room, and dining room that had been converted into my aunt and uncle's bedroom after the stairs became too much for them, a living room, and—

my favorite room — the library with a huge stone fireplace. There were four bedrooms upstairs and another full bathroom, and an attic above all that. I'd worry about opening those windows later if the storm passed quickly. I knew my old bedroom had a fan in the closet, so I wasn't too worried about musty air.

The realization of the house being stale reminded me there would most likely be nothing to eat here. I hadn't even thought about hitting town first to grab a few groceries, considering Aunt Agnes always had a well-stocked pantry. No doubt someone had come by and done the deed of cleaning out the perishables as a courtesy after she passed away.

A loud clap of thunder sounded just as my belly growled. Seconds later, the lights went out. The onslaught of heavy rain on the roof couldn't drown out my loud sigh. Retrieving the flashlight I'd set down, I went back around and closed all the windows I'd just opened, hoping this sour beginning wasn't a forewarning of my time here.

Chapter 3

Through the heavy downpour, I made out lights at the furthest rental cabin—the one closest to the lake. Since the power was still out, this puzzled me, but not as much as the fact that the place was obviously not vacant as it should have been. In the hall closet, I found my old raincoat and rubber boots. The light of my flashlight guiding the way, I ventured down the driveway toward the cabin, the massive pines standing sentinel on either side of me. I lurked around, scrutinizing the lit windows, trying in vain to spot someone. There was a truck in the driveway I didn't recognize, so someone must be inside. Despite my annoyance at them making themselves at home at Aunt Agnes's—now my—property, I found I was more cautious than put out.

Part of me was tempted to forgo the meeting I knew had to happen. I wasn't the confrontational type. More the simmer-in-silence type. But I was sure if I knocked on the door and perhaps inquired about the light in the darkness, it may, in a roundabout way, allow me to discover what this person was doing here.

So I ventured forward, hoping they weren't an axe murderer.

I had to knock twice since my first try was drowned out by a huge clap of thunder, causing me to duck my head. As soon as the door creaked open, I wanted to run away. Hide. Or both. It was Rory, whose handsome face greeted me.

"Thea?" My hood half obscured my face, so the question was fair.

I shoved the hood back with more force than necessary, perturbed with finding myself at a disadvantage. Silently, I cursed my curiosity, which had led to this unwanted and unplanned encounter — one I'd tried so hard for so long to avoid. The smirk on Rory's face when he took in my disturbed expression didn't help matters any.

"Whoa, it is you! What are you doing out in the rain?"

He let me stand there like a dolt while I decided on how to answer that question. Recalling my idea to ask about the lights helped me to find my voice. "Lights are out at the main house. Why aren't yours?"

He looked over his shoulder, then back at me, and shrugged. "Probably the battery backup power I installed kicked in. I thought the lights flickered earlier."

I pondered that statement momentarily. "You installed?"

He nodded. "Yeah. Seemed like a smart idea. The other cabin has it as well." He nodded in the direction of the smaller cabin I'd just passed to get to this one.

"You installed backup battery power in the cabins?" I reiterated.

He smiled that irritating, smug smile of his. "Yes. The batteries are charged with solar panels. It's pretty cool. Just in my two, though."

"In your two?" I felt like there was a punchline in there somewhere, and I had missed it.

He stared at me, and I noticed one of his eyes narrowed the way it did when he grew irritated or uncomfortable. "Yes, the two cabins your aunt left me in her will." He let the statement sink in a moment, along with the rain dampening my skin through my old worn-out jacket. "Maybe if you'd been here for the funeral and the reading of her will, you would have known."

I half expected him to slam the door shut to add emphasis to his remark, but he didn't.

So, confused and reeling, I turned around and stomped through the mud back the way I'd come.

Upon entering the house, I pulled off my jacket and boots and used my flashlight to guide my way to the living room and the hutch stocked with booze. Hunger forgotten, I reached for a bottle of red wine. Luckily, it had a twist top, so I didn't need to waste time searching for a corkscrew. Wine sloshed clumsily into the first glass I grabbed. I took a healthy swallow and another, willing my racing heart to calm.

Deep breaths, I counseled myself. Deep breaths.

The knock on the door a few minutes later didn't surprise me. Rory never could stand it when I turned my back on him and stormed off. He far preferred to talk things to death. The wine, combined with the rain and my tension, was already conspiring to give me a headache.

Taking another big swallow, I strode to the door and flung it open. Tempting as it was to stand there and let him get drenched as he had done to me, I couldn't bear the sight of him, so I turned and walked away. His stomping feet and the sound of the door closing told me he'd come inside. He had a flashlight, and the beam of light danced around the walls and floors behind me.

He found me in the living room, my fist wrapped around the neck of the open bottle of wine. Our eyes met, and I could see contrition on his face. I was too annoyed to care.

"I shouldn't have said that," he began.

"You think?"

He fiddled with his jacket, still undone in his haste to follow me. At least he'd removed his boots. "You look well," he said, changing tactics.

"Yeah? Well, you look the same. Judgemental and mean." He totally had that coming.

He winced. "T, I'm sorry. I'm sure you had your reasons

for not being here."

Yes, I did, but I wasn't in a sharing mood. I topped up my wine and presented him with my back.

Out the window, a flash of lightning let me glimpse Talon Lake through the trees. The lake was a decent size, not too big or too small. About a dozen cottages dotted the shoreline at the opposite end, whereas on this side, just three properties were tucked in around crown land. This was the only resort on the lake. It sat on three acres of land, a thousand feet of that being lakefront. The resort had five rental cabins. To the right of this house were two of them. To the left, another three. All of them were set near the water's edge, spaced out generously to allow privacy for guests.

Every summer, as far back as I could remember, my aunt and uncle lent out the two cabins on the right free of charge to a camp run by Hadleigh for underprivileged youth. Some of the kids had lived in foster homes or at the orphanage in town. Others had been sent to escape their troubled family lives for a while.

The furthest of the pair of cabins had three bedrooms, and the other one had two. Both had held several sets of bunkbeds in the bedrooms up until about seven years ago when the town council had set up a campground on another lake with a lodge big enough to hold up to fifty kids. So my aunt and uncle had donated all but two of the bunkbeds to the new camp and kept just one in each cabin. All the camp kids went there from then on, so I didn't have to worry about the future owner of this place not honoring the tradition.

I remembered those kids from summer's past. Some of them were shy, some sad, some angry, and most of them just happy to be out in the fresh air, swimming in the lake, hiking in the woods, and sitting around a campfire roasting marshmallows, hotdogs, and smores.

Rory had been one of those kids.

We'd met during his first summer of camp here. I'd been nine years old, he eleven. Recently uprooted from Scotland. I remembered how he fascinated me. How I'd followed him around when he argued with the other boys and stormed off into the forest on his own. I'd thought I was sneaky until, one time, he'd hidden and jumped out, scaring me silly. Then he'd laughed. Hard. And I'd found myself laughing with him. I'd loved that laughter. It wasn't often over the years I'd get to hear it. I'd try and come up with clever ways to amuse him, even just to see him smile.

He'd told me about Scotland. How his mom had moved there from Hadleigh when she'd been nineteen and fallen in love with his dad. They'd married, and he'd been born a year later. Then, his dad died in a work accident, and his heartbroken mom moved them back to Hadleigh. He'd confided how she started drinking too much, and even though he knew she loved him, no matter what he did, she always seemed sad. I'd shared with him my own troubles about my mom dying. How I'd felt the same way about my dad — like I was in his way. Just a painful reminder of the woman he'd loved more than anything and then lost. That no matter how I tried, I couldn't fill the void in my dad's life.

Rory and I shared a connection. Losing a parent and wishing the other one would notice us.

Every summer, he'd return. And every year, we'd grown closer.

Until things between us became complicated and exhausting.

Until he'd broken my heart.

While lightning flashed and thunder rocked the land around us, another storm was brewing inside.

"I knew you were close to my aunt, but I had no idea how much," I said, turning to face Rory. That was a lie, considering the visits and meals he'd shared here over the years, during summers and holidays. I knew from Aunt Agnes's letters even when I wasn't here, Rory had been. Filling a gap in their lives, I felt guilty for putting there.

His eyes narrowed. "I didn't manipulate her if that's what you're implying."

I raised an eyebrow and took another swallow of wine. His gaze lingered on my glass. He had never had a drink the entire time I'd known him. I guess because he'd seen what it did to his mom. How she'd died due to cirrhosis of the liver. Having my aunt and uncle in his life had probably been the closest he'd had to family. But it didn't give him the right to be critical of me. I felt bad enough for not being here much over the years. I'd had a career to get off the ground.

A broken heart to mend.

"I'm not implying anything. I'm just wondering how it came about that you now own two cabins at the resort, and I'm left with a huge mess."

"What mess?"

"The lawyer said I needed to be here in person to deal with surveyors and access roads and right-aways, and now I know why."

He smiled ruefully. "So you're angry everything isn't neat and tidy, handed over to you with a big bow attached."

"No, I'm angry that you've dragged me into something I didn't want."

That left him speechless for a moment.

"So why not just sell it off and be done with it?" he finally snapped.

I gestured with my glass and sloshed wine onto the floor. "That's what I wanted to do, but now I'm stuck here dealing with all this." *Dealing with you.*

"Well, I'm sorry your aunt passing away has been so

inconvenient for you," he said and then immediately looked guilty. Before I could say anything, he spoke up. "Sorry. Again. You have a way of setting me off —"

"I set you off?" I interrupted. "Oh, please…"

"No. It's true. I don't know why I'm angry, but I can't help it. We could have dealt with all this months ago, but you weren't here."

"I almost died, okay?" I revealed, recalling Jehrel's words.

"What? You almost died? How? Why?"

I set my glass down and didn't bother to refill it. I was always a lightweight when it came to alcohol, and I was already feeling the effects of what I'd drank. "I'd been on my way here for the funeral, but my appendix almost burst. I had to pull my car over and call an ambulance."

"Oh, T," he said, sitting down in an overstuffed chair by the fireplace.

"My car got ransacked on the side of the road while I was in the hospital, and my phone was lost — I never did get it back. It took me a long time to recover from the operation. I was staying with friends, and when I returned to my apartment, there was a notice to vacate, so then I had to move. I've moved quite a bit lately. That's why I didn't get the lawyer's letter for so long."

He stared at me, and I could see he was processing everything I'd said. "You must have known she'd leave you the place."

I sighed and went over to take the seat opposite him. "I assumed, but I dunno. Seeing it in writing made it feel more real. I guess I didn't want to face it," I admitted. To my embarrassment, I felt tears filling my eyes and my lip tremble. I forced myself to get a grip. Breaking down in front of him was not going to happen. Never again.

He reached out and took hold of my hand, giving it a squeeze. I let him comfort me for a moment, then pulled my hand away. A huge clap of thunder spurred me to my feet.

"I plan to take inventory of everything in this house and the cabins — well, the three I own — and list the items I don't want with the resort."

"We'll need to deal with the severance before you sell," he reminded me.

Just hearing him say it annoyed me. More problems to solve and more things to take care of. It'd take days, maybe weeks. Jake had dropped off a flash drive with the video of the reveal we'd filmed. Just thinking about how well it had turned out brought a glimpse of light in my present darkness. I was on the verge of making my company something. Everything else was just bumps in the road.

"I'm meeting with Mr. Bailey on Monday. We'll discuss what needs to be done then."

"Okay," Rory said, his tone dull.

"What's the matter?" I asked. "You probably want to get this over and done with as fast as I do."

He stood up and stared at me. "You seem pretty set on getting out of here as fast as you can. I dunno, I thought, maybe…"

I watched as he fiddled with his jacket again. "What?"

"Maybe we could spend some time together? We've both suffered a loss. I know mine is not the same as yours, but…"

His glance slid away from me, maybe from embarrassment. "You loved her too. I know. And she loved you." *Obviously*, I didn't say that out loud. I could see the pain on his face, even in the dark room. He would have felt the same way, regardless of whether Aunt Agnes had left him the cabins or not. I knew him well enough to know that. And honestly, I didn't begrudge him her generous gift. The thing I didn't like was being forced to spend more time here *with him*.

"I saw your suitcase by the front door," he said, breaking into my thoughts. "Do you want me to take it up to your room?"

Of course, he knew which of the rooms was mine. We'd covered the walls with those old velvet posters you color in yourself with markers, along with other pictures we'd made during rainy days. Most of them still hung there. At least, they'd been there on my last visit. I hadn't got a chance to look around much since the lights had gone out so fast.

"Okay," I said, telling myself it was because I didn't want to wander around in the dark alone and the bag was heavy. He gave me a nod and left the room. I could see where he was by the glow of his flashlight. When thunder boomed and shook the house, I swiftly followed him. Storms didn't really bother me. Or being in the dark. But the combination of both, plus the pall of loneliness cast over the place, made me seek out Rory's company.

He shrugged off his jacket and grabbed my suitcase. I trailed him upstairs and down the hallway to the last room. When he went in and put down the bag, he shone his light around the walls and chuckled when he saw the old pictures we'd made. Despite my embarrassment, I was glad they were still there.

"We spent hours on these," Rory said, moving closer to the one he'd colored of a tiger in the jungle—one of my favorites.

Though he'd been part of the main group of kids who'd come here each summer, he spent most of his time with me and my aunt and uncle. The camp leaders had allowed it, considering he didn't seem to enjoy the group activities they planned, and as long as they knew where he was and we'd not objected, they didn't see the harm in it. I'd been the same way, preferring the company of one or two close friends as opposed to a group.

The rain intensified suddenly, and the windows lit up with lightning flashes. The thunder was so loud I could feel it in my body. In the distance, I heard a loud crack and then what sounded like a huge tree hitting the ground. I had to raise my voice to be heard over the noise.

"Maybe you should stay," I offered. Not that it was a

long walk back to his cabin, but the storm did sound frantic and possibly dangerous.

Rory nodded. "Okay. Thanks," he agreed.

It wasn't like I didn't have the room, I told myself. Although I knew his consent was most likely for my benefit, not his.

Chapter 4

Rory settled into the room directly across the hall. He'd spent a lot of time in that room over the years. It was the same size as mine and just as cozy. Each of the four bedrooms upstairs had a fireplace. It had been built when there was no electricity. There'd been an outhouse, too, which had long since been filled in. Over the years, it'd been modernized — to a point — with electricity and plumbing.

As soon as we entered the room, Rory went to work, getting the fireplace blazing. The warmth quickly took the slight chill from the air. And although I objected, saying I could do it, he got one going in my room next.

"Least I can do since you're sheltering me from the storm, ma'am," he said, and we both laughed 'cause he'd said it in a cowboy accent you'd hear in a spaghetti western.

While he fiddled with the fire, I grabbed sheets and blankets from the hall closet and got our beds made up. It was a relief that, as far as I could see, things had been left as they were, not all packed up into boxes by someone who meant well. My aunt and uncle had been members of the church in town, and I had no doubt their friends and fellow parishioners had been anxious to lend a hand. Especially considering what a disappointment I'd turned out to be. They'd yet to learn how circumstances had plotted against me and my good intentions. This being a small town, however, I felt certain my presence here would soon spread like wildfire.

"All set," Rory said, as I daydreamed over the extra blanket I held at the foot of my bed.

"Thanks. I'm just wondering if I'll need this, but I doubt it.

He got to his feet from where he'd been tending the fire and brushed the soot from his hands onto his jeans. "Probably not. It'll heat up nicely in here quick enough."

He was right, of course, and it being so close to July, the weather generally would be quite mild. "I put an extra blanket at the end of your bed, just in case. You can toss it off if you don't want it."

"Well, you never know since I don't happen to have my jammies on me, and I may be forced to sleep in my skivvies," he said, and gave me a wink.

I hoped the room was dark enough to hide my blush.

He wandered over to linger by the door. "Well, goodnight. Sleep well."

"You too," I said, as he retreated into the hall and pulled my door shut after him.

I stared at the door for a minute, awed by this unexpected turn of events. Sheltering Rory had been the last thing I'd ever imagined I'd be doing tonight. I gave my head a shake, then grabbed my suitcase and put it on the bed. As I went about putting my clothes into the dresser, wondering how on earth the man I'd spent so much time avoiding was suddenly ensconced close by, my stomach growled, reminding me I'd yet to eat.

Finishing up my unpacking—I never could stand living out of a suitcase, even for a short while—I grabbed my flashlight and left my room. The creaky floor in the hall was mostly undetectable over the heavy rain as I crept toward the staircase. Downstairs, I headed to the kitchen, hoping there'd be something edible in the cupboards. There was no way I'd risk a ride to town in this storm. Tomorrow, I decided, would be soon enough to grab a few supplies. Not that I needed much, I reminded myself.

I wouldn't be here long. A vision of Rory's sad face when I'd made that announcement entered my head, and I quickly pushed it, along with the guilt it created, aside. How he had the ability to get under my skin after all this time amazed and annoyed me.

When I got into the kitchen, I saw the glow of a flashlight on the floor beside a pair of legs and a behind. Someone was bent over, looking in the cupboard. After a second of panic, I realized it must be Rory, no doubt having the same idea as me. I cleared my throat and winced when he bumped his head on the counter.

"Um, sorry," I said as he turned and got to his feet, his hand massaging his short brown curls.

"No. I deserved that," he said. "Serves me right for sneaking around."

"Are you hungry too? Find anything good?"

"Yes, and not really."

At least he was still dressed and not wandering around in his skivvies. Although, come to think of it, I was still wearing damp clothes. I should have taken the time to change, but the house wasn't overly chilly, and it'd slipped my mind when Rory arrived.

He had a tin of something in his hand. We both eyed it when he picked up his flashlight and shone it at the label. "There are lots of tins of stuff, but you can't heat it up here unless you want to use the fireplace. I could rig something over it. Or we could make a break for my place."

That last statement hung in the air between us.

He had power at his place because he owned it now, along with another cabin, and had made the upgrades. I felt irritated again, and I tried to blame it on being hungry, tired, and head-achy.

"No thanks." I couldn't keep the coolness from my tone.

To avoid looking at him, I went over and opened the fridge, which was dark inside, and now I was letting the cool air within escape, so I shut the door again. Then I felt embarrassed because I should have known better.

"I think I have an emergency candy bar in my purse," I said, still not making eye contact. I'd left my purse on the table by the front door. Turning stiffly, I made my way there, then set my flashlight down and began rifling through my bag. I saw the glow of Rory's light come up behind me.

"Any luck?" he asked. His tone was cautious, and I knew he'd felt that animosity earlier as well.

Part of me was tempted to sneer, 'What makes you think I'd share?' while another part of me wanted to tease him with the same line. I was so mixed up with emotions I didn't know how to act. How to feel. Everything I said or did felt wrong. There was no handbook on how to deal with heart-breaking exes who resurface in your life owning half your inheritance — well, almost half.

Then there, at the bottom of my purse, I found what I was looking for. I pulled out the plain, dark chocolate Hershey Bar and held it up. Rory smiled, possibly remembering how I loved plain chocolate the most. I did love nuts and caramel and all the other things you could mix with chocolate, but sometimes a girl just needed plain 'ol chocolate without the drama.

Before he could say anything, I pulled off the wrapper and split the bar in two, handing him half. He smiled at my gesture. I left my purse on the table and wandered to the library. Rory's light followed along behind.

This room was two stories, taking up part of the second floor to accommodate the high stone fireplace. Hundreds of books — many of them I'd read — packed tall shelves that you needed a ladder to reach the top ones. Another wall had large windows set facing the lake, offering up the best views. The windows hadn't always been so big. My uncle had reworked the wall to expand the view. Right now, it wasn't so glorious, considering the great flashes of lightning illuminating the ferocious storm outside. I moved back, recalling that sound earlier of a tree being struck and falling over.

Rory took a seat by the hearth, and I opted to do the same, keeping a wary eye on the storm.

"Sounds like there'll be some damage to clean up in the morning," he observed.

Was it perverse of me to hope that one of his cabins and all his precious upgrades lay crushed beneath the weight of a mighty pine? No, that's terrible, I silently chastised myself. If he was in the cabin, he'd be flattened like a pancake. Hmm, pancakes. My stomach rolled again.

It was going to be a long night.

"What're you thinking about?" Rory asked.

I quickly masked my expression, which was possibly gleeful, considering I'd just been thinking of a tree in Rory's living room. I'd also been thinking of pancakes, so I allowed myself to pretend that was where the glee was coming from. Not the fact that Rory could possibly resemble a pancake in the first scenario.

"Um, pancakes?"

"Really?"

There was no way he could read my mind, no matter how well he knew me. About as well as Jehrel, if not more. Although, Jehrel would no doubt know exactly what I'd been thinking. Jehrel knew me after The Jilt when I'd taken off my rose-colored glasses and looked at the world realistically with a touch of cynicism. Rory knew me before The Jilt. And him being the reason for the defining change in me only made this more awkward.

"I'm hungry," I said by way of explanation.

"You didn't stop on the way here?"

"Yeah, I did, but not for food."

He made a face. "It's a long drive from T.O.."

The fact that he knew where I lived didn't surprise me.

It'd been our dream for years. Both of us moving from our small towns to the big city and making our dreams a reality. Rory had always wanted to be a policeman, and what better place than Toronto? My dreams had included us getting married—he'd proposed during my last year of college—and me opening my own business.

Everything changed when I came for a visit to Hadleigh four years ago. I'd graduated, and Rory had put in for a transfer from Hadleigh's police force to T.O.'s. But when we'd met up to talk about our wedding plans—we were going to get married in Hadleigh and then move to Toronto—he'd been different. He no longer wanted to move. He'd withdrawn the transfer request without even talking to me first. There'd been a coldness about him I couldn't figure out. His demeanor was completely different from the last time I'd seen him. Like he was someone I no longer knew. I tried talking to him about it, but he kept insisting he'd never really wanted to move anyway. He'd just been going along with what I wanted. I'd asked him if he even wanted to get married, and he'd shrugged, not making eye contact. Hurt, confused, and embarrassed, I'd removed my engagement ring and put it on the table. He'd smirked. Hiding my tears, I'd told him, 'Fine, have a nice life,' and stormed off, determined to never lay eyes on him again. I'd gone to him excited to make plans for our future together, and instead, I left alone and upset. I vowed never to look back. Well, except for visits to my family.

"I had a couple of Cokes," I said by way of explanation. No way would I reveal my stomach had been in knots because of him. The fact I had been civil to him tonight was impressive, and I gave myself credit for being so mature.

Just then, the lights came back on.

We looked at each other and rushed back to the kitchen.

"Oh, what a relief," I said, snatching up the tin on the counter. "Now I can use the stove."

Rory opened another cupboard and grabbed a saucepan.

When I dumped the canned stew into the pot, it didn't look like much. "Is there more?"

He already had a wooden spoon in his hand and began stirring, so I went digging around in the cupboard myself.

"Success." I waved around a duplicate can. Opening that one, I dumped it into the pan as well. "That's better. Too bad there isn't some bread or rolls." It surprised me how hungry I was, especially considering I wasn't concealed by darkness any longer. My clothes were damp, my hair probably resembling seaweed, and no doubt the bit of makeup I'd applied today was either long gone or running down my face. I hadn't expected the lights to just come back on like that, though. And now, as I thought about it, I began to feel self-conscious. And then I wasn't very hungry anymore.

Rory, of course, looked perfect. Rugged, handsome, and totally at ease.

His mind, no doubt, wasn't running a mile a minute, analyzing everything he'd said and done in the past hour. And he certainly wasn't wondering how he looked after being soaked by the storm. In my defense, I'd also recently endured a long, long car ride. Not to mention the stress of having my ex-fiancé sprung on me, plus the fact he now partially owned my inheritance.

So there was that.

Tamping down my desire to rush off to check my appearance in the bathroom, I let him stir the stew, and I retrieved some bowls and spoons from the cupboard. As I grabbed the cutlery, I checked out my face in the reflection of the chrome toaster. My head looked distorted, and my eyes bulged, but my hair wasn't as bad as I'd feared.

We ate in silence, and I found I did have an appetite after all.

"I guess I can leave now that the lights are on?" Rory

said, phrasing it as a question, not a statement. I detected a slight gleam of what resembled hope in his expression. Why he wanted to spend more time than necessary together was beyond me. I thought he'd be as anxious to part ways from this awkward reunion as I was. Although, he had said something about sharing our grief.

I shrugged by way of answering. Plus, my mouth was full, so I swallowed. "It still sounds bad out there." It was true. The storm rushed around us, sounding like we were at the center of a busy train station. When he failed to say anything and continued to look at me, I said, "You should stay."

He smiled then, and I had to force myself not to melt. Had to remind myself how he'd jumped up and down on my heart like it was a trampoline. I didn't want to give him any credit for making me more determined than ever to succeed. And I had. I'd gone out on my own and, against all odds, started up my business. I'd worked my butt off leaping over all the hurdles in my path. Sweated, plotted, and pivoted many-a-times, perfecting my vision. And slowly, carefully, my dream was coaxed into being. Or, at least, it would be, with luck, as soon as I uploaded the video of the reveal. I had planned to do it tonight once I'd gotten settled in. But fate and nature had other ideas.

"So, what have you been up to?" I asked. *Besides updating your newly acquired property?*

Now, it was his turn to shrug. I got the feeling he wanted to omit the fact he'd spent a lot of time at his new cabins and the plans he had for them to spare us more awkwardness. "Keeping busy," he wound up saying.

"How're things on the force?" This was a loaded question I purposely posed to him. I didn't want him to know that I knew he'd recently left policing behind. Didn't want him to know I'd asked my aunt about him. Wanted him to think I didn't know, didn't care, what he'd done the past few years.

"Oh, um, I left," he admitted.

"Really? Why's that? I thought you liked being a cop." It was pretty much all he'd talked about growing up. Not long after he'd arrived in Hadleigh, a few policemen in town had taken an interest in him and his mom and their situation. Though he hadn't said it, I had a feeling the first few times he'd spent with those cops had been when his mom was drunk and disorderly or passed out somewhere, and he'd been left on his own. Even now, I could see painful memories cloud his gaze. He'd been comforted by those officers of the law. They'd made him feel safe. And he wanted to be one of them someday.

He became interested in his stew, though his bowl was almost empty.

I let him squirm a moment longer before I felt bad. "It's okay if you don't want to talk about it."

"Thanks. Really not much to say," he mumbled. He got up and took his empty bowl to the sink. After he rinsed it out, he said, "I think I'll head up." He retrieved his flashlight from the counter, knowing as well as me that lights here were temperamental during a storm. Just because they were on now didn't mean they'd stay that way.

He waited for me as I rose and followed suit. Soon, we were back upstairs. As we entered our rooms and turned to close our doors, our eyes met.

He smiled tightly. "Good night, T. I'm... glad you're here."

I returned his smile and gave a slight nod. Then, not knowing what to say, I shut my door.

After leaning against it for several minutes, I got ready for bed.

Chapter 5

Rory pushed a shopping cart in Hadleigh's main grocery store. Though it was early, he'd already checked in with his old partner, Glen, at HQ to see if there was any new information about a case of interest. There'd been nothing to update, and despite Glen's offer of going out for coffee, Rory had declined. He wanted to pick up a few things for Thea to make her stay here less of a bother. Considering his part in the unexpected inconvenience, he felt responsible for making it up to her. He'd also been tempted to stop by Waverly house and check on Gavin, knowing how storms could frighten him. But he knew if he wanted to make it back before Thea woke up, he had to get moving.

A short while later, he was on the roadway toward Agnes's — *Thea's* — house. Would he ever get used to the fact that Agnes was really gone, and Thea was here in her stead? The idea wasn't so much unsettling as it was unexpected. Of course, he'd always known this would happen. It was inevitable Agnes would pass away and leave the resort to Thea. But after six months passed, Rory had begun to think Thea would never return. He'd been so surprised to see her. Delighted and terrified at once. He'd ached to see her again. To hear her voice. To watch her smile. But at the same time, her presence, especially now, was bad timing.

He'd been aware whenever she'd come to town in the past, despite her trying to remain out of sight. At least out of his sight. But he had resources. Ways of knowing she'd arrived, except for this time. When he'd opened his door during the storm, he'd been caught unaware, and it'd taken everything in him to not pull her into his arms and kiss the frown off her face.

He knew she despised him.

As much as it hurt, it was necessary.

She would most likely never forgive him for hurting her. He'd never forgive himself for it, either. The look of betrayal on her face would be eternally etched in his memory. But despite how he'd hated himself, he'd known he had to set her free.

He couldn't leave town.

And he couldn't ask her to give up her dreams and stay.

One night that was carved in his memory and his nightmares eternally is what had changed everything for him.

With crystal clear recollection, he could play the scene out again and again, but every time, it always ended the same way. With his life changed forever.

And from that same night, a tiny light in the darkness had emerged. One which had set him on a new path. One which hadn't included Thea and the dreams they'd shared.

As he pulled up at the house, a face flashed in his mind's eye. One with a crooked smile, a smattering of freckles, and a mass of brown, uneven curls. *Soon*, Rory vowed. It'd taken months to pull this off, and all the while, Gavin had waited for Rory. Suffering in silence, confused, and afraid.

At last, everything would be in place to take the next steps. And nothing, and no one, not even Thea, would stand in his way.

~

The next morning, I woke up momentarily startled, unsure of where I was. Then, it all came flooding back. Sitting up, I stared at my bedroom door. Had I imagined everything? Had it been a nightmare? My gaze darted to the cooling embers in the fireplace. Sniffing, I detected the lingering scent of woodsmoke.

No such luck.

I hadn't lit the fire. Rory had.

Rarely did I light any of the fires here, inside or out, since I wasn't really very good at it. But, considering all the times I had to light them for Jehrel, who was completely out of his element with fire, I had gotten better. Water was more Jehrel's thing — he swam like a fish — but boy, could he scream if he thought something in the lake touched him.

Thinking of Jehrel, I reached for my phone, expecting there to be at least two dozen messages. I wasn't wrong.

Weeeellll?

Did you figure out anything? About the surveyor and stuff????

Helllloo?

OMG, you're with HIM, right?!!!

I mean The One Who Shall Remain Nameless.

Am I right??

Hellooo?

Answer me. I'm going nuts here!

And on they went.

I thought it best to just call him. At least the power had stayed on. My phone was fully charged, and it had been nearly dead when I'd plugged it in last night. That part I was crystal clear on. Oh yes, there had been wine. Hence, the slight pain in my head that was tapping out the beat to *Another One Bites the Dust*. As much as I wanted to call Jehrel, I had to see if Rory was still here. Talking about him while he was in the house wouldn't be ideal. There might be a lot of swearing. So I tiptoed across the floor and eased my door open. The door across the hall was slightly ajar, so I crept out and peeked into the room.

Empty.

I pushed it open more and saw the sheets and the extra blanket I'd placed at the end of the bed were all folded neatly, and sat on the chair.

So, Rory wasn't in the room, but it didn't mean he'd left the building.

Two choices presented themselves. I could venture down the hall, descend the staircase, and sneak around to see if he was still here. Or I could head to the bathroom first, check my appearance, brush my hair and my teeth, and perhaps change my clothes. Though the cute little shorts and tank top jammies I'd changed into last night did look adorable on me. I really did need to use the bathroom, so I opted for door number two. Rory — if he was still here — would just have to wait until I was ready.

Dressed, combed, and fresh-breathed, I descended the stairs. I was going to keep my jammies on until I realized I didn't want to be grasping my phone like a lifeline if I ran into Rory. So, now it sat tucked neatly in the back pocket of my cut-off shorts.

When I entered the kitchen, I was surprised to see the table covered with half-emptied bags. A moment later, the front door thumped, and I heard footsteps heading my way. Resisting the urge to check my appearance in the toaster, I stood my ground. Rory soon appeared, his hands carrying more bags.

"What are you doing?" I moved out of his way as he put the bags down on the table with the others.

"Sorry, I meant to have it all put away before you came down."

There had to be at least eight bags, four partially unpacked, the others full. I saw bread and milk, eggs, cheese, butter, pasta, sauce, apples, oranges, bananas, and a bunch of other stuff.

Rory began pulling stuff out of the bags and went back and forth to the fridge to put away the cold stuff while I stood there. "I wasn't sure what you're into nowadays, so I kind of just went with the staples."

It looked like he'd bought everything but staples. From what I saw, he'd covered all the things I liked, including my favorite oatmeal raisin cookies and chocolate mint ice cream.

"Um, why?" was all I managed to say.

He paused for a moment, hands full of canned soup —

cream of broccoli and chicken and rice, more of my favorites—
and looked at me. "There wasn't anything here to eat."

"Yeah, but I told you I wasn't staying."

Now his back was to me, and I thought I detected his
shoulders stiffen. "It could take a while to get things straightened
out."

Ah, so it was Guilt who shopped for me this morning.

"Anything you don't eat, I'll take off your hands," he
offered. "The canned stuff will keep if you need to leave and
come back. At least you won't starve."

"How much did you spend on all this?" Had to be over a
hundred dollars. "Let me pay for it."

He straightened and went back to unpacking. "Don't
worry about it."

That was Guilt's voice.

Okay, no problem. He's up two cabins, so he can afford it. That
ugly voice inside my head was at it again. *Just get over it already.*
What's done is done, I argued back silently.

My phone started playing YMCA by the Village People.
Without looking, I knew it was Jehrel.

"Are you gonna get that?" Rory asked. "It might be your
lawyer."

"He's not my lawyer." I pulled out my phone, pretending
to confirm who it was. I was almost tempted to say it was my
boyfriend. Technically, it wouldn't be a lie. Jehrel was my friend,
and he was a guy. But if I did say it and got no reaction from
Rory, my heart might fracture more.

"It's about work," I lied. "I'll talk to them later." Jehrel
tended to be loud when he talked. If I could see his words in
print, they'd be all caps and end in exclamation points. There was
no need for a speakerphone when talking to him, and I didn't
want Rory overhearing any sensitive information. Knowing he'd
not give up, I sent Jehrel a quick text. *Talk later. Yes, HE is here.*

That'd give him something to chew on while he waited. Then I shoved my phone in my back pocket again.

"What time is your meeting tomorrow?" Rory asked.

"He's coming out here around ten-ish."

"Okay, I'll stay out of your way. If you need to include me in any discussions, I'll be at the cabin."

I nodded, and seeing no way around it, I helped put the rest of the groceries away. I kept out bacon and eggs and a loaf of bread to make toast. Then I put on a pot of coffee and started making us breakfast. It was the least I could do, considering all the food he'd bought.

"How was it outside? Any damage?" *How's your cabins?*

"There was a bunch of stuff blown around and some smaller trees down. Nothing covering the roads here that I saw, but out to town, there were crews clearing with chainsaws and trucks."

"Wow, yeah, that was quite the storm." Then, I almost said; Thanks for staying with me last night. But I liked the idea that it was me who had been the magnanimous one.

Breakfast ready, we sat down to eat. Rory chugged a glass of orange juice—extra pulp the way I liked it—and then piled eggs and bacon onto two slices of toast, smothered it in ketchup, and squashed them together like I knew he would.

"Umm, good," he said, his mouth full of food.

"Gross."

He smiled and took another huge bite. I got up to scoop more eggs and bacon from the frying pan onto his plate. He reached for the stack of toast on the table and made another sandwich.

I ate, but not much. My belly was still in a jumble. Looking around the kitchen in the light of day, I distracted myself by noticing the updates Aunt Agnes had made over the years. I remembered how the kitchen looked when I was little—done up like the 50s—and that had been updated from an even earlier era. The table we sat at was still the old-fashioned chrome with a Formica top, along with the chrome chairs. But the range and the fridge had been updated from the older Tappan and Frigidaire to newer models, along with the small appliances I saw set out on the countertop. I made a mental note to check out the attic and see if there were any antique or retro items I could use for my business. My clientele mainly catered to the Gen X-ers, dating 1965-1980. But that didn't mean I'd turn away someone who wanted a '50s kitchen, which was becoming all the rage.

"Not hungry?" Rory asked.

"Just thinking about work."

He swallowed his next bite, then took a big swig of coffee. I poked a fork in my eggs, pushing them around my plate.

"Aunt Agnes said something about you running a restoration business for homes or something."

Oh, so he'd asked about me as well. "You could say that, though I think of it more as interior design and minor renovations if needed."

"Cool. Well, she was really proud of you," he informed me before taking another giant bite.

"Thanks." She'd told me as much the last time I'd seen her, but it was still nice to hear.

Despite the animosity with Rory over the cabins and our soured past relationship, I had to admit I didn't totally hate the fact we were together. This was going to be a hard weekend to get through. Actually, it may even turn into a hard week. I was glad I wasn't facing it alone.

Chapter 6

After Rory left, I locked the doors to prevent any surprise visits and headed up to the attic. I had a notepad and pen and my phone. The first thing I planned to do was call Jehrel. I knew it was cruel of me to keep him twisting in the wind this way.

The entranceway to the attic was the first door to the right at the top of the stairs if you stood facing the hallway. Beside that door was the guestroom, then the bathroom, then Rory's room. Across from Rory's room was my room, and beside mine was the master bedroom. I remember late at night, when Rory was over, and one of us couldn't sleep, we'd sneak into the other's room. We'd talk in hushed whispers, making sure not to wake anyone else up. Sometimes, we'd dare each other to go up into the attic with just a flashlight and bring back something as proof we'd not chickened out. The hardest part was getting down the hallway past my aunt and uncle's room without detection. Being in the attic at night was spooky, especially if there was a storm. But my fear of losing Rory's grudging respect for my bravery had always been stronger than any fear I had of boogiemen in the attic.

I opened the creaky door — one we'd always made sure to oil when we were young — and headed up the staircase. Having a long-time fear of being locked in, I left the door open at the bottom of the stairs, along with the door at the top.

The far end of the attic had a few old trunks set against the wall, one of them sitting beneath a little window. I switched on the overhead bulb, and the sun shining through the window lit up the area as well. As I wound around boxes and coatracks, old furniture, and rolled-up carpets, I made mental notes of what I could recall being stored amongst the dust and cobwebs. It looked like no one had been up here for years. Since Aunt Agnes's knees had been bad and her health not great over the past half-decade, I figured I was probably the last one to venture here.

Using an old scarf, I pulled off a coat rack, I dusted the top of the wooden chest beneath the window, and sat down. I pulled out my phone and called Jehrel. He answered on the first ring.

"Oh my God! Finally."

"Hello to you too," I said, smiling because I could picture the look on his face.

I heard a humph, and I knew he was annoyed with me.

"I'm sorry it took so long to call. My phone was nearly dead when I got here last night. You're never gonna believe what happened."

Silence.

"Just after I arrived, the power went out. And when I looked out the window, I could see a light on at the furthest cabin — the ones they used to lend out in the summer I told you about — anyway, I thought, 'who could that be?'." I waited a moment, letting my words sink in. Knowing Jehrel, I knew I'd got his attention. He never could resist a good story.

After a few moments, I heard a cool "Go on."

"So I pulled out my old raincoat and boots — did I mention the terrible storm?"

Another few moments. "No, you did not." Still cool.

"So I went out into the storm to investigate…"

"You didn't." Slightly warmer.

"I had to. Who was in the cabin? And why did they have light? It was a steady light, not the swinging around movement of a flashlight."

"At least tell me you took a flashlight and your phone," he

said drolly.

"Um, yeah, I had a flashlight, but like I said, my phone was on its last legs when I pulled up to the house."

He emitted a dramatic sigh, the kind that said, 'Whatever shall I do with you?'

"I crept up to the cabin and tried to get a look through the windows at whoever was inside. But I didn't see anyone. Until…"

"Yessss?" He took the bait. I could have bet he was sitting on the edge of a chair or a bed or something.

"I went up and knocked on the door."

"Oh! So brave."

Now I had him… "To my utter shock and dismay, it was *him* who opened the door."

"Ahhh—oh yes, you already told me you'd met up with *him*. Really, Thea. So dramatic."

I chuckled. "You love it."

"That's beside the point. Anyway, what *happened*?"

"He let me stand out there in the rain, getting soaked in my old jacket."

"The beast."

"I didn't know what to do. So I asked about the lights. Why did he have them and I didn't?"

"What'd he say?"

"He mansplained how he'd updated not just the cabin he was in but the one beside it as well. Something about battery and solar power that comes on automatically in a storm."

"All the rage."

"I asked why he'd done it, and what was he doing there anyway?"

"What was he doing there?"

Dramatic sigh. "You were right."

"I was?" His tone turned delighted.

"Yes. Aunt Agnes left him not one but *two* cabins. That's

what all the huff is about with the surveyor and the deeded access."

"Oh! I knew it." He loved being right. "Then what happened?"

"We got into it. Well, kinda. He was insulting, so I spun around and stomped back through the mud to my aunt's house."

"Now yours," he reminded me.

"More trouble than it's worth, I'm beginning to think. Especially now with *Rory* in the picture."

"What happened next? Did he come after you?"

A very unladylike snort. "Of course he did. I told you how he has to have the last word."

"Oh, was he doing that squinty-eye thing you said he does?"

"You know it," I confirmed.

"And…"

"Well, he pounds on the door, and I was tempted to leave him out in the rain the way he left me, but I'm so above that type of behavior."

"So above," he agreed.

"So I let him in, and by this time, I'd had a bit of wine…"

"Oh no, not wine. Honey, you know you and wine, and especially you and wine and him, don't mix well at all."

"I know, plus with the rain…"

"Headache," we said in unison.

"He knew I was annoyed about the cabins. Not the fact that Aunt Agnes left them to him—you know he'd been like family to her and Uncle Jimmy—it was more because now I had to deal with him. Him and the lawyer, and the surveyor, and all the legal stuff. It's going to make things so much harder to sell this place and get back to my life."

"So much trouble." He knew I didn't just mean all the legalities but also having to deal with the personal issues Rory's presence presented as well.

"I guess him owning two of the cabins makes you all the more anxious to sell?" Jehrel guessed.

"Yes. No. I don't know. We kind of worked things out last night."

"Oh! Do tell."

"He'd said something about how we could have dealt with all the legal issues months ago if I'd been at the funeral and the reading of the will."

"No!"

"Yes, that's what had set me off at first. But then, although I didn't feel the need to explain myself and why I hadn't been there, I wound up telling him, and then he kept apologizing, and I knew he felt bad."

"Okay."

"And the power was still out, and the storm was wild, so he wound up spending the night in his old room."

"Okayyy…"

Another snort. "It wasn't like that. It was dangerous for him to go outside. We heard lightning strike a tree, and it fell over. And…"

"And I know how you are when it's stormy." Of course, he knew.

"This morning, I came downstairs, and he'd gone to town and bought a whole bunch of groceries since there was like nothing here to eat."

"That was nice," he said grudgingly.

"I suppose. Though I think it was more like he felt guilty 'cause now, instead of me being here just a couple of days, it's gonna be a week or more to deal with all this stuff."

"There! You see, aren't you glad I packed you extra clothes."

"You were right."

"I'm always right. I wish I was there. If Alan didn't have to go on that ridiculous business trip, I would be. You know that, right?"

"Yeah." They had three cats, and one of them was nuts when it came to strangers. The only way they could leave town if I wasn't available to watch them was if Alan's mom came over. The cat loved Alan's mom since it had been his pet from when he still lived at home. But Alan's mom lived two hours away, so getting her to come would be a pretty big ask.

"Don't worry, I'll handle things and be home as soon as I can," I assured him.

"When are you releasing the tape?" He meant the reveal. I knew he was excited to view it, and I felt badly there hadn't been time for us to watch it together before I left.

"I want to watch it first. Maybe later today." I looked at the notepad I had put down on the trunk. "First, I have to make a list of everything here, deciding what to sell with the place. I'm hoping there might be some old stuff I can use for the business."

"Oh, could you do that, though? Wouldn't it be sentimental?" he objected, knowing I'd have to relinquish the items with the renos.

I shrugged even though he couldn't see me. "Maybe. But if there's any really old stuff, it would be up here in the attic — where I am right now — and I wouldn't have any attachment to it since it'd been packed away like forever."

"I suppose."

"It'll be fine. Well, I better get busy. I'll talk to you later, okay."

"Okay. Love you."

"Love you, too."

"Who?"

That hadn't been Jehrel's question. I'd heard the beep of the call disconnecting. When the coat rack in front of me began to move, I screamed my head off.

The next moment, I felt hands grabbing onto my arms. "Thea!" someone yelled in my face.

Wait. That was Rory's voice.

I opened my eyes, which had squeezed shut in terror a few seconds earlier. Once focused on the looming face in front of me, I saw him, concerned and confused.

"How did you get in here?" I demanded, annoyed now.

"I knocked first, but there was no answer. I have a key. Aunt Agnes gave it to me years ago, just in case, I guess."

"Oh." When he'd come in with groceries, I'd assumed with it being so early, he'd left the door unlocked.

He plunked down on the trunk beside me.

"You're sitting on my notepad," I informed him.

He wiggled around, reached under his leg, and pulled it out, passing it to me.

"Sorry, I didn't mean to scare you."

"What are you doing here?" I asked again.

His eye narrowed, and he looked away. "I dunno. I thought maybe I could help you."

"Help me?"

He gestured around the attic. "With whatever it is you're doing. You were saying you had a bunch of stuff to take care of."

"Oh."

"I feel bad. You know, adding to all the trouble. I know you have a life to get back to. Someone special back home who's missing you."

Ah, so he'd heard me say 'love you' on the phone, and now he was fishing for information. What was it to him anyway if I had someone special waiting for me or not? What did he care?

"What about you? Anyone special in your life?" I turned the question around on him instead of answering.

He shook his head. "Not romantically."

Looking at him sitting there so close, close enough to touch, I felt a heat well up inside of me. I recognized the sensation. He was like the sun. And I had been the fool who'd allowed myself to get too close and got burned.

I wouldn't make the mistake again.

Chapter 7

After I informed Rory that the stuff I needed to do inside would be personal, I asked him to make a list of things outside if he wanted to help. I'd pulled off a few sheets of my notepad and handed them over, telling him he could probably find a pen downstairs.

"Why don't I just use the notepad on my phone?" he'd asked, staring at the sheets of paper like they were foreign objects.

"Whatever's easier for you." I hadn't asked for his help. I'd wanted him to go away so I didn't have to think about him anymore. Concentration was needed for what I had to do next, and his presence made it harder. Already, I'd felt bombarded by old visions and voices from the past. Nostalgia could be an uninvited guest when it was your own you were dealing with. The look on Rory's face when I'd first told him I could handle things alone was my undoing. All that sadness tinged with what I guessed to be regret had eaten away at my resolve, and I'd caved. Getting him to take stock of outside items would get him out of my hair and get some work done.

An old shed outside contained items such as fishing rods, paddles, life jackets, and a net. I was sure there was a bunch of other stuff as well, plus there was a canoe and a paddle boat tipped over and covered with tarps near the dock, which could be listed with the resort. I really disliked the idea of someone else owning the things my family had used so much over the years, but I couldn't justify putting a pair of boats in my tiny living room at home, no matter how much I cherished them. There would have to be a lot of sacrifices made, and I had to prepare my heart to handle it.

Rory found me in the kitchen an hour later, crying over a potato masher.

Though I dabbed away the tears and shoved the tissues I'd used to swipe at my nose into my pocket, I couldn't hide my red eyes.

"What's wrong?" His tone was gentle, which only made me feel worse.

I waved around the masher as though it should speak up and reveal its part in my misery. "This. I could include it with the dishes and pots and pans and utensils and other cooking stuff, but the handle is burnt, so I should just throw it out, or maybe take it home 'cause it's still useful, but looks old and worn to someone else." My words ended with a sob I tried to contain but failed.

Rory reached out and took the masher from my hands. He inspected the burnt end and smiled. "I'll take it. Considering it's my fault it looks like this."

It was true. He'd wanted to help with dinner, and Aunt Agnes had let him take care of the potatoes. He'd peeled, cut, and boiled them, and as he'd gone to the fridge to grab butter and milk, he'd carelessly left the masher too close to the still-hot stove element. The handle had melted by the time he came back. Aunt Agnes had seen it, but too late. The damage had been done. I still remembered the smell.

"How'd you make out with your list?" I attempted to change the subject. If I could listen to him talk, it'd give me a chance to regain my composure. Getting through this whole ordeal would take me forever if I kept breaking down. The problem was every utensil, every piece of cookware, every chair, table, lamp, and book held memories. Even the walls and corners, doors, and staircase seemed to conspire against me. From a distance, my idea to itemize things and list most of them with the property to sell had seemed a daunting task. Up close, it was turning into a herculean effort.

"I made a list on my phone. I'll send it to you if you give me your number," he said.

I told him my number, and he sent me the list. Glancing at it, I could see it was detailed. "Thanks."

"You have my number on there now, just in case you didn't already."

"Ah, no, actually, I didn't have it." I hadn't listed him in my contacts when I got my new phone. If his number hadn't changed, then I still knew it off by heart, but I wasn't about to tell him that.

"Have you finished upstairs?" he asked, indicating my notepad.

"Yeah, I think so. I'll do another walk-through when I'm done and make sure I didn't miss anything." There'd been a bunch of antiques in the attic I was interested in keeping for my business. Most of the stuff up there had been stashed before I'd been born, so there weren't memories attached. I'd have to look into renting a truck to bring back the items I wanted with me and also a place to store the stuff.

"What about the cabins?" he asked.

"You mean the three I still own?" I said before I could stop myself. I could see my words wounded him. Oh well, I thought, he could share in this painful day with me.

"Do you want me to go through them and list the contents?" he asked, ignoring my jab.

"Oh, do you have a set of keys for them as well?" Wow, I was hot today.

He stared at me a moment, his eye narrowing. "I do. Considering I've been the only one around lately, it's probably a good thing."

Touché.

We glared at each other until he looked away. "How about you take one, and I'll take another, and whoever is done first can get started on the third?"

Whether I liked it or not, it still had to be done. "Okay."

He waited while I put on my shoes, and we headed out. I'd yet to venture outside and see the damage from last night's storm. As Rory had reported, there appeared to be little sign of the chaos we'd heard and witnessed. Mainly puddles and a few downed branches, but that was all. Rory noticed my assessing gaze.

"It's worse out toward town."

"So you said." When he'd gone out this morning and returned with his guilt groceries.

I think he was looking to fill the silence with idle chatter. If he felt awkward, though. I'd had some time to ponder how he responded to my question in the attic about not having anyone special in his life. He'd denied there being anyone.

Years ago, part of me had thought perhaps he'd driven me off because he'd found someone else. Maybe he had, but if so, I guess it hadn't lasted. My aunt had never mentioned him being with anyone else. But if he hadn't rejected me because he wanted someone else, then there had to be another reason for his behavior. If it'd been another woman, it would have explained it. If not, then maybe it had just been about him no longer wanting me. That I was lacking in some way. And that thought hurt more than if there'd been someone else.

After he'd left to go outside, I had dwelled on the end of our relationship. To him, the moment when he'd shattered my heart didn't appear to register on his Life Changing Events radar the way it did mine. To Rory, it was like something he'd done on a Sunday afternoon to kill time. Whereas for me, that moment had changed my life. It had spurred me into taking the leap to move away and then to open my own business. I had to wonder how my life would look right now if he hadn't broken my heart. We reached the first cabin.

"I'll take this one," I said, jangling the ring of keys I'd nabbed hanging on a hook at the main house. I didn't want to think about what might have been any longer. My life was fine, just the way it was. I was happy. I was fulfilled. And it was thanks to me, not him.

Giving a nod, Rory walked off to the next cabin, and I unlocked the door to this one after three attempts with different keys. I hadn't been in these cabins in a long time. Whenever I'd come to visit, I'd stay in my old room. Jehrel, whether he'd come with or without Alan, would always stay in the guest room. It was the second largest room on the floor, and he usually brought a lot of stuff with him and needed the space. We'd never felt the need for more privacy since we had the whole second floor of the house to ourselves. The cabins usually were rented out anyway.

Each cabin came with its own boat, whether it be a rowboat, canoe, or paddle boat. They were separate from the pair which belonged to the main house. I decided I would list all of the boats with the resort. Each cabin also had its own waterfront area with a small, dedicated beach and swimming spot, along with a shed that held lifejackets, oars, and other odds and ends I would need to go over and record. Each cabin was also fully stocked with kitchen items and small appliances, and there were sheets and blankets, and pillows as well.

After I finished with my list for inside, I headed down to the water's edge and unlocked the shed. I looked over and saw Rory was already in the shed of the second cabin doing inventory as well.

Funny, I thought, allowing my mind to wander once again.

If things hadn't changed that fateful day.

If Rory and I had stayed together like I'd planned.

If he hadn't broken my heart.

If we'd gotten married and had inherited the resort.

If we were getting things ready for renters for the season. Then things would be just like this. But there wouldn't be an ache in my chest and a hole in my heart that nothing seemed to fill.

So many ifs.

Things would have been so different.

In another life.

~

I sat on my bed, my finger hovering over the button on my laptop to click 'Load.' After three more deep breaths, I clicked it.

In anticipation of launching my reveal tapes online, I'd created a profile over a month ago on a streaming channel, and this would be the first upload of what I hoped were many. Doing it earlier in the day had crossed my mind, but I knew from research that late afternoon was the optimal time to launch.

While my video slowly uploaded due to the sketchy Wi-Fi here, my heart began to hammer in my chest in anticipation. Soon, my dreams would be out there for the world to see. To judge. To comment on. Once the upload was complete, I planned to share the link on several social media networks. I'd made accounts under so many that I'd had to list them in another notebook which I had open in front of me. One thing I did like to have on hand were notebooks. There was something comforting about putting a pencil or pen to paper that felt more real to me than typing words onto a computer screen, which could be lost in cyberspace at any time.

And then it was live.

I clenched my hands into fists to refrain from gnawing on my fingernails. Referring to my list, I logged into site after site and shared the video link. Then I closed my laptop and left my room. Making tea, I sat down with a hot mug at the kitchen table and called Jehrel. He didn't answer, so I left him a message, hoping he'd take the hint and go online to leave glowing positive comments on each site—I'd made him a list as well.

The doorbell rang, so I got up to answer it.

Rory stood outside, and I opened the door and stared at him.

When I didn't say anything, he said, "I didn't want to let myself in again."

Refraining from comment, I moved to let him in, and he followed me to the kitchen. Seeing my tea and the teapot on the counter, he made himself a cup and sat down with me.

"What's up?" I asked.

"There's been some inquiries about the cabins."

"What about? Not about selling them, I hope? I don't want to sell them off individually despite the fact you have two of them. It's going to be enough trouble with right-of-ways and surveyors and all that cr—."

"No," he cut me off. "I mean inquiries about renting them out for the season."

"Oh." I hadn't thought about that, but of course, it made sense since this was a vacation resort. I'd just assumed people would know my aunt passed away, and the resort would be in limbo while her heirs decided what to do with it. But then again, people who came here were from out of town and may not have heard about her passing.

"Calls have been coming in over the past few months. I've taken down names and contact information, but I also explained that Agnes had passed away, and I wasn't sure what was going to happen with the resort. I was going to update the website stating about her passing, but I didn't feel it was my place. Plus, I don't have the password to get in anyway."

"Oh," I repeated. "I can do it." I really didn't want to do it now, though. No way would I be able to keep from looking at the status of my video.

"What?" Rory asked. He knew me well enough to know something was up.

It was out there for the world to see now, so there was no sense hiding what I'd done. "Um, I don't really want to go online right now."

He stared at me, waiting for more information. When I remained silent, he said, "Because?"

"Because I won't be able to stop myself from looking."

"Looking at what?"

"My video status."

His face twisted in confusion. "Video status?"

I sighed. "I uploaded a reveal tape and shared it with the world, and I'm afraid to see what everyone's saying about it. Or if anyone is even watching it."

"Okay."

"Just okay? This is my life."

His tongue flicked out to swipe across his top lip. "Ah, what were you revealing?"

If he was being rude or ridiculous, it'd show on his face, and it wasn't. I knew he'd asked my aunt about me and my life, but that wouldn't automatically mean he'd know I was taping reveal videos.

"It's for my work. Upon completion of a remodel, I thought it'd be good publicity to tape the reveal to the owners. You know, get their reaction on film. Like those other home shows do."

He appeared to mull this over for a moment. "Yes, that does make sense. So this reveal tape you posted is your first job?"

"It's my first whole house remodel," I clarified. "All I'd done up to that point was mainly single rooms."

"Huh, it's strange people would opt to do just one room."

I shrugged. "Not really. I mean, remodels aren't for everyone. And even then, the people who want them the way I do it usually don't want to remake a whole house. Most of the time, it's just the kitchen or the rec room. Or a bedroom. I was hoping if people saw how it looked to have the whole house done, they'd be more inclined to jump right in. Just do it."

He mulled again. "Isn't it kind of weird to just do a single room? I mean, if some of the house is updated, the rest would look strange, don't you think? Unless it's a cost issue, which I understand. Then, one room at a time would make sense."

Now, it was my turn to be puzzled. "What is it you think I do?"

He shrugged this time. "I dunno. Renovations? Restorations?"

"Ah, okay. Actually, I think Aunt Agnes had trouble understanding my line of business as well. Especially since I've not run into anyone who remodels homes quite like I do."

"How come? What is it you do?"

Why did I suddenly feel more anxious about revealing the exact nature of my business to Rory than I did about releasing that video to the world? What did I care about his opinion? I took a deep breath.

"The name of my company is, You Can Go Home Again."

I could see him mentally tossing it around in his head. "Okay. Catchy. I like it."

"It means I put rooms, or in the case of my reveal tape, entire homes, back the way they looked. It's nostalgic." I stared at him a moment. "Get it?"

He nodded, still working it out. "So, like that old farmhouse in town people go through, you know, with the petting zoo out back? It's called the Homestead or something like that. From the early settlers."

"Ah, yeah—no. I don't go back quite that far. I think I'd need a history degree for that. What I do is mainly from about the 1950s right up to the '90s. Mostly, my clientele consists of Gen Xers. But I have done the odd room for Millennials."

Again, he stared at me, processing. Then he asked, "Really?"

His tone implied he was curious, not being sarcastic. "Yes, really."

He whipped out his phone and began thumbing through it.

"What are you doing?" I asked.

"Looking for your video, where'd you post it?"

I put my head into my hands to hide my embarrassment. "Everywhere."

"Oh! Here it is. Wow, look at all those—"

He was talking about the comments or the number of views. "No! Don't tell me. Especially if it's bad. I don't want to know."

Then, I could hear my voice over the speaker of his phone as he watched the video.

I had no clue what he thought, nor did I care.

I was too busy running from the room.

Chapter 8

My laptop lay open in front of me as I sat on my bed. I'd yet to gather the courage to turn it on. The website for the resort needed to be updated, I reminded myself. And no doubt there were lots of messages and/or inquiries about cabins from hopeful summer renters. I was strong enough to get online and not look at comments about my video. Of course, I was.

Another few minutes later, I turned on the computer. I had to initiate a search for the resort's site since I suddenly couldn't remember the web address.

As soon as I found it, I logged in. When I'd designed this site for my aunt and uncle, Rory and I were still a thing. But then we weren't, and I'd changed my log-in from TheaL*vesRory to C*ptainJerkW@d . I had no problem remembering that.

On the Home page of the site, I made a note about my aunt passing away and how sorry we were to not be able to offer any cabins for rent at this time. I said to please check back for any future updates on the status of the resort. Then, I went into the section for messages or inquiries that were sent to my aunt's email address. Being the webpage creator, I was able to access everything, and I spent the next ten minutes responding to individuals who had messaged. The calls Rory had taken had been from the dedicated landline at the resort. I hadn't checked that yet since he'd already said he'd been monitoring it.

Just as I was wrapping up, a knock sounded at my door. "Can I come in?" Rory asked.

Two beats later, I replied, "Okay."

From the look on his face, it was hard to tell what was going on with him. My pride prevented me from asking. He'd watched my video, embarrassing enough, and I wasn't about to beg for feedback.

"I'm finished updating the resort's site, and I've responded to all the messages. I've also listed my email as a contact, so you shouldn't be bothered anymore," I informed him.

He came over and sat on the end of my bed. "It was no bother. Thanks for doing that, though."

I bristled, not wanting his gratitude for something I should have thought to do months ago. "Well, I'm sorry it took so long."

He shrugged. "You've been busy."

It annoyed me how he let me off the hook so easily. He should be put out. But then again, he did score a pair of cabins for his troubles. I wasn't sure if I would ever reconcile myself with that fact.

"What?" I could feel him staring at me even though my gaze was directed at the fireplace.

"I don't know what to say," he admitted.

I looked at him then. "About what?" If he was going to tear my video to shreds, I wasn't prepared. I hadn't had time to create an invisible shield of armor. I only hoped my narrow gaze said, 'Go ahead, I dare you.'

"Your video—reveal tape—it was incredible. I've never seen anything so ingenious and original. It put a lump in my throat."

I begged him with my eyes not to tease me. "Really?"

He smiled. "Really."

Now, I had a lump in *my* throat.

"Where on earth did you come up with the idea? I mean, I've seen some home shows and reveals, but never anything like that."

"I—I dunno. It just came to me," I admitted. Maybe from all the years of longing I'd faced? Hoping, wishing, and praying things could go back to a time when my mom was alive. Every single modification made to our home over the years felt like an eraser on a chalkboard wiping away the pictures in my mind I had of her. Washing dishes at the sink, folding clothes from the dryer, watering the plants in front of the living room window. Each change banished her existence with every stroke until there was almost nothing left.

"I can understand what you were trying to explain now about the nostalgia. And I'm not the only one. There were a lot of great comments. This one guy, Jehrel, wow, he was really into it. Must have left three or four comments."

I snorted. "He's a friend of mine. Doesn't count."

"Well, there were dozens of others. More were popping up as I read them. Besides, friend or not, he's entitled to his opinion. So am I."

"Thanks for saying that. I'm glad you liked it. I only wish Aunt Agnes and Uncle Jimmy had a chance to see it."

"What about your dad? I bet he's proud of you," he rushed to say, no doubt seeing the sudden tears in my eyes.

"My dad's on a cruise with his latest girlfriend."

"Oh. Sorry."

Now, I shrugged. "Doesn't matter."

"I bet you get a slew of calls for renos from this," he predicted.

"I really hope so. That was the plan."

"The important thing is you're doing what you love. Not everyone achieves their dream. Savor it."

"Thanks. You're right. I will. Maybe just for a little while. Then, onward."

He was the one who looked sad now. "Take some time. Don't be in a rush to charge ahead."

I laughed. "I'm worried there'll be a hundred places who take my idea and run with it. Before you know it, I'll have major competition, and they'll probably have the bankroll to outdo me. I have to make hay while the sun shines, Uncle Jimmy used to say."

"I get it now. Why you're anxious to get going on selling this place. You need the capital for your business."

"Yeah."

He appeared thoughtful. "I'm sorry I'm causing you problems. It was never my intention to stand in your way."

"It's not your fault," I assured him, feeling suddenly magnanimous. "The lawyer will be here tomorrow, and hopefully, we'll get everything ironed out smoothly and quickly."

"Whatever I can do to help, just say the word."

"Thanks." He may be all dewy-eyed and kind right now, but I had a feeling he'd be all business once the lawyer arrived. He'd probably realized I didn't have the money to buy the cabins from him. Even if it had been an option, I wasn't convinced he was remotely interested in selling them. Despite the distance between us over the years, since I'd arrived here, he'd seemed all about reconnecting. Maybe it was his emotions over losing my aunt, who'd been like a mother to him? I had no idea. I wasn't about to delude myself with notions he wanted to re-establish things between us, as in more than just a friendship. I had no intention of us ever being a couple again. Not when he'd so callously tossed away what we had. No way.

Rory stood up. "I'm gonna get going. I have some stuff to do in town. Do you need anything while I'm there?"

I closed my laptop, still not brave enough to look at the comments. "You mean you didn't get all you needed this morning? Oh, I bet you didn't have enough room left in your new truck." The truck he had before was a single cab. The new one was a crew cab.

"Ha, ha. No, I have a meeting."

When I stared at him expectantly, waiting for him to elaborate, he dodged my gaze and walked to the door.

Well, that wasn't at all suspicious.

Probably had something to do with the cabins he now owned. The ones he'd already outfitted with updated emergency lighting and God only knew what else.

Whatever.

After meeting the lawyer tomorrow, my next step was listing this place with a realtor. I'd be home by the end of the week.

And despite the ache in my gut, I had no intention of ever looking back.

~

Rory didn't return home until late evening. I admit I may have looked in the direction of his cabins several times to see if I'd missed his truck going by. But after dark, I couldn't ignore the glow of headlights as he slowly rolled past the main house. I got the feeling the so-called meeting he'd had was more like a date. Probably why he'd acted so dodgy earlier. I checked the time on my phone and saw it was almost ten o'clock. I wondered if he may have brought his *friend* home with him. Maybe waiting for the cover of darkness?

What was a girl to do but go for a stroll?

It was a beautiful night, after all.

Ten minutes later, I wondered what was wrong with me as I lurked around the tall trees near Rory's place, hoping to get a glance at any *guests* he may be entertaining. I didn't see anyone. I'd no idea why it mattered to me if he did have someone in there anyway. Possibly because he'd said there was no one special in his life, and I wanted to prove to myself what an untrustworthy ratfink he was.

Sure enough, my suspicions proved correct.

Unfortunately, Rory's guest arrived at the cabin in their own vehicle, headlights shining right at me.

From the tree I'd ducked behind, I silently prayed they hadn't noticed my skulking form.

And after all that, it was a man who climbed out of the vehicle.

He was tall and wore a suit.

Purposefully, he strode up to the door with what looked like a laptop bag hanging from his shoulder. Before he could knock, Rory opened the door and invited him in.

It appeared the man had been unaware of me. There'd been no searching gaze sweeping the area when he'd climbed from the car. He'd seemed preoccupied with his mission. I wondered what type of business was being conducted under the cover of darkness.

Perhaps he was a lawyer?

The fact that Rory wasn't entertaining a woman eased my mind somewhat. But now I was full of curiosity at this new quandary. Not that it was actually a problem. And it certainly wasn't any of my business. I forced myself to rein in my curiosity and return to the house. After all, I still had a few emails and messages to answer.

During the wait for Rory's return, I'd gotten up the courage to go online and read many of the comments made on each forum about my video. I was pleasantly surprised and relieved most remarks were positive. And just as Rory had predicted, I did receive a handful of requests for quotes and even appeals to post more videos. I'd sent off a quick message to my video guys, thanking them again for their great job and promising to use them for my next reveal. Whenever that would be.

I'd called Jehrel as well.

We'd talked about the success of the tape, and we'd also discussed Rory. I'd admitted things had been going quite well despite my fears to the contrary. Jehrel had been quick to see every side of the scenario and used his imagination over time to think up several more. Such as… Maybe Rory and I were destined to be a couple again? Or maybe he'd never gotten over me and had lost his job after several warnings about being distracted and mopey? Maybe he'd turned to a life of crime? Or he was hoping to stall a smooth transition of fixing things legally, thereby stalling my plans to sell and leave? Or he was secretly married and had three kids? Maybe he was planning on moving to Toronto and setting up his own reno business? Or, he'd found gold at the resort and tampered with my aunt's will?

And on he'd gone until I'd begged him to stop.

I opted not to get back online. The screen time had started making my head pound, and I'd just gotten it settled down. I went around shutting off lights and making sure the doors were locked. Then I got ready for bed.

It felt strange being in the house alone.

It was the first time.

Even the night before, Rory had been here for company.

After peeking out the upstairs window facing his cabins, I climbed into bed. It still felt weird to think of them that way for a long while. Rory and I had referred to them as the Lost Boy's Cabins. Perhaps it was fitting he now owned them, considering how much time he'd spent there as a boy. What'd they call that? Serendipity? I'd switched on the bedside lamp before turning off the overhead light, and now I reached into the drawer of the end table and pulled out a book I was reading. I'd been reading it for about five years now. Whenever I came here, I'd read a bit more. Surprisingly, every time, after just a few lines, I was right back into the story again. Rory and I had still been a couple when I'd started the book, and I think part of me was afraid to finish it. Like it'd signal the end of an era or something.

After about ten pages, I returned the book to the drawer

and shut off the light. Tired, I closed my eyes, determined to sleep despite whatever was going on down the road.

Maybe Rory did have a lawyer over and was secretly seeing if he may be entitled to more than just a pair of cabins? Maybe he was after the whole shebang? He could claim abandonment, perhaps? I hadn't really been around a lot. That being mostly Rory's fault. But I'd still come by a few times a year. It could be the reason he'd been hanging around me since I got here. Scoping out the territory. Looking for an edge.

I let loose a big sigh. At this rate, I'd never get to sleep. I tried thinking of my next job—whatever it may be. Then I thought about the meeting with Mr. Bailey in the morning. If I didn't get to sleep soon, I may oversleep and not be prepared. Not that I knew exactly what I needed to prepare for. I grabbed my cell and double-checked it was charged up, and I'd set an alarm. I had. So there was no need to worry.

Then why couldn't I sleep?

The bed wasn't exactly comfortable. And despite having slept in this room like a million times, it didn't feel like home yet. From past experience, I knew it took me at least a couple of nights to warm up to sleeping quarters. Last night didn't really count because I'd had a bit to drink, and falling asleep had come easily since I'd had a long, eventful, exhausting day.

A loud squeak overhead made me sit upright.

Just when I laid back down moments later after dismissing it as the house settling, it squeaked again. And then again.

Like someone was working their way across the attic floor.
Squeak.

Logically, I tried to make sense of the sound. Had I opened the window when I'd been up there making my lists?

I couldn't remember.

Maybe I had, and the wind was blowing stuff around.
Squeak.

It had been slightly breezy when I'd been sneaking around outside Rory's place. That had to be it. If a monster was creeping across the floor up there, it would have made it to the door by now. It'd be coming down the stairs, then along the hallway toward me. Unless it opted to use the main staircase and head downstairs. The first floor was more appealing anyway. The kitchen was down there.

But monsters didn't eat food.

Squeak.

They ate people.

Good grief. What was I? Five?

If I was five, I wouldn't be here alone.

My phone started playing The Village People, and I grabbed it.

"Jehrel?" I said too loudly. At least it sounded loud.

"Oh good, you're awake."

He didn't sound like himself. Monster forgotten I asked, "Hey, you okay?"

He promptly burst into tears. A thousand scenarios galloped into my head. "What's wrong? Is it Alan? Your mom?"

"It's n—nothing," he insisted. "Alan called and is staying away an extra night. I'm lonely. There're only cats to talk to. You're gone. Alan's gone."

Despite the dramatics, I was thrilled to hear his voice. "Before you know it, Alan will be home annoying you. Then I'll be back, driving you crazy as well. Enjoy the silence."

He sniffled loudly. Then his nose honked as he blew it. "Silence. What's that? Meowing at all hours. Nonstop hissing. Cat litter flinging everywhere."

"Poor baby."

"What are you doing? Not hanging out with *him*, I hope?"

"No. Although something did happen tonight. I'd love to get your take on it. Let me tell you all about…"

"Were you in bed?" he interrupted.

"Yes. But never mind, let me tell…"

"Oh my god, you're all alone in that ginormous house all by yourself? And for the first time." He tutted a few times.

"So I was saying…"

"Are you afraid?"

"What? No. No way. I'm fine. There was some squeaking around in the attic, but I think I left the window cracked up there…"

"You mean tonight? You were in bed and heard noises?" he clarified.

"Yes, tonight, but…"

"Oh, honey, oh no. Not the monsters?"

I sighed and hung my head, vowing for the tenth time to never tell Jehrel anything ever again. "Do you want to hear about Rory or not?"

"All right, tell me all about it," he soothed, and we settled in for a nice long chat.

Chapter 9

My alarm woke me in the morning. Staring at my phone, I noticed the battery was almost dead since I'd spent half the night talking to Jehrel. It was nine, and I had just enough time to shower and dress, and grab some coffee before Mr. Bailey arrived. When I ventured down the hall, I looked out the bathroom window toward Rory's cabins. I only saw his truck, so his guest must have left sometime in the night. I plugged my phone into the bathroom outlet so I would hear if it rang. As I shampooed my hair and shaved my legs, I wondered for the hundredth time who the man at Rory's might have been.

Mr. Bailey arrived promptly at ten. I ushered him inside, and we sat at the table so he could spread out his papers.

"Coffee?" I offered.

"Yes, thanks." He didn't look up from the tidy stacks of sheets he was lining up.

His hair was shades of salt and pepper, and I pegged him to be in his late fifties. He had the bushiest eyebrows I'd ever seen. The constant smile he wore despite his business-like attitude made me see why Aunt Agnes had always spoken of him fondly. Carefully, I set down his coffee amongst the papers and sat across from him, my own mug gripped in my hand. Rory must have noticed Mr. Bailey's arrival, and I wondered if he would come by. Probably not without his lawyer — if that was who had been here last night. I strained my ears for the sounds of a car.

Mr. Bailey had placed the papers upside down to him so

I could read them. Color-coded tabs were inserted in the stacks, most likely to indicate where a signature was needed.

"I assume you're aware of the other beneficiary named in the estate?" he asked.

It was hard, but I refrained from snorting. "Ah, yes. We met up during the storm the other night. He's already outfitted his cabins with upgrades."

He cleared his throat. "Perhaps he might have waited to see if there'd be any challenges to the estate before he began modifications to the property. However, due to the length of time that has passed —"

"I'm not challenging his inheritance," I interrupted. "I would like to resolve any issues there are with severance and access or whatever else needs doing so I can list the resort as soon as possible."

He looked at me, his expression curious. "You're interested in selling?"

"Yes. I thought I mentioned that on the phone. Anyway, I run my own business, and I can't run this resort as well. Plus, I need the money," I admitted.

He looked even more curious at that. After shuffling around some papers, he placed a new stack in front of me. "The estate… It does come with a cash settlement included."

"It does? Oh, I wasn't aware." I'd known my aunt and uncle had been comfortable, but I'd assumed most of what they made from the resort went right back into the upkeep.

He used his pen to point out a place on the paper.

I looked, then looked again. "That says 500,000 dollars."

"Yes, that's correct."

"Wait. What?" I was sure my mouth was hanging open.

He aimed his smile at me. "It's a generous amount. They also left a sum of money to the Boys and Girls Camp of Hadleigh."

"Now, that doesn't surprise me," I assured him. But then

I had to ask, "What about Rory? I mean, the guy who inherited the two cabins?" He had been driving around in a newer truck.

He appeared puzzled. "Oh, no. He didn't receive any cash in the inheritance. Just the cabins."

That pleased me, but I wasn't sure why. "Does it say anywhere in the will *why* they left him two of the cabins? I mean, they must have known the trouble it would cause with all the legal issues involved." If they wanted to acknowledge him in the will, they could have left him some cash, which would have made things a lot easier on me.

"Ah, no. No explanation. Although, I do agree with you. The legalities will take some sorting out."

"Hmm, I wonder if I could offer to buy him out at fair market value. Then I could list the entire resort without having to get into the severance issues," I said.

"That's entirely up to you. The money is yours to do with as you please," he assured me. He shuffled the papers around some more. "Miss James, if you could please sign here."

After I'd signed all the necessary paperwork, Mr. Bailey left me a detailed outline of what needed to take place in order to sever the land legally and a list of contacts — if it turned out buying Rory's cabins wasn't an option. He also left me his card and told me I could call him any time with questions I may have. In turn, I gave him my banking information so the money I inherited could be transferred from the holding account into mine. The transfer, including interest, would be completed within the next 48 hours, he assured me. I stacked the papers he left for me, put them into a large envelope, and placed them on top of the fridge.

Just as I was showing Mr. Bailey out, I saw Rory strolling down the roadway. I waved goodbye to the lawyer and called out to Rory to come inside.

In the kitchen, I offered him coffee, and he sat down at the table.

"How'd it go?" he asked.

Placing his cup down, I took the seat across from him. "Better than expected."

"How so?"

I wanted to tell him about the money, but I didn't want to say how much I'd received. If he knew, I feared it may drive up his price.

"There was a sum of money included in my inheritance that I wasn't expecting," I said, still feeling surreal about the whole thing. I watched him carefully for any reaction.

He sipped his coffee and let the mug linger near his lips. "That's nice. What do you plan to do with it?" He sipped again and set his mug down. The way his gaze moved around the kitchen, I got the feeling he was looking for food.

"Hungry?" I asked, ignoring his question.

He shrugged. "A little. Did you eat yet?"

"No," I said, getting up and going to the fridge to pull out some eggs and milk. "No time. I got up at nine and had to get ready."

Grabbing a frying pan, I set it on the stove and went back to the fridge for mushrooms, peppers, and cheese, figuring I'd make omelets. While I made breakfast, Rory put on another pot of coffee.

"I don't want to tell you what to do, but if you inherited money, maybe you could put off selling the resort for a while?"

When I looked at him quizzically, he went on.

"I just mean, maybe you could think about it, you know? Spend some time here, perhaps rent out a cabin or two."

"I'm not interested in running a resort," I said.

"I could help you. In fact, I could run it if you decide to keep the place going."

Setting my attention on breakfast, I said, "Hmm," as though I was mulling over his suggestion.

After the omelets were done, I slipped them onto plates and brought them to the table, and sat down. Rory brought over our refilled coffee cups and reclaimed his seat. He ate while I stared at him. Initially nixing his idea outright, I now pondered his suggestion. Keeping the resort going had never dawned on me. I already had a business to run. But now, thanks to the inheritance money, I had options. I was suddenly humbled and grateful for the thoughtfulness of my aunt and uncle. Rory noticed when tears rushed to my eyes despite my attempt to hide them.

"Oh, I'm sorry, T. I didn't mean to upset you. Forget what I said before. I was being thoughtless. You've already come to terms with letting the place go, and here I am..."

"No," I interrupted. "It's okay. You didn't upset me. I just never imagined I'd be given a choice in the matter. Keeping the resort, it means so much..." Then I did cry. Sobbed right there in front of him despite my resolve to never do so again. Before I knew it, he'd come around the table, knelt, and gathered me in his arms. Even passed me a few napkins that were always kept in a cute little tray on the table. It took me several mortifying moments to compose myself. Finally, I pulled away, and he gave me a quick squeeze and kissed the top of my head like I was a child. Then he returned to his seat and tucked into his omelet like nothing had happened.

"Sorry," I began, seeing the dampness of my tears on his blue shirt.

He shook his head. "Nope, no apologies. We both knew this was gonna be a hard week."

"I... I'm overwhelmed by the gift of this choice I have now."

He smiled, and I felt guilty for spying on him last night and for having those terrible thoughts about him meeting with his lawyer to try and swindle me. And then, after hearing about my cash inheritance, my first thought had been about buying him out to get rid of him and about all the problems he was causing me by owning them.

Maybe I needed to stop and think for a moment. Think about why Aunt Agnes had left him the cabins in the first place. If I was being totally honest with myself, I knew I'd dumped a lot of my guilt on Rory. I'd blamed him as the reason I didn't visit my aunt so much and one of the main reasons I wanted to sell the resort. And his presence here did have something to do with it, but not as much as I'd made it out to be. After four years of heartbreak, hanging onto my anger proved harder to do. It'd been easier to blame Rory. Easier than owning the fact that I was putting my business first. Putting it before my family. And though it was true I needed more capital, I'd been running my business on a shoestring budget and doing all right for myself. I hadn't really needed to sell the resort. But the fact had also been true that I would have been torn between trying to run two businesses. And though I could have hired someone eventually to run the resort, it was easier to play the martyr, to blame Rory, and walk away.

But why had my aunt left him the cabins?

Had she been trying to send me a message?

"I think you need to figure out what's in your heart," Rory said. "If you want to keep this place, and you can afford to, then do it. If that's what makes you happy. If you choose to sell, then I'll be sad, but I'll understand. You also don't have to make up your mind right away. You can wait, take the summer off to decide, or a month, or a year."

"I don't know what to do," I admitted. I know I didn't want to suddenly ask him if he wanted to sell his cabins to me. Not when he'd been so kind. I did still intend to ask him, but I'd have to wait for the right time. If I kept the resort, the problems I faced with him owning two of the cabins would complicate things. Did I want that bother now? I needed to think. But sitting across from him wasn't helping matters. I wanted to be alone. And I wanted to call Jehrel. He'd know what to do.

I needed time. At least now I had that luxury.

After we finished eating, I bid Rory goodbye with a promise to give the matter some thought. Then, instead of being alone or calling Jehrel, I decided to go into town. It had been a long while since I'd done so. When Jehrel and I ventured there, it had always been a mission in stealth. The chance of running into Rory had been great, considering the shopping vicinity consisted of a few street blocks placed strategically and aesthetically around a large park. Hadleigh Park was the crown jewel of the town. Roughly two acres of grassland with winding pathways around huge oak and willow trees. Park benches and a few picnic tables dotted the area. Growing up, I attended many festivals there. The town of Hadleigh enjoyed a good get-together, and every few months, there was an annual event to celebrate. There'd also been several wedding receptions hosted there over the years since the charming white-sided town Chapel — the one I'd hoped to be married in — was just across the street.

My drive to town was uneventful. Any remnants of the chaos left by the storm had been cleared from the roads. There wasn't anything specific I required, so I parked my car on one of the side streets and headed over to the park. Strolling slowly, I allowed myself time to reminisce and enjoy the mild, sunny day. So much of my life had consisted of being here, endless memories of happier times.

And some not so happy.

I made a mental note to drive over to the cemetery on the outskirts of town and pay my respects to my aunt and uncle.

Now that I could explore the area at leisure, I noticed a couple of storefronts were different, like the bait and tackle store, which I recalled had moved to a larger location a year ago. A flower shop now occupied the space. There'd been a hardware store which had shut down and sitting empty the last time I'd been in town. Now, it appeared to have a new owner. Once I was close enough, I could read the sign, Let's Thrift Again~Antiques. *Cute.*

The urge to look around the shop was overwhelming. It helped that I now had a boatload of cash practically burning a hole in my pocket. Or at least, I would soon.

Then I felt guilty rejoicing over the money, considering it was inherited.

Out of the blue, my aunt's voice sounded in my head. *Thea, we love you, and we want you to be happy. Besides, we can't take it with us.* The ghost of her laughter washed over me. I froze, then peered around the park. Briskly, I crossed the street and entered the shop. An old-fashioned doorbell jangled, alerting my arrival.

A woman bent over a box on the floor and called out, "Hello," sparing me a smile and glance over her shoulder.

"Hi."

She stood up and turned around, brushing her hands down the front of her pants despite having a tattered apron on over her clothes. She looked to be in her mid-twenties, close to my age. Her blond hair was done up in a messy bun, and several strands lay damp on her face, showing she'd been hard at work. By the look of the half-empty shelves and display cabinets, I assumed she was still getting settled in.

"My name's Cassidy, I'm the owner. Is there anything I can help you with?"

She didn't extend her hand, probably due to the grime on it, so I refrained from the gesture as well. "Hi, I'm Thea. I'd just like to look around if that's okay?" Was it completely vain of me to think she might possibly recognize me from my video?

One day, I vowed.

She nodded once. "Sure. As you can see, I'm only about three-quarters unpacked, but the boxes are labeled, and most have been sorted into clusters of similar items, or at least by dates. If there's anything specific you're looking for, let me know."

"Okay, thanks." There didn't appear to be anyone else in the shop besides us. The building was two stories, and I knew there were a pair of apartments on the second floor the previous owner had rented out, I believe, even after the storefront was vacant. When I got to the back of the store, I saw a propped open door with a hall area and staircase beyond it. There was a sign on the wall by the door that said *More Items Upstairs*. Curious and slightly nosy, I peered around and didn't see any sign of Cassidy. I figured she was still busy unpacking. Since the sign clearly stated the store continued upstairs, I decided to look. In the hall area beyond the door and the stairs, I saw an exit leading to the parking lot out back. Occupants of the apartments could park their vehicles and then enter through the backway, bypassing the store. I noticed the stairway headed up and another one that led downward as well. There was no sign saying more stuff was below, so I opted not to descend despite my interest being piqued. I'd had no idea there was a basement under this store, but I supposed it made sense in terms of storage space.

At the top of the stairs was a hallway and four doors. The first door on my left was the only one open, so I stuck my head in there. More piles of boxes, some open and half-unpacked, sat on floors and tables. There were also items packed onto shelves and display cabinets, same as below. Toward the back of the room, I spied larger pieces of furniture, so I ventured in. It appeared I was in one of the apartments, now obviously vacant. It was small. A little kitchen area and what appeared to be a pair of bedrooms and a bathroom were situated off an alcove. What had been the living room now hosted the store overflow. I passed a table with an old rotary dial phone and a pair of antique typewriters. Sitting in the middle of the table was a Sony Walkman straight out of the eighties, complete with headphones. I picked it up and held onto it, knowing how hard they were to find. As a bonus, I found a Bon Jovi cassette tape still in it. Nothing appeared to have price tags. I'd have to ask Cassidy, careful not to appear too interested, of course. The penny pincher in me would be ever-present.

My phone started playing YMCA, so I pulled it out of my back pocket. "Hey."

"Hey, yourself," Jehrel replied. "Whatcha doing?"

"I'm thrifting and totally holding an '80s Walkman in my hands right now."

"Oh! You're in town? And you have a Walkman? Stellar day! How'd it go with your lawyer?"

"He's not my… Never mind. You are not going to believe it." I slunk toward the doorway, making sure Cassidy wasn't on her way up. It would kill any bargaining power I had if she overheard me saying I'd just inherited half a mil. The coast was clear.

"So, it appears there was also some money included in my inheritance."

He inhaled loudly. "Really? Do tell."

"Um, five big ones."

"I thought you only got three. Whatshisface got the other two."

"Wow, you're hot today," I informed him.

"Okay, all joking aside, what exactly does that amount to? Fifty-K?"

"Um, no. More like five hundred K." I pulled the phone away from my ear, bracing for the scream I knew was coming. I wasn't disappointed.

When he quieted down a bit, I put the phone back to my ear. I could hear gasping sounds. "Breathe," I urged.

Very quietly, I heard him hiss, "You got half a million dollars!" And then more loudly, causing me to arm-length the phone again, "and I had to WAIT TO FIND OUT? You went

SHOPPING INSTEAD OF CALLING ME?"

When silence reined, I moved it back to my ear. "I'm sorry. I had to process. You know I process by thrifting. Do you have any idea what this means?"

He ignored my question, rushing on with, "Did you tell *him*?"

"Ah, he was there right after the lawyer left." I was never going to hear the end of this. "But, I didn't tell him how much." Hopefully, that tidbit would deescalate any fits.

Silence.

"Rory said something which made me think. He asked if I wanted to rent out my cabins for the summer. You know, since I could maybe afford to now. He said he could run the resort for me if I liked. And that maybe I might reconsider selling. I... I have this beautiful, amazing gift from my aunt and uncle." I had to stop. There was suddenly a lump in my throat. While I talked, I strolled back through the room, eyeing the wares. Jehrel remained silent, but I soon heard sniffling.

"Are you crying?" I asked.

"I can't help it," he snapped. "It's all so beautiful."

I put the Walkman down on an end table so I could run my fingers over a portable record player from the '70s.

"What... do you think you'll do?" he asked with a hiccup.

I shrugged even though he couldn't see me. "Dunno. Take some time, I guess. Figure out what to do. It's not every day you're handed half a million dollars."

A gasp sounded, which hadn't come from over the phone. I looked to my right and saw Cassidy standing there. *Great*. So much for my bargaining power.

Chapter 10

"Oh, hey," Cassidy said.

"Lemme call you back," I said into the phone and hung up. "Hey," I said to Cassidy.

"Soooo, find anything you like?" The look on her face spoke volumes.

"Yes, actually, although there's no prices on stuff."

"Yeah, still need to get around to that. Need to finish unpacking, too. Technically, I shouldn't even be open right now."

Seeing the Walkman, I picked it back up, careful not to hold it in a death grip. "What's something like this worth?" *Did that sound casual enough?*

"Hmm." She appeared to give it careful consideration.

"There's still a Bon Jovi tape in it," I confessed.

"Oh, well, that changes things." She laughed when she saw what I'm sure was terror on my face.

"How's thirty bucks sound?" she asked.

It was in mint condition. She easily could have gotten double. "I'll take it," I said a little too loudly, not even bothering to haggle.

"Great. Is there anything else you need a price on while I'm up here? Or do you want to keep looking around?" She looked torn. Wanting to make sales, but also wanting to continue setting up.

"I think this will do it. I'll be back, though," I promised. "I'm not sure when since I don't know how long I'll be staying in the area."

"Ah, I didn't think I recognized you." She headed in the direction of the door, and I followed. "So what brings you to town?" She tossed the question over her shoulder as she went downstairs.

"Tying up some loose ends," I offered vaguely. At the bottom of the stairs, she paused to wait for me. "Never knew there were basements in this row of stores." Maybe she'd indulge my curiosity and give me a tour? My hopes were dashed when she shrugged and went through the doorway leading to the main floor of the store.

"Haven't been down there yet, believe it or not." She crossed the room and went around the counter to where she'd set up the check-out area. Then she reached under the counter to pull out a large black book.

I relinquished the Walkman, placing it on the counter. She ran her finger down a handwritten list of what I assumed was inventory, made a checkmark, and jotted down the price beside one of the items.

Eying the list, I commented, "Wow, you're so organized."

She smiled. "I'm old school, I admit. I love technology, but if the power goes, I'd be out of luck without this. I do have everything listed online as well, but there's something about—"

"Seeing it in black and white," I interrupted, then chuckled. "I'm the same way."

She put the Walkman into a small paper bag with handles while I pulled out some cash and paid. "You run a business as well?"

"I do," I said. "Right up your alley. It's a retro-reno-design business. I put rooms and recently an entire house back the way they looked in the old days, depending on the owner's request."

"Really? That sounds so cool."

From the look on her face, I could tell she was confused.

Most people were when I told them what I did. Like Rory had been, thinking I restored old houses.

"My clients are usually Gen-Xers. They like the old shag carpet, and stereos, and paneling. Reminds them of their childhood," I clarified.

"And Walkmans," she said.

"Yes. Definitely Walkmans." I held fast to the bag, worried she might change her mind on the price.

"That idea is amazing," she said. "I've never heard anything like it."

"Thanks, I was going for originality. I named it You Can Go Home Again."

She mouthed the name, testing it out. "I love it."

"Thanks. I love the name of this place. So original." I didn't feel like she was only humoring me to make future sales. We were almost kindred spirits in a way, considering our choice of livelihoods.

"Oh, thanks. Although," she said in a conspirative tone. "I have to warn you. If you're looking for new clientele here, most of the home décor I've seen is already in the past."

We both laughed.

"Hey," she said, looking at her watch. "How about going for a coffee, maybe a bite to eat? I could use a break. If you're not in a hurry, I'd love to hear more about your business."

I checked my watch as well, noticing it was getting near lunchtime. After eating with Rory, I wasn't hungry, but coffee sounded great. "Okay, sure."

Cassidy shed her apron, locked up, and we strolled down the sidewalk. I let her lead since she seemed to know where she was going. I recalled there being a donut shop in town that also sold other desserts and coffee. They had a few tables set up inside and out for customers. If I remembered correctly, though, it was in the opposite direction.

She noticed me casting looks behind us. "A new place opened up a few months ago. It's great. A bookstore cafe. They sell teas and pastries as well."

"Sounds great. There are a few places like that in Toronto, where I live. I have a favorite near my apartment."

"Sometimes they have an author come in and read from their book. They've hosted book clubs as well."

"I've thought about writing a book sometimes. It'd probably require a lot of patience, which I'm sadly lacking."

"Me too — both writing a book and lacking patience. Plus, I don't know when I'd have the time." She stopped before a store. "This is it."

The sign read NovelTea. *Also cute.* I pulled open the door, and we went inside. There was a cozy vibe to the place. Pairs of chairs with small tables nearby were placed around the floor space. A set of two easy chairs by the fireplace looked especially inviting. Bookshelves lined two walls from floor to ceiling with a rolling ladder attached. A spiral metal staircase allowed access to a balcony with more shelves set against the back wall.

"Oh, this place." I was at a loss for words.

"I know, right?"

Even the floors oozed old-time charm with the wide plank hardwood and a smattering of vintage rugs.

A counter was set up, and behind it on the wall were chalkboards with menu listings written in different colors. Jars sat upon a shelf displaying an array of flavored teas.

"Hi, what'll it be?" asked the girl behind the counter.

"Are you the owner?" I asked. She looked to be in her early thirties, petite, brown hair in a neat French braid down her back.

"Yes, I'm Genie." She had a friendly smile.

"I'm Thea, and this is Cassidy," I said.

Genie smiled. "I know Cassidy," she told me. "She haunts the place."

"Yep, that's me, the town ghost," Cassidy said.

"Ghosts aren't scared to go into creepy basements," I teased her. "Oh good, you have coffee. Can I have one of those cookies to go with it?" I pointed. "And I'll take the coffee black."

"Sure can. For here or to go?"

"We're staying," Cassidy said, giving me a narrow look for my earlier comment. "I'll have my regular."

Genie used tongs to snag a peanut butter chocolate chip cookie and slip it onto a china plate decorated with little blue flowers. She filled up a large ceramic mug with coffee and slid both items across the counter to me. When I went to grab some cash from my wallet, Cassidy was already handing over a twenty-dollar bill.

"It's on me," she said.

"Really? Thanks," I told her, feeling slightly guilty since it was probably one of the bills I'd given her for the Walkman.

While Genie made up Cassidy's order, I picked up mine and wandered over to the chairs by the fireplace. It wasn't lit, but I loved the cozy vibe. I remained standing in case Cassidy had a favorite spot, but she soon came up beside me and nodded at the chairs. We sat down, placing our orders on a little end table between us.

"So?" she asked and took a big bite of her cheese muffin.

"You were right, I love it."

She smirked and swallowed. "Thought you might."

"I'm surprised it's not packed."

She took another bite before responding to my comment. "It'll fill up. When they have an event, it's sometimes standing room only."

I raised an eyebrow, impressed.

"I'm not scared, you know," she said, turning her interest to her coffee.

Now, it was my turn to grin. "Oh, let me guess. You've

been too busy to go into the basement? If you want someone to hold your hand, I'm your girl."

She smiled and sipped from her mug. "Okay, you got me. I'm a little freaked out. It's just that... Oh, yeah, you're not in town much, right?"

"Not lately."

"Well," she looked around before she spoke. "Someone died down there." Her voice was low.

I paused mid-sip. "You're kidding."

"Nope. There used to be tenants upstairs."

"I figured. I knew there were apartments over the store."

She nodded. "Well, when I bought the building, only one apartment was rented out. A woman lived there. She was old and kind of feeble. Her name was Elaina. She'd been there a long time, apparently. I'd decided I would keep her on as a tenant if she wanted to stay. Anyway, the stairs had got to be too much for her, and she was going into a nursing home in town."

I knew the place. It was nice, backed onto the narrow river which wound through town.

"Well, one night, she came down the stairs and headed into the basement. The cops thought she got confused and started down there instead of going out the door into the parking lot. They found her dead at the bottom of the stairs."

"Oh, no. What a shame."

"It was. I didn't know her, but still, what a terrible way to go. And I feel bad even saying it, but it delayed things a bit with me taking possession. You know, with the investigation involved and all that."

"Yeah." I knew all about delays. "Though, why does an elderly woman falling down the stairs need to be investigated?"

"Well, apparently, the way they found her was suspicious. Like she hadn't just fallen. They suspected she'd been pushed."

"Pushed! Really? How terrible. Who would do such a

thing?"

She shrugged. "Hence, the investigation."

"So what happened? I mean, you took possession, so they must have solved the mystery?"

She made a face. "No. It's still ongoing."

"Wow. I hope you changed all the locks and stuff?" That made me think about Rory and how he had a key to my aunt's — *my* place. He was a cop. Well, he used to be a cop. I wondered if he knew anything about what had happened.

"Yes, of course. I mean, there could be a killer out there wandering around town." She visibly shivered.

"But I doubt they're hiding out in your basement," I said teasingly.

She narrowed her gaze at me. "Thanks a lot. Makes me nervous enough worrying about ghosts, never mind thinking the killer is lurking around down there. Especially when I'm trying to sleep upstairs."

Ah, that explained what was happening with the other apartment. It made perfect sense for Cassidy to live on-site. I laughed at the face she was making. "I meant what I said. I'll go down there with you and check it out. When we leave here even, if you like."

"Why do I have a feeling this is about more than you just wanting to help me get over my squeamish-ness?"

"Okay, you got me," I admitted. "I'd love to see what's down there. You must be curious?"

She sipped her coffee. "I guess. I've been so busy unpacking I haven't really thought about it. I assume it's empty."

"Oh, well, we can leave it for another day, then?" As much as I wanted to go exploring, I still wanted to head out to the cemetery, and I was also anxious to get back to the resort. There was so much to do and to think about.

"Give me your number," she said, pulling out her cell

phone. "I'll call you when I'm ready to go down there. If you'll still be around, that is?"

Now, it was my turn to make a face. "Yes, I'll be around for a while. Longer than I expected." I got my phone out, and we swapped them so we could enter our contact information, then switched back. "Cassidy Daniels. Nice to meet you."

"You too, Thea James," she said.

I almost said, *my friends call me TJ*, but I refrained. The only person who ever really called me that was Rory. Over the years, he'd dropped the J and just kept the T.

"So, tell me all about your business. What made you come up with such an idea? Was it all the new series streaming which have scenes flashing back or set in the '70s and '80s?"

I finished off my cookie and sipped my coffee. Then, I settled in to talk about my favorite subject — my company.

Chapter 11

At the cemetery, I stood looking down at the graves set side by side. My aunt and uncle. Together in death as they were in life.

"I'm sorry, Aunt Agnes," I spoke quietly. "Sorry, I wasn't there in the end. If I'd known how sick you were, I never would have left. And please know I tried to make it to the funeral. Fate just seemed to have other plans for me. Although, I have a feeling you know all that now."

I paused and swallowed over the lump in my throat.

"I want to thank you both. For loving me and giving me a place to belong. For making me feel safe and being the family I needed. Thank you for all your guidance and patience over the years. For encouraging me to follow my dreams and make them a reality."

I took a deep breath and let it out slowly.

"And thank you for leaving me the resort. And the money. I wish... I wish you both were here so I could say goodbye in person. Hear your voices and hug you one last time." I felt a tear slip down my cheek, and as I wiped it away, I could almost hear Uncle Jimmy's chuckle and hear him say, *Now, now, little miss, what can I do to make it all better?*

"You can't this time," I whispered. And as much as I wanted to ask why they'd left Rory those pair of cabins, I didn't. Deep down, I felt I already knew why. Rory had been like a son to them. And those cabins had such special meaning to my aunt and uncle and to Rory. It had been the right thing to do, and I could no longer feel annoyed or inconvenienced by it.

I pressed my fingertips to my lips and blew on them lightly in the direction of the graves. "I'll visit again soon." I couldn't say goodbye.

Once behind the wheel of my car, I gave in to the tears. When they'd run dry, I used the scrunched-up napkins I grabbed from the glove compartment to blow my nose. This would be the last time, I vowed, I would allow myself to wallow in misery. Though I'd never felt more alone, I took strength in knowing my aunt and uncle would always be with me.

Shortly after, I pulled up in front of the main house at the resort. When I grabbed the bag with the Walkman, I smiled. It had been a good trip into town. I'd paid my respects to my aunt and uncle. I'd made a friend, possibly two. And discovered a pair of shops I could look forward to visiting again.

Inside, I put the bag on the counter and made up a pot of coffee. I had a feeling Rory would be back, no doubt hoping for an answer to his suggestion. Despite wanting to think things through, I hadn't had the chance to do so. Outside, mug in hand, I headed toward the lake. I took a seat at the end of the dock, setting my mug beside me. Pulling off my shoes and socks, I dangled my toes in the water.

As I knew he would, Rory found me about fifteen minutes later.

Just like when we were kids, he plunked down beside me and soon had his feet dangling in the water, too.

"Sooo," he began.

"How much do you want for your cabins?" I cut to the chase. Having some time to think, I figured the easiest and fastest way to solve the issues I faced would be to buy back the cabins. Doing so, the way would be clear to either sell the resort or hang onto it and rent it out.

"What? I don't—"

"No, listen," I cut him off to forestall an argument. "I know you don't want to sell, but honestly, to me, it makes more sense to sell the resort as a complete package or to rent it out like you suggested." I took a breath and charged on before he could get a word in. "And, if I decide not to sell, and you're still interested in overseeing the rentals, then the job is yours. You could live in the main house. For free, of course." I figured that was more than generous.

He was stunned into silence.

"I know it's a lot to think about. Just take some time, but not too much, please, and get back to me." It felt good putting some heavy decisions on him. Like I'd lightened my burden.

"T, I don't need time to think. What you're offering is very generous, but—"

"But?" I didn't like where this was headed.

He stared into my eyes, and I could see he was confused and maybe a little hurt. "When your aunt and uncle left me those cabins, I was so moved. Like, they got it. They knew what they meant to me. All those years growing up, coming here, it was a place I felt I belonged, you know?"

I feared I'd made a terrible mistake. "Rory, I'm sorry. I know what it was like for you. I was there. It was the same for me—in a way. Like this place was our salvation. It wasn't just a pair of cabins, though. It was the whole place. That's why I thought you could let them go. That if you stayed in the main house, it would be the same."

"But it isn't," we both said.

"To me," Rory said, "the cabins represent a turning point in my life. A time when I had nothing and no one. But then, like a lifeline, I finally found a place I belonged and a family who cared about me. Owning them, it's like… coming full circle, you know? All the sad stuff from my past—I haven't buried it. I've reconciled it. Laid it to rest. Finally."

I nodded, knowing exactly what he meant. I'd felt the same when I'd done that last job, a total renovation. As though achieving my dream had been worth all the sacrifices I'd made.

"Okay, then," I said. "We'll figure it out. All the legalities, the severance, the right-away stuff."

"You're not upset? I know it's a hassle for you."

"It's okay. I shouldn't have asked," I assured him. "Come to think of it, there's an idea I've been tossing around. You making those changes to your cabins got me considering it."

"You want to upgrade your cabins with backup power? I could do that."

"I'm thinking about doing more than power upgrades. I was tossing around the idea of remodeling each cabin in an era theme. A '50s, '70s, and '80s style. That way, I could have functioning showpieces for my company. I'd have them photographed and featured on my website. People renting out the cabins could experience an era of their choice. Maybe it would drum up some clients for me or at least make people aware of what I do."

Rory appeared to mull over the idea. "I like it," he said. "And you can write off the cost of the renovations as a business expense. It's a great way to advertise your business while still earning income from the rentals."

I was impressed with his comments. "You've got a good head for business."

He flushed a little at my compliment and smiled. "Thanks. Since I've been trying to get my own thing going, I've learned a lot."

"Oh, you're starting up a company? Is that why you left the force?" When he bristled, I knew I'd pried too much.

He turned his gaze away and pulled his feet from the water. "I thought I wanted to be a cop, and it was a good job until it wasn't. I wanted to do something else." He spoke while putting his socks on. Since his feet were still damp, he struggled a bit.

"It's okay. You don't owe me any explanations." I appeared to be asking him all the wrong questions today. I pulled up my feet, resting them on the dock for the warm sun to dry.

After tugging on his shoes, he got up and looked at me. The expression on his face seemed to imply he wanted to explain his actions. Maybe even explain why he broke my heart four years ago. Then, the moment passed.

Turning my gaze away, I stared out across the lake. In the distance, I made out a few canoes, and closer to shore were a pair of loons. Summer season would soon be in full swing. If I wanted to rent out the cabins, it might not be a good idea to begin renovations right away. At least not on all the cabins. It appeared I'd concluded I was keeping the resort for now. I reached for my socks and tugged them on, followed by my shoes.

"When do you think you would like to start renovations?" It was as if he'd read my mind.

"Since we're at the end of June, things will get busy at the lake fast. I think I'll reach out to some of the people who emailed the website inquiring about renting this summer. I could rent out two cabins and start work on one. How does that sound?" He reached out his hand and helped me to my feet. I bent and grabbed my empty mug.

"Good. And I could rent out one of my cabins as well to make up for the loss of one of yours," he suggested.

I stopped myself in time from blurting out it would hardly make up for the loss, considering the revenue of that one cabin would be his. I didn't want to be petty. Especially when I remembered the large sum of money I'd inherited.

"It's a good idea," I said instead. "So what is it you're doing now?" If it took up too much of his time, he might not be able to oversee the resort. Although he'd been the one to suggest it.

"Oh, it's nowhere near the scale of what you do," he assured me. "But I started doing power upgrades to homes and cottages. I have a website, and I showcase the pair of cabins I did—that's how I know you can write this stuff off. I've got a great accountant."

"Oh, is that who you had over last night?" I asked and then almost bit my tongue off.

He looked at me a moment, that one eye of his so squinty it almost shut. "No, that was, um, my lawyer."

So, I had been right.

"Your lawyer?"

"Um, yeah. You know, for business stuff." he then got fidgety and wouldn't make eye contact.

Yeah, sure.

I laughed uneasily, trying to lighten the sudden tension in the air. "It's okay if you were seeing your lawyer about the cabins," I assured him.

He did look at me then. "Honestly, T, it wasn't about that."

"Okay." I waited for him to elaborate. When he didn't, I began walking back toward the house. He fell into step beside me.

"Oh, I was in town talking to the antique shop owner, Cassidy. She bought the old hardware store. She said something about an elderly woman falling down the stairs."

"Oh?"

"Yes, the police were investigating because they'd suspected she'd been pushed." I watched his expression to see how he reacted.

"Hmm," he grunted, his face remaining blank.

"Cassidy said there was a delay in taking possession of the property due to the investigation. Of course, she felt terrible for the woman—Elaina. She's also kind of freaked out to go into the basement of the place."

"Why's that?"

"It was never solved. Murderer still on the loose."

"Oh," he repeated.

We were close to the back door, and Rory stopped walking when I started over to the house. He probably hoped for an invitation to come in. If I wanted to learn more of the story, I suspected I'd have to comply.

"Do you want to come inside? We can talk about our plans for summer?" Since I no longer had to worry about taking inventory and preparing to sell, the summer suddenly loomed before me, filled with possibilities. Of course, there were still the legalities of Rory's cabins to deal with. The weight of that no longer overwhelmed me. Rory, nodding at my offer, followed me inside. We went into the kitchen, and he sat down while I put my mug in the sink and opened the fridge.

"I can make lemonade?" I recalled seeing a few cans of frozen concentrate juice among the groceries.

"Sure," he said.

While I grabbed a pitcher and began making the juice, I casually continued with the topic of Elaina. "Oh, I was telling you about the woman who fell and how the police suspect it was murder." When he remained silent, I continued. "It was months ago, and I guess you'd left the force by then, so you probably don't know anything about it?"

When I looked over at him, he shrugged. "I may have heard some talk about it around town," he replied noncommittedly.

"Yes, people talk. Especially in small towns. And a murder must have got a lot of attention." I stirred the juice and then pulled out a couple of glasses. I poured the lemonade, and took both glasses to the table, and sat down. He still hadn't commented.

"You still have friends on the force you talk to?" I tried to sound casual.

He shrugged. "They're not allowed to comment on an

ongoing investigation."

"It's kind of a cold case now, apparently. Cassidy has moved in."

"The woman who's afraid to go into the basement?"

"Yes. I offered to go with her."

That earned me a snort from him. "Cause you're so brave."

I took a few swallows of my drink to cool my temper, then made a face. "Ugh, too much water."

"It's fine," he assured me after taking a swallow of his. "So why are you so interested? Just because your friend is spooked?"

I took another sip and made another face. "Yeah, I suppose. I feel bad they haven't caught whoever did it. And to think there could be a murderer wandering around —"

"Sorry, I don't know anything," Rory interrupted.

"Okay," I relented. "I'm going to grab my laptop from upstairs so I can get in touch with renters."

"Good idea," he said, smiling. Whether he was relieved I was letting go of the whole murder mystery thing or because I had decided to move ahead with rentals, I'd no idea. I got up and put my glass in the sink, opting not to finish it.

"Back in a sec," I said, and left the room. When I was halfway back downstairs, I heard Rory's cell ring. Silently, laptop in my grasp, I waited on the steps to eavesdrop. Maybe it was his lawyer? Or his girlfriend? I'm not sure why I cared if he did have a girlfriend. It wasn't any of my business. It wasn't like he'd asked me to rekindle things. Not that I would, anyway. And what was up with him and his lawyer? What had been so important he'd had to come by after dark? Rory said it had nothing to do with the cabins, so maybe it was about his business? But I had a business as well, and I didn't need a lawyer for that. Straining my ears, I snuck down another couple of steps since his voice had dropped low. If he hadn't been so shifty when I'd asked certain questions, I wouldn't have to resort to such lengths to gain information.

"I thought I signed everything last night," Rory said.

After he paused, I assumed to listen, he continued. "Why does that matter? Yes, it has only been a few months, but I've been busy with clients. Do I need to supply the judge with names and phone numbers?" His voice had grown louder and agitated.

"Yeah, I know," he said with a sigh. "Okay, let me get back to you."

When all remained silent for a few moments, I snuck back upstairs and called down, "Hey, was that my phone I heard?"

"No, mine," he called back.

"K. Thanks." I had left my cell downstairs so my question would seem legit to him. When I returned to the kitchen, he had one hand clenched around his glass and was staring off into space.

"Everything okay?"

He shook his head to break the spell. "Yeah. Fine."

Reclaiming my seat, I itched to ask him why he'd demanded to know if he had to supply a judge with his client list. He'd said it sarcastically, but why say it at all? Was he in trouble? Is that why he'd left the force? Had it been what his meeting with his lawyer was about?

So many secrets. And despite my offer to him to run the resort and stay here, in this house, I was suddenly uncertain. Years ago, he'd acted completely out of character, tossing away our long-made plans and our engagement as though they were nothing. His betrayal had been so cold and shocking it had made me wonder if I'd ever known him at all. Of all the years I'd known him, we'd spent only the summer months together, except the odd long weekend or holiday. The other ten months of those years, he could have been a completely different person.

The past four years, we'd been estranged. Maybe he had secretly married and was getting a divorce? Perhaps he'd had to prove his income to make alimony payments. Maybe he'd left a steady-paying job out of spite?

"Are you going to check the website?" Rory's question made me realize I was now the one staring off into space.

"Yeah, right." I set the laptop down on the table and got it started. It took a while to get online and to the site. "Slow internet," I muttered.

"That's something else I could probably help with."

The website came up, and I logged in to see the messages I'd received and responded to already. There were four new ones, but I thought it best to go back to the oldest requests and start with those.

"Weekly rentals should be prioritized over weekends and single nights," I said.

Rory nodded in agreement.

"Oh, here, the Tallmons. They're repeat renters the past few years." I'd set up the site to highlight guests who were frequent flyers—as Aunt Agnes liked to call them. There was a page as well where notes could be logged about guests. Things like very neat, forgetful packers, enjoys the water, loses things, never around, always around, loud, quiet, friendly, too friendly, and so on. It helped when deciding when and where to place guests. It wouldn't do at all to have Mr. Cole, the quiet, always-around writer, next to the cabin with The Tallmons, a rowdy, super friendly, busy family of five. Aunt Agnes said it was all about balance and harmony, so everyone's experience here was a good one.

"Since we're only renting two of my cabins and one of yours, it's going to tighten the list of who we can take on." Seeing Rory make his apology face again, I rushed to add, "It's fine, though. Considering this is the first time for both of us having a go at running a resort. It'll be good to take things slow and easy."

"Oh," Rory said.

"What?"

He looked embarrassed suddenly. "Are you going to help with the resort as well?"

"Wait, you're right, I'm going to be too busy doing renos on the cabin—I think I'll choose the one at the far end, beside Crown land—so you'll be on your own, for the most part. I'll help whenever and wherever I can. I can give you access to the resort website as well." *First, I have to change the password.*

He seemed relieved. Maybe he *was* supporting an ex-wife and needed a second job?

"You know, my offer for you to move in here still stands. I mean, it's a big place, plenty of room for both of us, and I'll only be here until the renovations are done. In fact, I'll hardly be in the house at all. I'll mostly be down at the cabin, and if you like, I could just move all my stuff down there?" All the cabins were winterized, and usually, one or two of them were rented out quite regularly. Hadleigh offered a bunch of winter activities, such as snowshoeing, ice fishing, tobogganing, and skating, along with snowmobiling. Running the resort could easily be a year-round job.

"I don't want to push you out of here," Rory insisted. "I can just stay in my cabin."

"It's okay, I don't mind," I assured him. There was another reason I wanted him close. It wasn't because I wanted him back. I just didn't like these secrets between us. Something was going on with him, and if I was going to entrust him with my family's resort, I wanted to know what it was before I left town.

The fact that there'd been a murder in Hadleigh, and he was being all shifty, and had left the police force, and had a lawyer, and was talking about a judge, should have put me on edge. But it didn't.

Not really.

Maybe just a little.

Chapter 12

That night, I curled up before the fireplace with a big mug of soup for dinner. Rory and I had worked out most of the details of the summer rentals. Guests had been chosen, and emails sent. A young family anxious to secure a place had even sent a deposit. We had the rest of the week to air out the cabins, make sure everything was well-stocked, wash windows and bedding, shake out mats, and plump pillows. Rory would go over the boats and make sure the lifejackets, oars, anchors, fishing supplies, etc., were in good working order. The gardens needed to be weeded, the firepits raked, the picnic tables and outdoor chairs and tables wiped down, and the trees and brush around the shorelines trimmed. It suddenly felt like a million things to do with little time to do it. How had my aging aunt and uncle pulled this off every year? Although Rory and I had been there to help out many times in the past. We knew what needed doing and how to do it. We'd had good teachers.

After making lists of to-dos and details, we parted ways. He'd had something going on in town—didn't elaborate—and I'd opted to carry on with my pad of paper and pen in the library. The bulk of the work would be at my two cabins since Rory had already seen to his. Making it ready for guests, however, would take a bit more finesse. He'd been so kind as to cut the grass and keep the weeds at bay at the main house during my absence. Awkwardly, I thanked him for that. And although he'd waved off my appreciation, I felt slightly appeased, making it up to him with the offer of bedding and towels and whatever else he needed for his cabin.

Sipping my soup, I gazed into the fire I'd lit with little trouble. Despite the mild evening, the sight and sound of a fire comforted me. Through the screened windows, I could hear the hum of mosquitos and catch the scent of the lake carried in by the slight breeze. I felt closest to my uncle in this room. The dark wood, the hearth, the smell of the old books, the worn leather of the chair beneath me, I'd always associate with him. Whereas my aunt had been all about the kitchen. The bright colors, the old-fashioned appliances, the smells, and the tastes. Thinking of them didn't give my belly a pang this time. I had a feeling it had much to do with my decision to stay. No longer did I have to decide what to let go of. This time, my lists were a blessing, not a burden.

The Village People jolted me out of my reverie, and I made a dash to the kitchen to grab my phone. "Hey."

"Still waiting to hear back from you," Jehrel said with a huff, the sound of his fingernails drumming in the background.

I plunked down on the kitchen chair. "I know, I'm sorry."

His annoyance no doubt battled with his desire to know what was happening. "What did you decide?" he demanded, desire winning out.

"I may be here a bit longer," I eased into breaking the news.

"Why? Have you decided not to sell? Or is it because *whatshisface* is making things difficult?"

"Actually, I asked him to run the resort."

"YOU WHAT?!"

I had to pull the phone away from my ear from his outburst. "I decided to keep the place. But you know I'm not about to live here. I have a business to run and don't have time to run two of them."

"What'd he say?"

"He agreed. Actually, it was his idea to begin with since he knows I'm anxious to leave. I also asked him to sell me back the other two cabins, then I totally regretted it."

"How come?"

"He just reminded me of how much they mean to him."

Jehrel sighed. "So, if he's agreed to run the place, what happens with the cabins? You can only rent out your three, then?"

In the background, I could hear loud meowing. "I fed you!" Jehrel screeched. "All of you. Stop stalking me." A door slammed.

"Are you hiding in the bathroom?"

"I swear they're plotting my demise. They think I've done something to Alan, and they want revenge."

"He's coming back soon, right?"

"Not soon enough. They stare at me like I'm a giant tuna."

I knew he'd be looking in the mirror, making sure his expression displayed the correct amount of angst.

"Hey, I have an idea. When Alan gets home, why don't you see if his mom could watch the cats for a weekend or—*hint, hint*—longer, and you two can come here. Sooner rather than later."

"You want me to bring you more clothes." It wasn't a question.

"Bingo. You guys don't have to do any work. Just come out and enjoy the boats and the water, hang around town, see the sights."

"Get eaten alive. By something other than felines."

I snorted. "The bugs aren't that bad."

"You just say that because they don't love you. What is it with me being so delectable to everything?"

"Because you're fabulous." I could picture him preening before the bathroom mirror.

"You're just buttering me up."

Then I remembered Cassidy and the mystery. I made my voice low, "Oh, I have to tell you something,"

"What is it?" he attempted to lower his voice as well and failed.

"Oh, wait. Before I tell you that, I have to tell you—"

"Noooo. Tell me the juicy thing first," he insisted.

My turn to sigh. "Okay. Well, remember I told you about the new antique store in town?"

"The Walkman, yes."

"Well, the owner, Cassidy, is super nice, she and I went out for lunch. Actually, coffee. There's another new place in town. NovelTea. It's so great—"

"Get to the point! You're like a runaway freight train."

"Is that a crack about my caboose again?" When his response was only huffs, I continued. "So, Cassidy tells me she was delayed taking possession of the building. It's the old hardware store that has two upstairs apartments."

A heavy sigh.

"Apparently, an elderly woman lived upstairs. She was moving into a retirement home soon. She was found at the bottom of the basement stairs. Dead."

"Oh! How terrible. There's a basement in that place?"

"Yes. And why she was headed down there in the middle of the night is anyone's guess. But—wait for it—she didn't just fall down the stairs. She was pushed."

"No!"

"Yes! So, they opened up an investigation into it but never found out who did it. Cassidy's too afraid to go into the basement. I offered to go with—"

Now, he snorted. "Cause you're so brave."

"Have you been talking to Rory? Anyway, that's the mystery."

"Did you ask *him* about it? Like he is — *was* — a cop."

"I did. And he denies knowing anything. He was real shifty about it, too. But, before I get into that more, I want to tell you what else I planned to do." I took his silence as an invitation to continue.

"I want to renovate each of my cabins in an era. Of course, since I'm renting them out, I can only work on one this summer. I'm thinking of starting with the cabin beside Crown Land, doing it up '50s style. I'll rent my other two cabins out for now, but then when the first one's done, I'll start to work on the next era. I'm thinking about doing a '60s and '70s, or maybe an '80s. I haven't decided yet. Oh, and Rory said to make up for the loss of one of my cabins, he can rent out one of his. But also — get this — I offered him the option to stay here at the main house so he could rent out both of his cabins." I dropped my voice another octave. "I think he needs money or something. I overheard him on the phone…"

"Wait! Stop. Stop the train!"

"What? Am I going too fast? I can't help it. There's so much I still need to tell you."

"Let me process this for a second." The line was quiet for a moment, only broken up by intermittent sounds of his deep breathing, muffled meows, and hissing — Jehrel's.

"Is Rory going to move into the house with you?" he finally asked.

"No, he declined."

"Oh. Okay. So, if you're planning on doing all these renovations, I take it you're not staying for just a week or so?" was his next question.

"Um… I've been so caught up with making plans I haven't really thought about it. But, yeah, now that you mention it, I might be gone a while longer," I admitted.

"How much longer?"

I shrugged even though he couldn't see me. "Dunno. I

don't have anything else on the go at the moment. All the inquiries I got for estimates after I released my reveal video are set for fall. Summer's kind of dead for renos, I guess, since everyone wants to get away. And judging by the number of emails we had for rentals, I can totally see that. And as for doing up that cabin, Cassidy has some great stuff, from what I've seen. Not to mention all the stuff here in the attic. I don't think getting what I need will be a problem. Oh!"

"What?"

"I wonder if I should get those guys up here and tape the actual reno *and* the reveal since our last video — *my* only video — seemed to do pretty good. Thanks for your reviews, by the way. I haven't checked the status of it lately, though..."

"You're crushing it," Jehrel admitted.

"Really?" I gushed.

"You know it, girl." I could practically hear his eyes roll, but I was thrilled. "I hate to burst your bubble, but a bunch of comments are about the film crew."

"Really?" I repeated. "But they're not even on there. They're behind the cameras." I tried to recall when they'd been in any of the video but failed.

"It's because they also shared the link on their site — they're quite popular, you know."

"Huh."

"Well, it's probably a good idea," Jehrel admitted. "And it might not be a bad idea to have someone else at that resort with you."

"What do you mean?" I had a feeling I knew where this was heading.

"You know exactly what I mean." He tried to lower his voice and again failed. "Since Rory could be a murderer!"

"He is not! That's not what I was implying," I insisted.

"You said he was being shifty and did not elaborate, which

makes my mind go to all kinds of places."

"Well, reel it back in! I simply questioned him about the investigation, and he denied knowing anything and changed the subject."

"He's the killer!"

"Don't be ridiculous. The only thing Rory's killed up here are mosquitos. And possibly a few fish over the years. Although..."

"Yesssss?"

"I overheard him on the phone with his lawyer. And he did admit to me it was his lawyer who'd been here last night, but he said it wasn't to do with the cabins."

"So what did it have to do with? Keeping him out of jail for *Murder*?"

"Knock it off. You just want me to invite the camera dudes up here so when you arrive, you'll have something else to look at besides Alan. Don't deny you were stalking their page," I said.

"Don't try to make this about me."

"Anyway, I overheard Rory on the phone, and he was talking about having to supply a client list for a judge."

"Client list? JUDGE?!"

"Yes." I pulled the phone away from my ear again. "Apparently, he started his own business since leaving the force—he didn't get into why he left. The only reason I can think of why he'd have to supply a client list for a judge is to see how well his business is doing. Maybe he's in the middle of a divorce? Maybe he has to pay alimony?"

"Oh! That does make sense. Not as exciting as him being a murderer, but still..."

"If you call him a murderer when you're here, so help me..."

"Don't get your panties in a bunch. I won't."

"Good. And don't pass your theories around to anyone

else up here either."

"I won't," he promised.

"Good." I got up and wandered back into the library to settle down in front of the fire again.

"Soooo."

"What?"

"Are you spending another night in that big 'ol house all by your lonesome again?"

I sighed. "Yes. Don't start."

"You're the one..."

"I know! But I don't want to talk about it, okay?" Sometimes, I regretted telling him everything.

"Okay. Let's talk about what you're going to do with all that money you inherited. I think we should start with a new wardrobe. Although, we'll have to shop when you get home. I can just imagine what kind of fashion is going on in that small town."

"Don't be a snob."

"Oh, darling. I don't think even Toronto will be the place we need—"

"I'm not taking you to Paris," I interrupted.

"But, just think about the fabrics and the styles—"

"No way. Just put it out of your head. I'm using this money wisely. I'll probably invest most of it—"

"Oh! I don't even know who you are anymore. I better go. The cats are quiet, and I can just imagine what they're doing."

I laughed, picturing the look on his face. "Okay. Think about what I said. Come here as soon as you can. And bring Alan. And more clothes."

"All right. As soon as I can," he promised.

We said goodnight, and I put my phone aside and reached for my soup. It'd gone cold. Now, all I could think about was spending another night alone in this big house.

And — thanks to Jehrel — wondering if the guy I'd known most of my life was a murderer.

Chapter 13

Rory sat across the table from an attractive older woman at NovelTea. Erika had suggested they meet there to talk about options over coffee. Genie came by their table and topped up his mug.

"Sign out front says there's something going on here next weekend?" Rory said.

Genie smiled. "Yes. I put the sign out this afternoon to give a fair warning. There's a movie crew coming to town in the middle of the week. Someone was here about three weeks ago scouting out filming locations. They called today and confirmed. I have to shut the place down from Friday night till Monday morning so they can set up, shoot their scene, and then tear down the set. It's a lot of work — for them. I just need to be on-site, being the owner of the building, for insurance purposes, apparently. At least what they're paying is generous, so I won't take a hit on sales."

"Sounds exciting," Erika said. "Any stars in it we might know?"

Genie shrugged. "Not sure. The movie is one of those small-town romance films with a bit of mystery, I believe. The scout didn't elaborate on the details. I got the impression they like to keep things hush-hush, considering it's the start of the season, and they don't want a crowd forming."

"Think they'll block off the street?" Rory asked, his mind already three steps ahead of what needed to be done for crowd control and setting up a perimeter.

"Not sure. I think they're filming in the park, too." She indicated Erika's empty mug. "Did you want another latte?"

Erika shook her head and began putting her papers into her case. "No, thanks. We're wrapping up here."

"I'm gonna hang around for a bit," Rory said to Genie.

"Sure, no problem," Genie replied and walked over to another table.

Erika gave Rory a hard look before she rose to leave. "Remember what I said. Your intentions are great, and you have a good chance of making this a reality. But what you plan to take on is a life-long responsibility. It's not going to be easy."

Rory's grip on his mug tightened. "None of this has been easy," he replied. "But nothing is going to change my mind."

Erika gave him a tight-lipped smile. "Okay, I'll get these to the judge and see what happens. For the record, I'm rooting for you."

Rory's smile was guarded. "I appreciate it."

Erika left, leaving Rory to contemplate their meeting.

He closed his eyes tight for a moment, then opened them when he heard a woman's laughter across the room. Finally, he thought, things were coming together. Maybe once Gavin was settled in, he could put the past behind him and start looking toward the future. It was going to be difficult, especially now that Thea had decided to stay. Despite the obstacle her being here presented, he wouldn't let it deter him from his course. It'd taken years to right a terrible wrong. Maybe once he had achieved his goal, he could finally let go of his guilt. His burden had been a heavy weight to bear. Not only because of Gavin but also because of what he'd been forced to do to Thea. Breaking her heart had not been a single tragedy. He'd broken his heart as well in the process. But having her here again had awakened all the memories and the longing he felt. Their future had been so bright, so filled with promise.

Until that terrible night.

For weeks, he hadn't been able to get the sounds out of his head. The yelling, the breaking glass, the gunshot. It all happened so fast. He'd been a rookie cop, not experienced enough to assess the situation, and had charged in thinking he could handle things. There were so many what-ifs afterward. What if he'd called for back-up? What if he'd waited for his partner Glen to realize what was happening inside the store he was in? What if he hadn't pulled his weapon? Would he be the one who was dead now? Or Glen?

He'd been acquitted of any wrongdoing in the internal investigation, but the impact of his actions had been far-reaching. Lives had been irreparably changed. Not just his. The man—Darren—who'd held up the store at gunpoint and ultimately been shot and killed by Rory, had a family in Hadleigh. A mother and a son. Gavin was only two years old at the time. Darren's mother had seemed older than her sixty years from endless worry and regret caused by her son's bad decisions. Rory had gone to them and broken the news of Darren's death, feeling it was his obligation. When he'd seen the older woman—aged even more so by the news he delivered—hug her grandson tight, he'd known he couldn't just walk away. Despite his plans with Thea, he had to make things right. He'd known all too well how life could be with no father and an uncertain home life. He wouldn't allow the past to repeat itself with Gavin.

Knowing what he had to do—though he hated himself even more for it—he'd broken things off with Thea. Over the next few years, he'd been a big brother to Gavin, becoming the father figure he'd taken from him. He'd also helped Gavin's grandmother around the apartment, completing small jobs that Darren had never gotten around to doing. He'd helped financially whenever and wherever he could. And just as Rory had been like an extended family member to Aunt Anges and Uncle Jimmy, he became an extension of Gavin's family, too.

When Gavin's grandmother's health took a turn, and her infirmity had forced her to give up the child, Rory had gone to Hadleigh's social services department to inquire about formally adopting him. Erika, Gavin's case worker, had suggested Rory find a different job to increase his chances. The twelve-hour shifts he worked at a dangerous occupation and the fact that he would be a single dad would present challenges. Rory had given his notice to the force the following week. Then, he'd started up a business doing power upgrades to homes and cottages in the area. A week before Elaina Caddel, Gavin's grandmother, had been set to move into a retirement home, she was found dead at the bottom of a staircase. Why anyone would want to push a frail old woman down the stairs was beyond Rory's comprehension. Gavin had taken the loss hard. Rory had grown close to Elaina over the years, and together, he and Gavin had mourned the loss.

When Thea had questioned him about Elaina's fall, Rory had been shocked into silence. Though he was no longer part of Hadleigh's police force, he had taken a personal, unofficial interest in investigating the accident. Some members of the force, who'd known Rory for years, had supplied information of what they'd learned as much as they were able. But the case remained a mystery. Rory had piled the failure of bringing justice to Elaina on top of the guilt he had already carried. He had vowed to Elaina at her funeral to find the perpetrator but, as yet, failed to do so.

While he and Thea made plans regarding the resort, he sensed an uneasiness about her. It was obvious his answers to her questions had been evasive. Although she'd put the matter aside, it remained between them like an obstacle in the room. The fact that she'd invited him to move into the main house had taken him off guard. If things went his way, Gavin would be living with him within a matter of weeks, hopefully. How could he possibly expect her to take on the added responsibility of a child underfoot? Not to mention, it would lead to a whole slew of questions. Ones that he'd avoided for years, not even telling Aunt Agnes or Uncle Jimmy. If Thea knew what had transpired four years ago and how it had led to him breaking her heart, it could do irreparable damage to their mending relationship. He knew she would be angry that he'd not given her the chance to decide how to move forward. He'd taken that away from her when he ended things with no explanation. And now it was too late.

Rory left the coffee shop and drove back to the lake. As the truck rolled slowly past the main house at the resort, he could see a couple of lights on. He had a feeling Thea would be curled up before the fireplace in the library. He also knew she would be uncomfortable being alone in the house. Maybe that had spurred her invitation to him?

He parked his truck in front of the last cabin and headed inside. In the kitchen, he grabbed a frozen dinner from the freezer and set it in the microwave. He'd have to spend more time cooking, he realized, if Gavin moved in with him. It wouldn't be fair to serve him reheated meals and fast food—a staple of Rory's daily life. A few minutes later, he was seated before the television, watching the Cooking Channel as he dug into his meal. He'd offered to take Erika out for dinner, but she'd declined, and they'd settled on meeting in the coffee shop instead. He'd not had much of an appetite anyway.

The guy on TV was using a slow cooker to make beef stew, extolling the virtues of the appliance for busy individuals and families.

Rory made a mental note to pick one up the next time he went to town. With luck, he'd get the chance to use it soon and often.

Chapter 14

I was on my third cup of coffee when I heard a knock on the door just after nine the next morning. The night had been slow to pass and full of squeaks and groans from the attic. I remained seated at the kitchen table, knowing it was Rory, and suspected he'd let himself in since we'd made plans to meet this morning. Sure enough, I heard the front door open, followed by the heavy tread of footsteps a moment later.

"Morning," he said, leaning around the doorframe as though too bashful to enter. "I let myself in, okay?"

"Sure." Considering I'd asked him to move in here, I felt the time for formality was over.

He headed straight for the coffee pot. Eying the almost empty carafe, he turned his gaze on me. "Rough night?"

I shrugged. "Old house, lots of settling, I suppose."

He poured the last of the coffee into a mug and sat down across from me. "Could it be that monster in the attic?"

I scowled at him as I lifted my mug to my lips. "Ha ha." Like Jehrel, he knew me too well.

"How was your night?" I asked, wondering if I'd get a straight answer.

"Fine." His shifty gaze told me I would get no more from him.

"Did you eat?"

"No. You?"

"No."

He was back on his feet and at the fridge in a flash, already pulling out bacon and eggs. Ripples of guilt rose in me, but I pushed them down. I was tired and didn't feel like cooking. Besides, Rory seemed to enjoy it. At least making breakfast. I didn't think I'd ever really seen him make anything else except for mac and cheese, grilled cheese, or heat up frozen or canned stuff. Before long, he placed two plates of food on the table, one in front of me, and started eating. Surprisingly, I had an appetite.

"Where do you want to start today?" he asked between mouthfuls.

"I can take indoors if you want to take outdoors?"

"Sure. I'll start with the boats since I cut the grass on Saturday, the day you arrived. I knew we were in for a storm, and that one was a doozy."

The storm that had knocked out all the lights except for his cabins. He'd spent the night, and I'd been glad for his presence despite the animosity between us. We'd seemed to put our differences aside. I never in a million years thought I'd be spending time with him here, never mind asking him to run the resort. A lot can happen in a few days.

He picked up his half-empty plate and went back to the stove for more food before reclaiming his seat. "Want more?"

I looked away from him since he'd already shoveled some eggs into his mouth when he asked me. "Gross."

He shrugged. "Oh, hey, get this. They're making a movie in town next week."

That piqued my interest. "Really? Where? About what?"

Another shrug. "NovelTea had a sign outside saying it'd be closed for the weekend. They're filming there and possibly in the park. Genie didn't have many details. Apparently, the movie company likes to keep things on the downlow so the area doesn't get overrun with lookie-loos."

"Oh, are there any stars? Or did they not tell her that

either?" I didn't ask how or why he was on a first-name basis with Genie. Though, to be fair, it was a small town.

"Not sure."

"Bummer. I'd like to go and watch — if there's time."

He waved his fork at my plate. "Then finish up, Cinderella. Lots of work to do first."

He was right. Hopefully, when the movie crew started taping, we'd be finished and could spare some time to watch them.

"I'm so excited they're making a movie here. The attention will spur interest in Hadleigh, and hopefully, some of it will spill over onto cabins I'm remaking. I wonder where the crew and actors are staying and for how long?"

"Could be. And I have no idea. At the hotel, I'm guessing. And maybe some B and Bs." That eye of his squinted. "I know what you're thinking, but we're already booked solid for July."

"Not your cabin," I reminded him in a sing-song voice. "If you move in here, you could rent it out."

He was about to retort but paused in thought. "Well, it's not like I'd need to move out. There are extra bedrooms. Maybe if some starlets need a place to stay?"

"Ha ha." I rolled my eyes dramatically.

"Just being neighborly," he insisted.

"Well, if it came down to that, I could lend out a few rooms here since you're so opposed to moving in. Although, a couple of my friends from the city may come for a mini vacation. If they can get away. And convince Jehrel's mother-in-law-to-be to watch the cats."

"Cats?"

"Yes. Three of them. He's alone with them right now while Alan is away at work." I smiled when I recalled our conversation. "If Jehrel and Alan know a movie crew is coming to town, I have a feeling they'll be here." Knowing Jehrel, I'd bet money on it. I made a mental note to call him as soon as Rory left.

Rory stirred some sugar into his mug. "Soooo, who is Jehrel?"

"My friend from the city. My very best friend," I added and basked in cool comfort from the way Rory flinched. He looked about ready to remind me that *he* was my very best friend, but then thought better of it. He no longer possessed the honor of that title, and he knew it.

Rory rose and grabbed both of our empty plates, and put them on the counter. "I'm going to get started."

"Me too," I agreed.

And then, with long, fast strides, he was out the door again. Two seconds later, I was on the phone with Jehrel.

~

Rory found me a couple hours later standing on the deck of one of the cabins, shaking out the couch pillows. I'd been dusting and vacuuming and had all the windows open in each cabin, airing them out. When I'd gone to Rory's rental cabin, loaded down with cleaning supplies and fresh linens, I'd felt a little weird. As though I was intruding on his space. He'd made a few changes along with some upgrades, which I'd had to admit improved the appearance of the place. Even though I had every intention of retro-designing my trio of cabins, I was still interested in investing in the power upgrades Rory could do. We'd discussed it briefly yesterday, and he'd assured me it wouldn't compromise the nostalgic look I was going for. Being immersed in time-capsule cabins didn't have to mean they wouldn't also be equipped with all the amenities. After all, if another storm knocked out the lights again, I was sure the backup power would be appreciated. Unfortunately, those things took time. And they'd have to wait until the busy rental season was over. Rory had assured me that after we had everything in ship-shape for our guests, he would start at the main house with the upgrades. He'd warned me of the expense, even though he'd magnanimously added he'd do the install for free. Then he watched my face carefully for a reaction. I knew when I hadn't batted an eye over the cost, he'd pondered just how much money I'd been left in the will. I'd taken perverse joy out of leaving him to wonder. Two could play the shifty game.

Rory joined me on the deck and leaned against the railing. "How's it going?"

Bits of grass were on his clothes and even in his hair, while smudges of dirt were on his face. "Um, good. What've you been up to?"

Self-consciously, he ran a hand through his hair and then noticed the grass as it floated to his feet. "I had the weed-whacker out doing some edging around the beach areas. I also went through the sheds and pulled out the gear to check everything."

We'd looked in the sheds to do the inventory but hadn't done more than list items. Buckles and straps had to be inspected on life jackets, and other safety checks had to be carried out on equipment. During my younger years, I'd always hoped my aunt and uncle would get a jet ski or a motorboat so we could go waterskiing or tubing like some other people did on Talon Lake. Now, I understood the ramifications of such dangers. Especially when it came to insurance issues with the resort.

"I stocked your cabin with fresh linens and towels and went through the bathroom and kitchen cupboards to see what was needed." After I spoke, we shared a glance, and I felt strange. Maybe because I'd referred to it as *his* cabin so easily, without any tinge of animosity, which I admit I'd been doing before. And while I was admitting things to myself, I realized I'd taken stock of a lot more besides the things the cabin needed. Being in there, I could mentally strip away time and see it as it appeared years ago when we'd been kids. So much time we'd spent together, sharing everything. The summers always seemed to last forever back then. During those months, I'd lived more than I ever did the remaining months of the years. When we'd meet up again each June, it was as though I'd never left. Sometimes, when I was lonely, I'd picture Rory being here, frozen in time, waiting for my return so he could come alive again. We'd known each other so well. Our thoughts, our dreams, our moods. Everything. And I'd loved him more than anyone I'd ever known.

But when things suddenly changed, I'd been so stunned, so hurt, that I hadn't even paused to think why he had done a one-eighty on all our well-laid plans. We'd envisioned our lives together, down to how we'd decorate the home we would one day live in. It'd started off as a pretend game between us, but as we'd grown older, it'd become more real. Attainable.

So what had happened? What could have possibly changed his mind? Had the reality become too much for him? Was he scared of leaving Hadleigh? Were second thoughts bombarding him?

I didn't know because I'd never asked.

As much as I'd loved him and wanted that life of ours together, I'd turned my back and ran without another thought, with hardly any questions or arguments. I'd let him go as easily and quickly as he'd let me go because of my pride. But had it been my pride, or was it something else? It'd been easy to play the martyr and lay the blame at his feet. But why hadn't I fought for him? Was it fear?

I sensed that Rory picked up on my confusion.

My glance slid to view the lake. Right now, it was so calm it appeared like polished glass displaying the reflection of surrounding trees and white fluffy clouds in a deep blue sky.

"Sometimes I forget how much I love it here," I admitted.

Rory's body shifted smoothly into place beside mine. He smelled of soap and grass and pine — an intoxicating blend delighting my senses. The heat of hard work radiated from him, mingling the scent of sweat into the mix. Deeply, I inhaled and closed my eyes for just a second. They say nothing is stronger than the sense of smell. Just like the whiff of candy canes took me right to Christmases past, and the sweet aroma of roses made me think of my mother, who I barely remembered, and the smell of pine took me right to this place, Talon Lake. And to Rory.

Rory turned his head to regard me the exact moment I turned mine. Inches separated my face from his chest. The rise and fall of his breaths were heavy and fast. Tilting my head, I sought his eyes, and when we connected, I was lost in them. Again, the years peeled away, and he was no longer the shifty, familiar stranger who'd broken my heart. He was my Rory. My heart. My other half. My love.

As though an invisible string bound us and pulled us together, our lips met in the softest brush. Then, boldly, his mouth moved more urgently against mine, silently answering my unasked questions.

Do you love me still?

Can I ever trust you again?

How could you break my heart?

That last question made me freeze in awareness of what was happening. Bracing my hands on his chest, I broke the kiss and pushed him away.

"Stop," I said. Though he'd already backed up.

"T, I'm sorry," he said. "I never meant..."

Anguished, I stared at him. "We can't. I can't." I forced my voice to steady and my gaze to harden. "That must never happen again if we have any chance of succeeding in running this resort."

He stared back at me hard, as though he'd break the cage around my heart with brute force, but then, slowly, I saw resignation light his face. He nodded once, not trusting himself to speak.

"I'll get back to work," he said. And then he was gone.

His scent lingered on the breeze before it too reluctantly followed him.

I bent and picked up the pillows I'd hastily dropped at my feet and hurried inside before the tears began to fall.

Chapter 15

Rory sat before the television, eating a warmed-up tin of clam chowder for dinner. Despite having no appetite, he forced himself to eat. For the hundredth time, he ran through the scene of him and Thea kissing. *How in the world had that happened?* Not that he regretted it, but never in a million years had he suspected it would occur. Things had been firmly put in the past between them, and though he still loved her as much as he ever had, he knew things could never work out. Her life was in Toronto. His was here. And when the summer was over, Thea would leave. He would run the resort and his other business, and she would get back to her career. Sure, she was planning to work here now, but it wouldn't be for long. It wasn't like she'd ever consider a permanent move to Hadleigh. All her life, she'd wanted to move to the city and follow her dreams. He wasn't about to be an obstacle in her path.

A future scenario kept running through his mind as well. The one where he explained to Thea why he'd adopted Gavin—if all went well with the judge. He had no idea how she would react. Introducing them would have to happen eventually, whether he was granted custody or not. Now that summer had almost arrived, Gavin would be spending time here with him. If he wasn't granted custody, he still had no intention of giving up visitation. He was sure he wouldn't be denied the option. He'd been part of Gavin's life for years. And he knew no one else had come forward with hopes of adopting the boy.

Rory was sure things would go in his favor. At least, now

he had another job to add to his resume. At his meeting with Erika, he'd told her he would be running the resort. He'd not had many details about pay or whether he'd move into the main house after Thea left. But Erika had seemed happy with the news, and Rory found that encouraging. Hopefully, the judge would as well.

Gavin's face flashed in his mind, and Rory smiled. He'd watched the youngster grow from a toddling two-year-old to a precocious, imaginative boy. Despite losing both his parents and the tragedy involving his grandmother, Gavin had remained strong. Stoic even. Rory had worried when he heard the news about Elaina, concerned Gavin would bury the pain or possibly break. How much could such a young child bear? When Erika had gently told Gavin about the loss, Rory had been there. Gavin had cried, as expected, but Rory was relieved to see the tears. Too many times, he'd seen kids and even adults bottle up their feelings, and Rory knew all too well the outcome of that. He'd done it himself after the death of his own father. It'd been compounded by the neglect of his mother. The feelings had festered inside of him until he couldn't stand it anymore. Luckily, he'd been able to talk things out with Thea and her aunt and uncle. The unburdening through conversations had eased the pain in his heart.

At the end of the week, school would be over for the summer. Rory hoped he may then be granted custody of Gavin. He'd petitioned the court months ago to have them allow Gavin to live with him as a foster. But he'd been denied despite his lawyer's and Erika's arguments in Rory's favor. At the time, the family court felt Gavin needed to remain a ward of the county and stay in Waverly's care. Allowing Rory temporary guardianship could have proved to be another upheaval in the boy's life. Especially if Rory wasn't ultimately granted permanent custody. Put in those terms, Rory understood the judge's decision, but Gavin's constant requests to be with Rory had been heartbreaking.

Tomorrow, Rory was determined to continue work to ready the resort for occupants. He also needed to have a sit-down with Thea to discuss the terms of his employment and his pay. Erika had asked him to obtain a written agreement signed by Thea so she could present it to the judge. That, along with the client list he'd supplied, should help his case.

Rory got up and put his bowl in the sink, and wandered over to the bedroom he'd chosen to be Gavin's. There was a double bed, a blue comforter with dinosaurs on it, curtains displaying the solar system, and an area rug over the hardwood floor where Gavin could sit and play with an assortment of toys that lined the shelves. There was also a bookshelf filled with storybooks. Rory loved the room. It was warm and inviting and something he would have loved as a boy. This room was one of the reasons he'd turned down Thea's offer to stay at the main house. Another reason was he wasn't sure how Thea would feel about Gavin. She may not appreciate having a young child underfoot. Rory knew Thea had a huge heart, and he hoped she would welcome Gavin with open arms. But he had to be prepared for another reaction. Thea had a plan on how her summer at the resort would look — with her elbow-deep in renovations. Gavin's presence might be considered counterproductive to Thea's plans. Rory knew she would never make a child feel unwelcome, but he didn't want her to feel put out. Maybe, after Thea left, Rory might consider moving into the main house. He could just imagine the fun Gavin would have racing around in there just as Rory and Thea had done.

Rory got swept along when his mind began to daydream. He pictured himself, Thea and Gavin, and another child, maybe a little girl. He and Thea walking hand in hand, watching the children scamper over the trails in the forest. A family living the happily ever after Rory had always dreamed of. Then his thoughts shifted back to the kiss he and Thea had shared.

Maybe it wasn't such a faraway dream as he'd imagined?

~

The next morning, bright and early, Rory joined Thea for coffee in the kitchen of the main house. He'd knocked on the door this time, not wanting to let himself in, not knowing what kind of reception he'd get.

"Hey." Thea had greeted him when she opened the door, then she turned and walked off, not making eye contact.

Rory had followed her to the kitchen and helped himself to the coffee. He took a seat across the table from her.

"Hungry?" she asked, still not looking at him.

"Sure. What're you in the mood for?" He hadn't meant to ask the question with provocative banter. The weird vibes he'd picked up on had made him nervous.

She did look at him then. Just for the barest of seconds before she dropped her gaze, cheeks flaming.

"I mean eggs. Omelet? Scrambled? Over easy?" That last one made her blush deepen.

Thea got up. "How 'bout French toast?" she suggested, her back swiftly turned as she went to the fridge and began scrounging around.

"Okay," he agreed.

They managed to cook breakfast without conversation or looking at each other. Rory was sure Thea felt as uneasy as he did. Soon, they were sitting across from each other again, both staring down at their plates while they ate.

"Hey, I need to get something from you if I can?" Rory finally broke the silence.

"What is it?" her voice sounded guarded.

"I need a letter of employment from you, laying out terms and stuff." Now, it was his turn to blush.

"Okay. Can I ask why the sudden need for formality?" Thea asked. "Don't you trust my offer?"

"No, no, it's not that," Rory rushed to assure her. Then he sighed and put his fork down. There was no way around it. He was going to have to tell her something.

He took a deep breath before explaining. "My lawyer suggested I have a client list on file, and if I were to obtain another source of income, to have an employment agreement on file."

"That sounds ominous," Thea observed.

Rory smiled, trying to lighten the mood. "I know. And this will probably sound even worse when I mention it's for a judge." He prepared himself for her censure.

Thea merely raised an eyebrow.

Rory figured her mind was probably going to all kinds of dark places, and he knew he had to say something to ease her concerns. "It's nothing bad, really. It's a venture I'm involved in. An acquisition of sorts."

"Requiring a judge?"

"Yes."

When he failed to elaborate, Thea did look at him then. Long and hard. Then she sighed and got up, reached on top of the fridge, and grabbed a pad of paper. She retook her seat and began writing.

"Whatever you have going on is your business. I'm not going to press you for information," she said as she wrote.

"I appreciate that." He would have attempted to explain further but figured it was best to leave it alone for now. Soon enough, she would know what was going on.

She paused and looked at him again. "Just please tell me if you're in some kind of trouble. If you are, maybe I can help."

Rory ducked his head to hide a swell of gratitude over that statement. After all he'd done, all the hurt he'd caused, she still had his back. When he lifted his gaze to hers, he'd composed himself. "I swear, this isn't about me being in any trouble."

Thea's eyes bore into his, searching for answers, for truth, before she gave up.

"There." She passed him the paper. "These are the terms of employment. I've mentioned in here that you may live in this house as a condition of running the resort if you choose to do so. The resort can remain open all year. I will continue to be responsible for any and all costs pertaining to running the resort, for my three cabins, and also for the care and expenses of this house. You, in turn, will be responsible for seeing the upkeep of the property is ensured, and the rental amounts are collected and deposited. If you incur any costs for repairs or such, you are to notify me in writing if the expense is over three hundred dollars. Otherwise, I'll leave it to your discretion."

Rory looked over the paper and noted there was a more than adequate salary included along with the use of the main house. "This is very generous. Are you sure you're okay with it?" He knew she'd been granted a cash amount along with the resort, but he had no idea how much, nor did he care to know.

"I know you love this place. And since you also have a stake in the resort, I know there's no one more qualified or invested besides me in seeing it succeed than you. I'm glad you agreed to take this on. You have no idea how it eases my mind knowing you'll be here to oversee everything," Thea said.

Again, Rory had to duck his head and compose himself. When he looked up, Thea was smiling at him.

"Now," she continued. "If you're ready to get started, we may just be finished before the renters begin showing up."

Rory smiled as well as they headed out together.

Chapter 16

"Yes, a movie. They're filming here right now." My voice was low, and if anyone was watching me, I admit, I looked suspicious.

"Oh, my gawd!" Jehrel screeched. "Do you see anyone famous?"

Craning my neck around the corner of the store again, I searched the faces I could make out. "I dunno, it's hard to tell. They're wearing costumes and make-up. And there's snow!"

"No!"

"Yes, all over the sidewalk. On my way into town, I saw lots of snow and movie equipment set up in the park as well. They're probably headed there next."

"Alan! We have to visit Thea right now!"

For the third time in the last five minutes, I had to pull the phone away from my ear since making the call. When I drove through town this morning, the only thought on my mind was *full steam ahead* on the cabin reno. Rory and I had finished readying the resort for guests by noon Friday. That had given me the rest of the day to draw up a preliminary sketch of what I planned for the reno and to go through the attic. I'd marked the items I wanted to use with Post-its. As soon as I was ready for them, Rory had offered to help me bring them down. Now, I planned to go through Cassidy's shop and see what she had from the '50s era.

My other two cabins were rented for the upcoming week. Rory's second cabin was rented for the entire summer. We decided to put Mr. Cole—the quiet writer—next to Rory. The Tallmons—friendly family—were placed in the cabin next to the one I would be renovating since we both would be generating a fair amount of noise. In the cabin on the other side of the Tallmons, I'd place a young couple in their mid-twenties. They were new to the resort, so I didn't have any notes on them. I hoped Mr. Cole would be far enough away from all of us, considering the main house separated my trio of cabins and Rory's pair, acting like a buffer.

"Oh, I think the hero just came out of the coffee shop," I said into the phone.

"Whatshelooklike?" Jehrel shrieked.

The sun was shining in my face, so I had to squint. I hadn't thought I'd be needing my sunglasses since I was supposed to be inside right now. Instead, I was giving Jehrel a play-by-play of the movie being filmed. I couldn't blame him for that since I'd been caught up in the excitement and called him.

"He's tall. Dark hair, not wearing a hat, but a long coat and scarf. Kinda looks like Damon from Vampire Diaries." Then I had to pull the phone away when Jehrel shrieked again. There was a bit of a tussle on the line, then I heard Alan's voice.

"Thea! What are you doing to Jehrel? He's scaring the cats with all that screaming."

Hearing hissing in the background, I wondered if it came from Jehrel or the cats. "Hi, Alan. They're filming a movie in Hadleigh."

"What? Ohmygawd!"

I laughed. He was as bad as Jehrel when it came to celebrities. "They're supposed to be filming all around Hadleigh over the next few days—at least from the gossip I heard going around town."

"We're on our way," I heard Jehrel holler, followed by more tussling on the line.

"Settle down!" Alan insisted. "Thea, is it okay if we drive

up? We don't want to impose."

"Thea already invited us up, and we're not imposing!" Jehrel shouted in the background.

"Wow, he's really wound up," Alan said.

"Yeah, I know, I can hear him," I said. "It's okay, it's exciting. And no, of course, it's no imposition."

"Jehrel said you were renting out cabins? I thought you were selling?" Alan said.

"I'm no longer selling. I am renting out the cabins, but there's plenty of room in the main house. You guys are welcome to stay as long as you like. Honestly, I can use the backup."

"Oh. Rory. Has he been around? Is he bothering you?" Alan asked. Obviously, Jehrel hadn't brought him up to speed on Rory and the resort.

"Yes. No. I dunno. It's complicated. I really could use my friends up here. But I understand if you're busy." Even if I planned to work, I hoped they'd come. Jehrel was great for bouncing ideas around with. And Alan had a level head that I could desperately use right now.

"We'd love to come, but I'll have to see if Mom can watch the cats," Alan said. By his tone, I could tell his mind was already three steps ahead, making plans.

"Okay, great. If you do come and I'm out, the spare key's in the same place." We had one hidden in a fake rock in the garden next to the front door.

"All right. Talk to you soon. Love you," Alan said, and hung up.

I watched the movie crew for a few more minutes until I saw Alicia Gains. She was watching the excitement as well, so she hadn't noticed me. Plus, she was ahead of me. Seeing her took the fun out of it, so I ducked back around the building and headed to Cassidy's store. Eventually, I knew I'd run into Alicia. It was inevitable, this being such a small town. And, of course, she'd demand a full accounting of why I'd missed Aunt Agnes's funeral. Then she'd probably have a zillion questions about the resort and other stuff — or a certain person — I'd rather not discuss with her. Actually, I resented the whole idea of having to tell her anything.

I soon reached Cassidy's store, and the bell clanged when I went through the door. My eyes adjusted to the darker interior while nostalgic scents rushed to greet me. I didn't see her, and I guessed she was still busy unpacking. Judging by the amount of boxes there'd been on my last visit, it might take her a while to organize everything.

"Hello?" I called out, not wanting to startle her in case she hadn't heard the bell. My steps made the floorboards groan as I walked to the check-out counter in the center of the space. Nothing. Winding around more displays, I moved toward the rear of the store and went into the back hall. The sign was still posted on the stairwell, so I headed up. The door to the apartment was open where Cassidy had set up the overflow inventory. Browsing, I noted more items displayed, most of the boxes having disappeared.

She had an area set up with old glassware and cooking utensils, along with some small retro appliances that would go great with my plans for the cabin. The kitchen and dining area in the cabin was open concept, overflowing into the living room. It was a great set-up since the view of the lake was clearly visible through the large living room window. Each of my three cabins had open-concept layouts, three small bedrooms, and one bathroom. I planned to remake the entire cabin. First, I'd have to pack up furniture, window coverings, carpets, throw rugs — everything.

Inevitably, people love the idea of a retro-design until it becomes inconvenient. If they couldn't watch the shows they wanted, or listen to the music, or be entertained the way they'd become accustomed to in this world of instant gratification, then the retro concept was no longer ideal for them. For this reason, I opted to hide modern conveniences around or within the folds of the designs I created. I'd gotten quite creative in my disguises so as not to take away from the effect of the retro-era. Guests would undoubtedly bring along their own devices, such as cell phones, iPads, or computers. The cabin would still have modern electrical outlets and Wi-Fi, and eventually, the power upgrades Rory planned to install.

Looking around at the displays and thinking about what I had planned was exciting but also a little overwhelming. Having to find wallpaper, and window coverings, lamps, and light fixtures, pictures, and other art, along with knickknacks and niche items. I realized I'd have to make a list of what I wanted from Cassidy's store along the same lines as I'd done with the items in the attic of the main house. I couldn't possibly begin to put things into the cabin until I tore everything out. A lot of the furniture and other things that I couldn't use I could donate. Maybe Cassidy had an idea of a place I could take the items to, and I'd also need to see about a rental truck.

Mind spinning, I decided to head back downstairs and see if I could find Cassidy to discuss my plans.

A quick glance of the main floor told me she hadn't returned. That left only one more place she could be—the basement.

I returned to the stairway and peered into the dark depths below. There was a dim light, as though it came from the other end of the space, the glow barely viable. A window, perhaps?

"Cass?" I descended a few steps. "Hello?" A few more steps. "Anybody?" Now, I'd reached the bottom.

Unlike the top floor, there wasn't a bunch of rooms branching off a hall. It was more like the first floor—a cavernous space that would probably echo if I yelled. This didn't seem the place to raise a voice. It seemed more like a place where whispers and secret steps moved about in the shadows. Determined, I delved deeper into the room, skirting around shelves and boxes of stuff that must have been left behind by the previous owner. What if Cassidy was hurt? Lying unconscious somewhere, not able to call for help? Or maybe she'd been silenced.

"Hello?" I whispered, recalling there was still a murderer on the loose.

Cassidy had been afraid to come down here, and she'd promised to contact me when she decided to explore. What would possibly entice her to descend into the depths?

"Hello?" a voice responded. It hadn't come from the basement, however. It'd come from the stairway.

"Cass?" I croaked. My throat was suddenly dry.

"Thea? Are you in the basement?" Closer now. Must be descending the steps.

"Yes. It's me. I'm down here."

Now I could see her. Steadfast, I worked my way over. Soon, we stood face to face.

"What are you doing down here?" She looked more bemused than annoyed.

"I… Couldn't find you. I thought you were down here," I said.

"Why? Did you hear something?" her voice was quieter now, and she peered around, eyes wide.

"No. Nothing. The light's on, though." It wasn't just natural light from windows, I'd ascertained.

"It's always on." She didn't elaborate.

She began to head back up the stairs, so I followed, no longer finding the basement so enticing.

"Where were you?" I asked.

We got to the hall area, and I noticed the door to the parking lot outside was propped open. *Of course*, she'd probably been outside.

"Getting some stuff from my car," she said.

"Oh." Now, I felt nosy and dense.

Her laughter made me feel somewhat better. "I really admire your bravery, going down there solo." She stood at the open door, and I figured she hadn't finished what she was doing.

"Need a hand?" I offered.

"Sure." We went out to her car, where the open hatchback displayed some boxes. Passing me two smaller ones stacked together, she removed the last larger box and put it down by her feet. She closed the hatch and picked the box back up. We headed inside.

"These just go on the main floor," she instructed, going over to the checkout desk.

We set down the boxes behind the desk where there were more boxes.

"Did you come in for something?" she asked, as though suddenly remembering I was a customer.

I moved around to the other side of the work area. "Yes. I've decided to stay the summer."

"Oh, great," she said, grabbing her handwritten notebook from under the counter. She opened it up and then bent to inspect the boxes we'd brought in.

"So, I'm looking for items from the '50s for a cabin I'm renovating. It's one of the cabins from a resort I inherited."

"Okay. That'd be upstairs then, where you got the Walkman. Everything from the '50s to the '80s is there."

"Yes, thanks. But actually, I was hoping if I jotted down a quick list, you could put stuff you come across aside for me? I have to do a tear-out of the cabin interior before I begin the reno, so it's not a big rush."

"Sure, make the list." She put a pad of paper in front of me and a pen on top of it.

"Also, I was hoping you might know a place I could donate the stuff I remove?"

She pondered my question a moment, and her face lit up. "Oh, I know. There's a home for kids. They're always looking for stuff."

I knew where she meant. "That's a great idea. I should have thought of that. My aunt and uncle used to give them a pair of cabins to use free of charge every summer for the kids. Then, when the home wound up building their own lodge, they donated most of the bunkbeds from the cabins to them."

"Oh, that's so nice of your aunt and uncle," she said. "You said you inherited the resort?"

I nodded.

"I'm sorry, they've passed away then."

"Yes, my uncle a few years ago, my aunt this past January."

"That was nice of them to leave you the resort."

"It was. But there are five cabins that came with it, and I only inherited three of them." I let her chew on that for a moment.

"Did they leave the other cabins to the home for kids?" she asked.

"No. They didn't."

"Who then?"

"My ex-fiancée."

"Oh, wow, that must be weird? Is that why you originally said you weren't here for long? Did you work things out then since you've decided to stay?"

"Yes, we called a truce, and I actually asked him to run the resort for me. And since things are kinda slow business-wise right now, I decided to reno the cabins. I'm still renting out two of mine, and Rory — my ex — is renting out one of his. I think since it's quite an involved project, I'll probably just do one cabin each summer."

"You're doing retro-themed on each of them?" she

clarified.

"Yes, starting with the '50s. The others I'll maybe do in '70s and '80s styles. They'll be like themed getaways and show pieces for my business as well, so I can write off the expense."

"That's awesome. I'm so happy to have a part in it, even slightly."

"Thanks. Hey, would you mind if I left some of my business cards here? Having a movie filming practically outside your door may entice some of the crew to come in and browse around."

"Sure. Are you hoping to score a job, possibly?"

"I'm not opposed to it. That would be fun. But realistically, maybe they'll want to check out my cabins as filming locations once they're completed. You know, if they're doing anything retro." I reached into my purse and took out a bunch of my cards, which I always kept handy.

"Yeah, that'd be right up your alley. Could you imagine your cabins being used in movies? Like, how cool would that be?"

"It'd be great. But, in the meantime, I'm going to concentrate on getting at least one of them completed. It would be good to have something to show in case someone did ever inquire about my work."

Cassidy took the cards and placed them on display on the counter. Concentrating on my list, I wrote down several items that came first to mind. Both of us worked in silence for a few minutes.

"Okay," I said, sliding the pad of paper over to her. "This should do for now."

Cassidy checked out the list and nodded. "Great. I think I have some of this stuff."

"Okay, perfect. If you could maybe take pictures of items you have and send them to me, I'll let you know if they'll work.

If so, you can just put sold signs on them, okay?"

"Sure. Hey, downstairs, there was a lot of stuff," she said suddenly.

"Yeah, there was." I shivered involuntarily.

"Great. Something else to add to my workload. It was supposed to be empty." She laughed lightly, but I got the feeling she wasn't too happy about it.

"Well, maybe you'll find some stuff that's useful, or maybe you can have a sale out front?"

"Maybe," she said.

"Okay, well, thanks. I better get going. I think I'll swing by the children's home and see if they want my stuff."

"Good luck," she said.

"Thanks." I turned and headed to the door, calling out, "Talk to you soon. Don't work too hard." As I walked out, I found myself face to face with Alicia Gains.

Chapter 17

Rory headed over to the main house at noon. There was still time to finish up any last-minute tasks before guests arrived. Check-in time was four o'clock. Surprisingly, he was nervous. Granted, it was the first time he'd ever actually run the resort. He and Thea had helped out before but never had the job of overseeing every little detail. Last night, they'd gone through each rental cabin for one last inspection. He'd suggested leaving a vase with fresh flowers on each kitchen table, thinking it might be a nice touch, but Thea hadn't agreed. She'd reminded him how Mr. Cole was allergic to several things, no doubt flowers being one of them. And although the Tallmon family had never reported any allergies, they didn't know much about the young couple due to arrive. She'd said it was better not to put out welcome food or gift baskets or flowers in anyone's cabin—just in case. Seeing the wisdom in her decision, Rory had agreed. He'd marveled over how many things there were to know about the hospitality industry and about how much he still needed to learn.

Thea had been great through it all. Never lecturing him or making his ideas or questions seem unwelcome or dumb. He knew he could learn a lot from her, and he was relieved she'd be here this first summer with him. Although, she'd mentioned the idea of renovating a cabin of hers each summer since the season was slow for her workwise. In a way, it would be like when they were young and could spend two whole months together, as opposed to just a weekend or holiday here and there. The idea of seeing Thea here each summer was bittersweet. Though he longed to reveal the truth of what had happened to end their relationship, he knew he never could. And just how would Thea feel about spending any time here at all if — or, hopefully, when — his adoption of Gavin happened? In the past, when they'd daydreamed together about their future life, there had always been children. He knew she wasn't opposed to the idea. But how would she feel about a child he may suddenly have with no offer of a reasonable explanation of why? What could he say?

When Rory reached the driveway up to the main house, he paused when he heard a vehicle approaching. It was too early to be their guests. It could be one of the cottage owners on either side of the resort. Otherwise, only guests or people who were lost or curious traveled down this roadway.

As the vehicle came into sight, Rory was surprised to recognize Erika's car. Seeing him, she pulled up beside him and stopped. He waited as she put down her window.

"Hi. Is everything okay? I'm surprised to see you out this way on a Sunday," Rory said politely. Actually, he was surprised to see her out this way at all. She'd rarely come by the resort after doing her initial home evaluation when he first applied to adopt Gavin.

Erika nodded in the direction of the backseat. Gavin was seated there, and beside him was his backpack. Shyly, he smiled at Rory.

"Hey, kiddo." This wasn't his visitation day. Rory, though delighted, wondered what their visit was about.

"I've been trying to get a hold of you," Erika said, her voice a bit strained.

"Is everything okay?" Rory repeated.

"It might be better if we can talk at your cabin?" Erika suggested.

Rory's stomach sank. Had things gone badly with the

judge, and to soften the blow, Erika brought Gavin along to break the bad news? Maybe for one final visit? Instead of answering, Rory nodded his assent and turned to travel back the way he'd come.

Moments later, as he got to his cabin, Erika pulled up out front. Rory waited by the door for them to exit the car. Despite the anxiousness he felt, he smiled at Gavin.

Instead of coming directly inside, Erika went to the rear of the car. She opened the trunk and called over to Rory.

"Want to give me a hand with these?"

Rory walked over to see what she was talking about. When he looked inside the trunk, he had to swallow over the sudden lump in his throat. Eyes stinging, he stared at Erika hopefully. She beamed back at him.

"Like I said, I tried to reach you."

Rory pulled out his phone and stared at the screen. "Oh. Our first guests are due to arrive today at four. Yesterday afternoon, I was doing last-minute resort stuff, and my phone was almost dead. I turned it off to save the battery until I could charge it. I guess I never turned it back on." He rambled on as he attempted to get his emotions under control.

When he heard Gavin chuckle, he looked over at the boy. Again, that nervous smile greeted him, and Rory knew Gavin understood what was happening. He was worried about Rory's reaction.

In three quick strides, Rory was in front of Gavin. He scooped up the boy with his hands and swung him around before hugging him tight.

"Is it okay that we're here now?" Erika asked. "We could wait if you're busy. I could call back and arrange a time that's better for you?"

"No!" Rory insisted, putting Gavin down and looking into his eyes. "We've waited long enough."

Gavin smiled, and nothing was more important to Rory in that instant. Not the resort, or the guests, or all the things he needed to do. Not Thea's reaction or how he would explain things to her. All that mattered was, at long last, he and Gavin were together.

Rory went over to grab one of Gavin's bags. "So, this is it? The judge granted me custody?" He needed to hear it. Fearful, it would just be another delay and another hasty visit. Although, Gavin had never brought along luggage before.

Erika smiled at him, and Rory thought he detected a few tears in her eyes as well. "You've been granted full custody. Rory is your son, now and forever," she confirmed.

Rory felt like taking Erika into his arms and swinging her around as well. He swallowed hard and smiled again.

"Do you hear that... Son?" he said, looking at Gavin.

Gavin grinned and nodded. "Yes, I do... Dad."

Both Rory and Erika had to duck their heads to hide the rush of tears.

Once they'd composed themselves, Rory led the way inside. "Let's put these in your room," he said to Gavin.

Ten minutes later, Gavin was settled in and sitting on the bedroom rug, building with Lego. Rory made up coffee and sat down with Erika to go over the paperwork.

"Everything has pretty much been done," Erika said, getting Rory to sign one last paper.

"So, there's no changing their minds?" he clarified.

Erika shook her head. "No. Of course, there'll be follow-up visits, but other than that, it's over."

"I can't believe it," Rory said. From where he sat, he could see Gavin in his room. Besides a look of concentration crossing the boy's face now and again, there was a steady smile on his lips. Never had he seen Gavin so content. Nor had he ever felt the same. As though he could finally let go of the breath he'd been holding for so long.

Chapter 18

It felt like someone had kicked me right in the gut.

Barely making it to the deck, I sunk down, pulled my knees up to my chest, and held on for dear life. I may have rocked a bit as well. Desperate for a distraction, I tried to focus on yesterday when I'd run into Alicia.

That had been something else.

Not quite sure how she found me and timed our run-in so perfectly. Unless she'd seen me on the street and followed? And me thinking I'd neatly avoided her. She had given me that pursed-lipped, narrow-eyed look of disappointment. Without words conveying what she thought about me missing my aunt's funeral. *How dare I?*

I shivered, and I wasn't sure if it was from the lingering effects of the chill she'd given off or my current dilemma.

Alica hadn't jumped all over me right away. It wasn't her style—I knew enough about her to know that. No, like a spider, she'd spun a web of pleasantries around me, lulling me to relax, before she went in for the kill.

"Thea! It's been so long," she'd purred.

Gathering my wits, I'd replied, "Hi, Alicia. How have you been?"

We'd bantered back and forth until the look on her face changed abruptly, and I knew the steak knives were coming out. But before she could strike, I'd leapt in her path and halted her advance. "Oh!" My right hand had gone to my side.

Startled off balance, she taken in my wince of pain. "Wha...
What's the matter?"

I'd held up a hand to stall her concern. "Nothing. Really.
Just some lingering pain. The doctor assures me it's just scar
tissue, but it really does catch me off guard sometimes."

"Scar tissue?" she'd ventured, and I knew I had her.

Sadly, I'd nodded my head. "Appendix. I had to have
emergency surgery."

"How terrible."

My eyes teared just slightly—I admit, it's a gift I have.
"The worst part was I'd been on my way to Aunt Agnes's
funeral when it happened. After all this time, whenever the pain
strikes, it brings me right back to that day. The terrible guilt I
feel..." Indeed, I had begun to feel guilty over the underhanded
performance I was putting on.

Her hand moved to rest on my shoulder. "My dear girl,
don't you dare do this to yourself. You are not to blame for
circumstances beyond your control. And your dear aunt would
understand. Why, when you didn't appear at the funeral, I told
anyone who said otherwise there was undoubtedly a reasonable
explanation."

Uh-huh.

So that particular inquisition neatly avoided, she'd
changed tactics.

"I assume you inherited the resort? Such an undertaking
for a single person. Are you planning to sell?" There'd been a
gleam in her eye, one that made me think of a hungry cat.

"Uh, no. I'm opening up the resort this summer." I'd burst
her bubble.

"Really?" Her eyebrows had shot up into her hairline.
"But your life isn't here. You moved to the city?"

"Business is slow in the summer, so I'll be staying."

"And then what? Will you sell?"

"No. I've decided to keep the resort running. I've hired someone."

"Who?"

Here we go…

"Someone from town," I'd hedged.

"Then I must know them," she'd insisted.

Once I'd caved and told her it was Rory, the claws had really come out. She'd questioned me relentlessly, determined to know every detail. I'd held my ground, equally determined to give up as little as possible.

In the end, I'd said Rory and I had come to an understanding, and there were no hard feelings between us. I hadn't divulged the fact he owned two of the resort cabins, and it still amazed me she didn't know. However, Rory had always been discreet. If he'd been the one undergoing the interrogation, he'd have shut it down long ago.

Thankfully, The Village People saved me.

"I'm expecting an important call," I'd made the excuse while scrambling for my phone. "I have to take this," I'd said, smiling bravely. "So nice to see you." And I'd fled.

My cramping limbs brought me back to the present. Gently, I relinquished the vice grip on my lower legs and eased them out to rest on the step. From here, I could look out across the lawn to the lake. The gentle lap of the water against the shoreline bringing me comfort. Fleeing to the dock had been my first inclination, but I feared I'd not make it before my legs gave out. At least from here, I could rush inside if I saw someone.

I had to move. Had to check the time. But I'd left my phone inside.

Guests were due to arrive, and I had to pull myself together. But I couldn't get the image out of my head.

Or the words.

Last night, I was sure I'd asked Rory to meet me for lunch

here. When he failed to arrive, I'd second-guessed my offer, wondering if maybe we decided to meet at his place instead. So, I turned off the coffee pot, got my shoes on, and opened the door. There, at the end of the driveway, I saw Rory, and he wasn't alone. He was talking to someone in a car. When he moved aside, I could see it was an older blonde lady. Attractive.

No biggie.

But then, he'd turned around and headed back to his cabin, and the car had followed him.

Since I already had my shoes on, I decided to let my nosiness win out, and I'd crept after them. Stealthily, moving tree to tree to keep from sight, I neared Rory's furthest cabin. The one that wasn't rented out for the summer.

I got close enough to see them but not quite close enough to hear them clearly. The woman and a child got out of the car, and the woman went around to open the trunk. Rory joined her there. They spoke, but I couldn't make out the words. Then Rory's face lit up like a Christmas tree. He strode over to the child—a handsome little tyke around five or six with a mop of brown curls. He picked up the boy and swung him around. I had no idea whose child this was. Rory didn't have any siblings, so it couldn't be a nephew, and he'd never mentioned any relatives. It was possible he was the child of one of Rory's friends or someone he'd worked with on the force. Since I hadn't heard my aunt mention any child before, I was in the dark.

Rory went back to help the woman lift some bags out of the trunk. I presumed they were staying. And then, after talking to the woman some more, Rory looked over at the boy. He spoke a few words, and though I didn't catch all of them, I distinctly heard him say, 'Son.' I wasn't sure until the child returned the sentiment and shouted out, 'Dad.'

That was when I took off.

Thoughts swirled around my head as I ran. Was this the

reason why Rory had broken things off with me four years ago? Granted, the boy appeared too old to fit the timing. If that woman and Rory had been together and she'd gotten pregnant, the child would be three or thereabouts. But what if they'd been together before he broke up with me and decided he could no longer keep them secret?

It was a pretty big thing to hide in a small town—having a lover and a child.

Surely, I'd have heard something? Some gossip, at least?

But I hadn't. No hints, no signs. Nothing.

Scenarios bombarded me, but I forced myself to look at this logically.

Maybe something else was going on? Maybe there was a perfectly reasonable explanation? To be honest, I feared hearing it. What if the things which first came to mind were true? What if I'd been a fool for years? What if I'd not been enough? What if Rory had never really loved me?

"T?"

Hearing his voice made me shake from my trance.

Barely five feet away from me, he stood. And he wasn't alone.

The child was with him. Staring at me wide-eyed like I was an anomaly. Rory stared at me as well, and for a second, I worried I'd been speaking aloud.

"Are you okay?" Rory asked, and I realized I must look like I'd seen a ghost. Or something just as terrifying. Maybe I had. Maybe the proof of my naivety now stood there staring at me.

Pull yourself together!

I remembered the vow I'd made to myself years ago as I'd put the shattered pieces of my life back together.

This is not my fault. I am enough. If he can't see that, he is the fool. Not me.

Three times, I silently repeated the words before I found my voice.

Instead of looking at Rory, I looked at the child. In his hands, I noticed he clutched a small plastic dump truck. "Hello." My voice sounded strained. I attempted to smile.

The boy ducked behind Rory's leg.

Rory looked at me funny, so I stopped smiling. "Thea, I'd like to introduce Gavin. My son."

To appear surprised, I opened my eyes wide and formed an O with my mouth. Gavin peeked at me and quickly hid again.

Oh, come on! If anyone had earned the right to hide, it was me.

I guess my expression demanded an answer because Rory dove right in.

"Before you ask, I didn't say anything because I was afraid I'd jinx it. Remember me telling you about an acquisition? I meant the adoption. It's why I needed the letter of employment, why I left the force and started another job. A job where I wasn't out on shifts and doing dangerous stuff. I needed to show I could offer stability."

"Wait." I held up my hand to stop the deluge of words he was dumping on me. "You adopted a son?"

Rory ruffled the boy's hair. "Yes." He stepped to the side, leaving the youngster exposed. Seeing me watching, he froze like a deer in headlights.

"Hi, Gavin. That's a nice truck you have there." Though a million questions swam through my head, I recognized the rush of relief coursing over me. Rory hadn't been having an affair. He hadn't had a child with someone else. That woman I'd seen must have something to do with the adoption. I hadn't been a fool.

Gavin broke from his trance and tilted his head to stare up at the house. "Is this your cabin?" he asked shyly, his voice in awe.

"It's the main house of the resort," I told him. "Rory — I mean, your dad — has two of the cabins that my aunt and uncle used to rent out to guests."

"Remember I told you I was going to work at a resort? This is where I meant," Rory said.

Gavin shot a look at him. "You're not gonna give someone my new room, are ya?"

Rory bent down to be at eye level with him. "No. No way. That room is yours, buddy. I'm not renting out my cabin. The one beside it is going to have a nice man stay in it for the summer." Then he turned and took a seat on the bottom step of the deck. "See those cabins over that way?" He gestured to my trio. Gavin nodded. "Those belong to my friend Thea, along with this big house here."

Gavin peered in the direction of my cabins for a moment, then looked toward Rory's pair. "How come she got more than you?" he asked.

Rory grinned, and I could see he hid a chuckle. "Well, that's because Thea's aunt and uncle left the resort to her. They were very generous and thoughtful to leave two cabins to me as well."

Gavin nodded solemnly. "That was nice."

"They left them to me because I've known Thea for a long, long time. Since I was just a little bit older than you are. You see, when I was little, I used to come here in the summer. Remember I told you how I used to live in the same home as you did in town?"

"Yes. Your mom was sick," Gavin clarified.

A shadow crossed Rory's face for the briefest of seconds. "That's right. She was sick a lot, so I would stay at the home, and they'd take care of me."

"Just like me," Gavin said.

"Yes. And in the summer, before the home built their own

campground and lodge, they used to come here. Thea's aunt and uncle would let them use the pair of cabins that I have now. The bedrooms used to be full of bunkbeds."

Gavin appeared to think about that for a moment. He looked up at me. "You and my dad played together when you were little?"

I swallowed over the sudden lump in my throat. Now everything made perfect sense. Somehow, Rory had crossed paths with Gavin. Seeing himself in the boy, a child lost, and alone, they had forged a bond. Then he decided to adopt him.

"We did," I confirmed, and stared into Rory's eyes when he turned and looked up at me. "We were the very best of friends."

"Sorry I'm late for our get-together this morning," Rory said. "Erika was just coming down the roadway when I reached your place.

"You don't say," I said innocently.

"Yes, I hadn't realized she'd been trying to reach me since yesterday. My phone was dying, and I'd turned it off while we were finishing up. I forgot to turn it back on. So, she came by with Gavin and the news that the judge had decided to grant the adoption."

The look on his face was pure bliss. I could see how happy he was.

"That's wonderful," I said. *That's why he was talking about a judge. And Jehrel thought he was a murderer!*

"This won't affect my ability to do my job if you're concerned," Rory said.

"No, I'm sure it won't." I looked at Gavin. "Hey, I was just gonna make up lunch. Are you guys hungry?"

Gavin looked at Rory before he nodded shyly.

"Okay, great. What do you like to eat?" I asked. Gavin shrugged. "I can make grilled cheese? Soup? PB and J? Tuna?" I tried to remember everything in the cupboard. That reminded me that I needed to shop again. Especially if Jehrel and Alan were going to come up.

Gavin looked to Rory for the answer, but Rory didn't say anything, which I appreciated. When I was little, my dad always spoke up for me when an adult asked me a question. Like I had no opinion of my own, or I was too dull-witted to understand the question or even know what I wanted. I'd told Rory about this during one of our many heart-to-hearts.

"I like grill cheese," Gavin offered.

"Great choice," Rory said. "I happen to love them, myself." He winked at me, and I smiled.

"Let's go in, shall we?" Getting to my feet, I gestured for Gavin to join me on the deck. He snagged Rory's hand as he came up the pair of steps to follow me inside.

~

While Gavin sat at the table with a glass of milk, Rory and I worked together to make lunch. I turned the coffee back on and made us each a mug while Rory grabbed the bread, cheese, and butter. Using two frying pans, we quickly made up a bunch of sandwiches. Rory put the platter down on the table, and I laid out plates and set out ketchup, knowing Rory refused to eat grilled cheese without it.

"Wow, you guys are fast," Gavin said, looking impressed.

"We work well together. Always have," Rory said.

"There's time to show Gavin around the house before the guests arrive," I offered.

"Great idea. Would you like that, sport?"

Mouth full, Gavin nodded. At least he hadn't picked up Rory's bad habit of showing off the contents in his cheeks.

Gavin swallowed and contemplated me. "Do you live here? All by yourself?" he asked, eyes wide.

I reached over with my napkin and dabbed a bit of ketchup from his chin. "Yep. Sure do. At least, for the summer, I do."

"Aren't ya scared?" Gavin asked.

Rory and I exchanged a look, and I warned him with my gaze not to dare say yes. "No. There's nothing to be afraid of," I assured him.

"I used to see a woman come in my room," Gavin said in a hushed tone. "I could see right through her, so I think she was a ghost. I haven't seen her for a while, though."

"You were probably just dreaming, buddy," Rory assured him.

Looking unconvinced, Gavin took another bite of his sandwich and quickly washed it down with a chug of milk. I made a mental note to add milk to my grocery list.

"Oh," I said. "You're going to need to go to town and grab groceries, I bet."

Rory looked panicked for a second. "Oh, geesh, you're right." He looked at Gavin. "I only have old people boring food at my house. We'll make a list together, and you tell me what you like."

"Okay," Gavin agreed.

I had a feeling, despite the great job Rory had done shopping for me, that his own freezer consisted of a staple of frozen TV dinners, and his cupboards held only tins of soup and Ravioli and boxes of mac and cheese.

"It's only just after one. Why don't you make up a quick list while we're eating, and then you can pop into town?" I suggested. "Gavin can stay here with me if he likes, and I'll give him a tour of the house."

"Oh, really? But our guests...?"

"Not due for hours," I assured him.

He looked between Gavin and me uncertainly. "I dunno."

"We'll be fine," Gavin said, making my heart melt a little.

"Sure we will." I got up and reached on top of the fridge for a pad of paper and a pen.

The pair began making their list, and I offered up a few suggestions as well.

"Okay, that's good," Rory said. "I'm sure as I go along, I'll see stuff to add." He looked at his watch. "I should head out. It's the start of tourist season, so I can imagine the crowd."

"Yeah, and not only at the grocery store," I added. "The streets will be busy."

Gavin, sitting close to Rory, gestured at him to bend down. Rory complied, and soon Gavin was whispering in his ear and giggling.

Rory smiled, and I swore his face went a bit red. "No, Thea is not my girlfriend," he confirmed, avoiding eye contact with me.

"Too bad," Gavin said to him. Then he looked at me. "You're nice."

Now I blushed. "Thank you. You're nice, too." Then I remembered why Rory and I had decided in the first place to get together for lunch.

"Oh, I made up this info sheet for the guests and printed off copies." I sprang to my feet to reach on top of the fridge again and grabbed a small stack of papers. I passed a sheet to Rory. "I'm surprised the ink still worked. The printer's a relic."

Rory looked over the short list of specifics for the guests, containing pertinent phone numbers, instructions for the cabin and boat equipment, information about the lake and the area, and some highlights about town and tourist spots, and some other stuff. I had gone over Aunt Agnes's original handout and just did some updating.

"Oh, there's a map, too," I said, rifling through the papers in my hands. I'd copied Uncle Jimmy's sketch that they used to pass out to the guests. Not much had changed with that.

"These are great," he said.

"If there's anything you want to change or add, let me

know. Oh, maybe grab some printer ink while you're in town, just in case?"

"Sure thing." He smiled at Gavin as he got to his feet. "You're sure you'll be okay?"

Gavin nodded.

"Good. Finish up your milk, buddy. Thea's gonna walk me to the door and be right back." Rory gave me a pointed look.

"For our tour," Gavin said.

"Yes, our tour," I agreed.

At the door, Rory paused. "Are you sure you're all right with this? I can take him with me if you're busy. He can have a look around here another time."

"No, no," I assured him. "We'll be fine. Don't rush. Get what you need."

Still looking uncertain, Rory left just as Gavin came to join us. Wearing a milk mustache, he watched after Rory. He was headed toward his cabin to grab his truck.

"He won't be long," I assured Gavin, gently guiding him away from the door. "Are you ready for a tour?"

The grim line of his mouth curled into a smile. An arm came up to rub across his upper lip. "Oh, yeah. Do you have an attic?"

Great.

"I sure do."

"Awesome!" he said. "Let's start there."

Chapter 19

Rory estimated ten thousand people were in line at the grocery store. And only three cashiers. Not to mention the million tourists who had flocked into town, swarming the shops and bottlenecking the roads. As much as he wanted to sigh in frustration, the elderly couple in front of him didn't deserve his impatience. Shopping had taken twice as long as it should have, with carts lining the isles like they'd settled in for a drive-in movie.

He took a deep breath and looked at his watch. Two-thirty. Despite the fact he'd been in line for a hundred years, he was making good time. Upon arrival in town, seeing the horde, he'd opted to stop in first at the Drug Mart and grab the ink Thea requested. Now, all he had to do was check out, drive home, unpack, and be ready for guests in an hour and a half. *Piece of cake.*

Gavin's face flashed in his mind, and Rory smiled.

He still reeled from this morning's events.

It was over. All the hoops he'd jumped through had not been in vain. Just the look on Gavin's face when he saw his bedroom had made it worth it.

And then there was Thea.

Knowing it was best to just rip off the band-aid, he'd walked them down the road and made the introductions. Things couldn't have gone better. Thea had accepted that he'd adopted Gavin, no doubt due to the bond she'd known he and Gavin shared over their similar situations. Granted, she may ask for more details later, he would fill in the blanks as best he could.

Without revealing the whole truth.

That would be disastrous not only for Thea but for Gavin as well. Rory was determined neither of them would learn about the part he'd played in Gavin's predicament. Gavin was far too young. Once he was older, Rory would have to tell him. But not yet. Rory hadn't been the one to put the boy into the home in town. Not directly. But he'd played a part in it. And even though he was no longer on the police force, he was still determined to solve the mystery of Elaina's murder. He had a theory about what had happened. But he'd yet to find any concrete proof.

Rory knew from Darren's rap sheet that he had a history of gang ties. He wouldn't put it past him to have attempted robbery to solve a larger problem. Gangs, never mind gang violence, were unheard of in Hadleigh. But Darren had relocated here with Gavin from the city when Gavin was very young. Down on his luck, he'd moved them in with his mother. If Darren had failed to make good on a debt to the gang, it might be possible they had come seeking reparation. Had Elaina been unfortunate enough to get caught in the fallout? But Darren had died years before Elaina's untimely demise. The gang theory was far-reaching, but it was all Rory had to go on.

Mechanically, Rory moved through the line, his mind deep in thought.

Instead of dwelling on things he couldn't control, he thought instead about the summer ahead. He and Gavin, and Thea would be together at the resort. That thought made him tingle. Gavin had already taken a liking to Thea, as he knew he would. And he suspected Thea wasn't averse to Gavin's presence. In fact, it appeared the pair had already begun to form a bond. It reminded him of how he had taken to Gavin so quickly years ago. A fierce protectiveness had come over him that he could only describe as paternal.

After Elaina's declining health and Gavin being moved into Waverly, he began the adoption process. For him, there'd been no other option. Having lost his own father at a young age, he'd worried about being a good dad. But then he recalled all the guidance and love he'd received from Uncle Jimmy. He'd been like a father to him, and the pain cut deep when he lost him. A similar pain rocked him when Aunt Agnes had died. When his own mom passed away from a drug overdose when he was fifteen, Thea, Jimmy, and Agnes surrounded him with their love. They saw him through it, making a difficult time somewhat easier to bear. His story would be very different if he hadn't had them in his life. He'd hoped when Agnes died, Thea would come right away and stay, even for a while. Even if she didn't want him around, knowing she was close would have made things easier. When she failed to arrive at the funeral without a word, he was confused, then frustrated, then sad. Logically, he knew something must have happened. He'd tried to call her, but her phone had gone directly to voice mail every time. He figured she was ignoring him. There'd been no other choice but to wait. And when she'd finally returned, he'd been so happy to see her. Initially, he botched things due to his lingering frustration, which had come out as snarky comments. He fixed that, though.

Never had he imagined they would wind up spending the summer together at the resort, along with Gavin. Despite the underlying secrets he hid, Rory couldn't be happier.

Suddenly, the world felt like a new place. There were so many things to do and experience now that he had Gavin to share them with. Seeing old sites through Gavin's eyes would make them new again. He remembered all the places he and Thea had discovered on their many hikes, first with her aunt and uncle and then when they were older, on their own. He smiled, recalling the summer he was seventeen, only a year away from being able to move out of Waverly.

He and Thea had ventured out onto the vast trails around Talon Lake. With him, he'd carried some basic supplies in a backpack, and they'd each had a canteen. From experience, both of them knew these little adventures could turn into hours. Sometimes, they would leave after breakfast and return to the resort by dinner. Uncle Jimmy would just shake his head and smile, and Aunt Agnes would be waiting with a hot meal and a lecture. This one particular time, he recalled, hadn't turned out so smoothly. In fact, Rory had been surprised Thea's family hadn't called the sheriff and rallied a search party to look for them.

Starting out, they'd had no idea things would be so different between them once they made it back...

"Come on, slowpoke," Rory called over his shoulder to Thea. Seeing her bent down, tying her bootlace, he paused. He uncapped his canteen and took a small swallow, rationing his water.

"Okay," Thea said, standing up and walking over to join him. She looked at her watch. "How far did you say it was?"

He began walking again, and Thea kept pace with him. "An hour or so to get there. We can spend the day and be back by dinner."

"I've heard that one before," Thea muttered.

Rory smiled, knowing she was just annoyed he'd found another cool place without her. Hiking these trails when she was back at home made him feel close to her. It also gave him the chance to share them with her when she returned. He knew she loved these excursions as much as he did. And despite hearing a lecture now and again, he appreciated Uncle Jimmy and Aunt Anges trusting him to bring Thea home safe. Those lectures were ones he'd endured solo. Not the shared ones they had to sit through whenever they arrived home later than expected.

In spite of the bugs being pests, the weather was warm and sunny. A beautiful day for a hike. The camaraderie they shared made the silence easy, neither feeling the need to fill the air with idle chatter. Both knew it was better to save their breath for the large hill. Out of habit, Rory took Thea's hand as they started up the steep incline. This was the hardest part of the walk. And even with them being in excellent shape, they both were breathing heavily by the time they reached the top. They stopped to catch their breath and take a cool drink before continuing. Another twenty minutes later, Rory turned off the trail.

"How're we gonna remember the way back?" Thea asked.

"Don't worry," Rory assured her. "I've come here a few times already. I know the way."

"I've heard that one before, too." Her comment had been quiet, but Rory had heard it.

The trees up here past the ridge were spaced wider than below, allowing the trunks to grow thick and tall. The wide canopy of leaves blew in the gentle wind, letting shafts of sunlight pierce the ground. The floor of the forest was carpeted with years of downed leaves cushioning the tread of their boots. Boulders, resting for eons, were scattered about like large dice tossed by giants. Some had moss growing on them, and some had indents shaped like steps or ledges jutting out over small openings. Some housed small animals, the telltale piles of leaves and twigs shoved into the shallow curves made smooth over the years by the elements.

"How's school going?" Thea asked.

Rory shrugged. "It's okay." He knew he was lucky to do well in school despite his circumstances. It helped to keep his mind focused on his goal of becoming a police officer.

"You're lucky you're going into your last year."

Her tone of voice surprised him. "I thought you liked high school? How they treat you more grown up."

"Yeah, I guess. It's just harder than I thought. The work and the social stuff."

"What about your friends? How're they doing?" he asked. She'd told him about Ava, Megs, and Lyla. They'd been friends since grade seven.

"We're not all in the same classes anymore. We see each other at our lockers and at lunch — if we have it in the same period. But they're all making new friends, going to the mall and out for coffee, and even parties without me. Sometimes I'm invited, but not all of their new friends get along with my new friends."

"Oh. So, you're making new friends as well?"

"I guess. It's not the same, though. I'm not close to them like how I was with my old friends. Sometimes, I want things to go back to the way they were, with us all together. I hate how everything changes."

Rory reached out and took her hand again, giving it a squeeze. "I know you do. Well, I haven't changed. Still the same old boring guy in the same old boring small town."

Thea smiled at him. "You're not boring. And I love Hadleigh. I don't want to live here when I grow up, though."

"Oh? Where do you want to live?" Rory asked.

Thea's face became animated. "I've been thinking about starting my own business once I'm done school. I'm not sure what it will be yet, but I do know I want to move to Toronto."

"What's wrong with Oshawa?"

She gave an unladylike snort. "Like I said, everything's changing. Not just the people but even the town itself. Buildings are going up in fields where fall fairs used to be set up. They're paving over everything, or expanding, or renovating. All in the name of progress."

"Don't you think everything will be expanding and progressing in Toronto?"

"Yes, of course it will. Inevitable, I guess. But I didn't grow up in Toronto. It's not my parks and schools and neighborhoods that are being torn down and being paved over or built up bigger.

I won't have an emotional tie to anything there. Maybe it will hurt less."

Her last few words were whispered. Rory thought maybe she hadn't meant to reveal them. If she had, he was honored she'd shared them with him.

"Well, maybe I'll move to Toronto one day, too," he said.

She turned her gaze to him and smiled, giving his hand a squeeze in return. "Really?"

He shrugged again. "Sure. A town that big will no doubt need another cop."

And then he was leading her through the last few paces toward his surprise. When they turned the corner around a huge boulder, Rory felt his hand tug as Thea paused mid-step.

"Oh! Wow," she gasped. "You were right. This was definitely worth the walk."

Before them was a lake about a third the size of Talon. The shape was oval, with the ends curling into mini bays to explore. All around the shoreline were brush and tall trees. Not a cottage or manmade structure in sight. The best aspect was the island sitting smack dab in the middle of the lake. Beneath their feet was a smooth rock face angling gently toward the water's edge.

"Wait a minute," Thea said, moving closer to the shore. "Is this the elusive Charlotte Lake?"

Rory joined her at the edge. "I can't say for sure. But I believe so."

"No way. I can't believe you found it. We've searched for years."

Rory swung the bag off his shoulder and placed it down away from the water. "The legend said something about an island. This has got to be it."

"The legend," Thea laughed. "You mean the boozed-up old guys you overheard talking about it? What were you doing outside the bar anyway?"

Rory laughed as well. "Just walking by. They were the ones who mentioned Charlotte Lake and the supposed treasure. So when I asked around at the library the next day, Miss Robinson brought up the story on microfiche."

"Yeah, the good old days," Thea said. "I don't remember that part of the story."

"Two years ago, I wasn't going to admit I'd gone searching for answers in a library," Rory said.

"You'll make a good detective one day," Thea told him.

"Thanks. Anyway, I thought if someone's going to bury a treasure, it would probably be on the island."

"Makes sense. But how would she get out there?"

"This was like a hundred years ago. Remember the old settlement we saw last year? It's not far from here." Thea nodded, so he continued. "Charlotte — the young woman the lake's named after — might have lived there?"

Thea didn't look convinced. "I dunno. I thought you'd overheard that she was supposed to have come from a rich family. How'd she end up in a tiny settlement in the middle of the forest?"

"How else? Love. She left her family in Hadleigh, which back then was the equivalent of a big town, to be with a man."

"Oh yes, that's right. You said something about her running away?"

"Yes, and when her family tracked her down, she took off into the lake and swam for the island to escape them. Initially, when she'd run off, she'd brought with her a bunch of gold nuggets her prospector father had gotten from workers in his mine to start her new life with her love," Rory said. "I wonder if he really loved her or if he just loved her gold?"

"So, weighted down by the gold nuggets, she barely makes it to the island," Thea continued. They both laughed.

"The nuggets probably would have fit in her hand," Rory

scoffed.

"Well, my way sounds more dramatic."

Rory shook his head. "So she makes it to the island and stashes the gold nuggets, determined to one day return for them and her love."

"But a few months later, her dad shuts down the mine, and the family sails back to England."

"Broken-hearted, the young man names the lake after her. And to this day, it is known as Charlotte Lake," Rory concluded. "But the story never revealed if the gold nuggets were ever recovered."

"Maybe they never existed? Or she dropped them on the swim across?" Thea guessed. "They'd be worth a fortune nowadays with the price of gold."

Rory pulled off his shirt. "Exactly. So, what are we waiting for?" He stripped down to his boxers, and Thea, more demure, left her t-shirt on to cover her bra and panties but took off her jeans.

Easily, they swam through the water to the island and, for hours, searched for gold nuggets, losing all track of time. Then, they sat by the shoreline and shared their first kiss.

Hand in hand, they returned just as the sun was going down, finding the resort in a frenzy over their whereabouts. They endured an hour-long lecture while they wolfed down their dinners. And though Uncle Jimmy had joined in on the lecture this time with Aunt Agnes, he'd still shook his head and smiled at them when he left the room.

"Hey, you're up!" The voice jolted Rory from his reverie.

"Oh, thanks," he said to the guy behind him in line and started loading his groceries onto the rolling counter.

Bags packed into the backseat, Rory climbed into the front of his truck. The time on his dash said three o'clock.

Moments later, he was rolling down the road back to the

resort.

Chapter 20

Gavin loved the attic. Especially the trunks of old clothing he insisted I open to prove there wasn't treasure inside of them.

"You see?" I said as he dove his hands in amongst the old pants and shirts and dresses.

"Yeah, just boring clothes." He pulled out an old fedora that Uncle Jimmy used to wear. Giving me an impish grin, he put the hat on his head and proceeded to waltz around the floor, snatching up an old cane along the way.

I couldn't help but laugh at his antics. "Oh, you think you're funny, do you?" I reached into the trunk and pulled out a feathery boa, which must have been from a costume. There was also a jaunty little hat that I pulled onto my head. Next was a long, shimmery cardigan that almost reached my knees.

Flinging the boa over my shoulder, I winked at Gavin. "Well, hello, darlin'."

He burst into laughter.

Soon, we had the other trunks open and clothes flung about as we each sought to outdo the other with ridiculous ensembles. The honk of a horn interrupted our game.

"Oh no! It can't be someone here already." I rushed to the window, hoping to see down to the driveway. And then the doorbell rang.

"Somebody's here," Gavin informed me.

Without baring a thought, we both hurried down the stairs. I flung open the door and lit up with delight.

"Ohmygod, Jehrel!" I grasped him tight in an embrace.

He gave me a squeeze and then stepped back to hold my arms. "Look at you! You're fabulous!"

I realized Gavin and I were still dressed up. "Oh, we were trying on old clothes from the attic," I explained.

Jehrel's gaze took in Gavin, who was barely visible behind the bright green dress and high black boots I wore. "Oh, you must let me go through those trunks," he insisted.

"But of course," I promised. I encouraged Gavin to come out, guiding him with my hands. "Jehrel, this is Gavin. Rory's son." The pointed look I gave him relayed he was not to question me further.

Jehrel bent down. "Hi, Gavin. And who are you wearing?" He posed the question like a red carpet host.

Gavin giggled. "I'm not wearing a who. It's an old jacket and tie."

"Don't forget that fabulous hat," Jehrel said, indicating the fedora Gavin still had on his head.

"Are you going to stand there yapping all day, or are you going to help me?"

All eyes turned to Alan, who had the four doors of the car open along with the trunk.

"Alan!" I said, rushing outside to grab a suitcase from his hand. "I'm so glad you guys could make it."

Each holding a bag, we embraced awkwardly. "Jehrel said you were in dire need of clothes, and I can see he wasn't kidding."

"Ha ha." I recognized a couple of my bags from home. "Thanks for bringing my stuff."

"Our pleasure, hon," Alan replied.

Jehrel joined us by the trunk of the car.

"No," Alan insisted, seeing his intent. "Take Lully inside first. Put her in the bathroom until we're settled in."

"You brought Lully with you?" I gasped. AKA ferocious

feline.

"I'm sorry, hon," Alan said. "I hope it's all right. The neighbor refused to watch her along with the other two. And my mom is having trouble with her hip again."

"Oh no, I'm sorry to hear that." *Great.* "It's fine. She'll have the whole upstairs to roam around. You guys okay setting up in the guest room?" It's where they always stayed.

"Certainly," Alan agreed.

"Okay, let's get you settled. Rory and I are expecting our first guests to arrive any moment now."

"Oh, we better clear out then," Alan said, grabbing another bag. Jehrel was already on his way inside. I could hear Lully wailing and hissing in annoyance from being jostled around.

"It's fine," I assured him while we both walked to the door, Gavin trailing my every step. "Rory will be back any moment to help."

"Where is Rory?" Alan asked pointedly, his gaze lingering on Gavin.

"He had to stop by town to pick up a few things." We began up the stairs in a line. Jehrel was waiting on the landing outside the guestroom.

"Lully's secure," he said.

We all entered the bedroom, which had a queen-sized bed in it and a fireplace. The view was the same from Rory's room, facing the lake, whereas mine faced the driveway and road in.

"Sorry, the bed's not made up, but all the stuff is in the hall closet, along with extra pillows and towels," I said.

"We know the drill, honey," Jehrel said. "So, is Rory and Gavin staying in the main house since he's running the resort?"

"No," I responded. "Rory's renting out his extra cabin to the writer who comes up every year. Rory and Gavin are staying in Rory's cabin."

"I have my own room," Gavin informed him.

Jehrel, who adored children, smiled at Gavin. "And I bet it's fabulous."

Gavin giggled, already taken with Jehrel, his exuberance having that effect on people. Alan's expression aimed at Gavin displayed he was equally impressed.

We left the bags and went back to the driveway just as a minivan pulled in. The Tallmon's piled out of the car, and Mrs. Tallmon, seeing me, immediately rushed over to pull me into her arms.

"My dear sweet girl," she said. "I'm so sorry about your aunt." I had to fight the urge to sneeze when her strong perfume overtook me. She released me, and then Mr. Tallmon was there extending his hand to take mine.

"So sorry for your loss," he said.

"Thank you both," I replied, swallowing over the lump in my throat. I'd forgotten that many of the frequent flyer guests would be mourning my aunt's loss. Many of them had mourned Uncle Jimmy's passing as well.

The Tallmon's three children, daughters Willa, ten, and Sydney, eight, and son, Mason, six, crowded around us like little ducks. Gavin bumped up against me, having taken cover behind me again.

Reaching for his hand, I guided him to the forefront. "This is Gavin." The other three children stared at him a moment, then, after their parents extended a greeting, introduced themselves.

"Won't it be nice to have some kids to play with?" I said to Gavin, who still hadn't uttered a word. He seemed fascinated by Mr. and Mrs. Tallmon.

A horn honked, and I saw Rory's truck stop on the roadway before the driveway.

"Excuse me a moment, please," I said to our guests. Taking Gavin's hand, we went over to the truck.

"Hey, how'd you make out?" I asked.

"Hey. Hi, Gavin. Having fun with Thea?" Both of his eyebrows arched as he took in our outfits.

"Yeah, she's fun. We played dress-up," Gavin said.

I looked down at the dress and boots I had on and blushed bright red. I'd greeted the Talmons dressed like this, and I was surprised they hadn't jumped back in their car and left.

"I can see that," Rory said. Reaching over to the passenger seat, he passed me a small bag. "Ink."

"Great. Thanks. You better go unload your stuff before it melts," I suggested. And before he could ask, I said, "Gavin can stay with me. He'll have some friends to play with, I think." I smiled at Gavin, but he was looking over at the Tallmon girls, who were pushing their brother back and forth between them while their parents talked to Alan and Jehrel.

Rory followed my line of sight. "Who's that?"

"Ah, that's my friends, Jehrel and Alan. They're staying with me for a bit. They brought up more of my clothes."

"They have a cat! It hisses like a snake," Gavin told him.

"Does it?" Rory looked at me and smiled. "I better get going so I can get back and help."

"Okay. I'm still expecting Mr. Cole and the young couple."

"Right. I'm off." Rory waved at us and rolled down the roadway toward his place.

Alan had his hands full again, and Jehrel was leaning into the backseat. I went over to the Tallmons, who were trying to break up the shoving match all three kids were in now.

"I'll run in and grab your key," I told them. I didn't have to look behind me to know Gavin was right on my tail. I headed into the kitchen and grabbed the key ring for the Tallmon's cabin and also a copy of the papers I'd printed up.

"Busy place, eh, Gavin?"

"Yeah. When can we go play again?" he asked as we got back outside.

"As soon as I get everyone settled, we can finish your tour," I promised him. Passing the papers and keys to Mrs. Tallmon, I smiled at her.

"I don't usually dress like this," I assured her. "We were in the attic playing dress-up with the old clothes." I really hoped she wouldn't start asking questions about Gavin.

Thankfully, she just beamed at us. "That's lovely. Isn't that lovely, Frank?" she said to her husband.

He nodded and smiled as well. They'd corralled their kids into the car, but since the windows were all down, we could hear them arguing. As they pulled away to park at their cabin, a sleek black sports car pulled in.

"Cool!" Gavin said.

Alan and Jehrel, who were on their way inside, paused to admire the car. After a quick look from me, they bustled inside.

Mr. Cole got out of the car and stretched. "Always forget how long that drive is," he complained.

A nice-looking man in his early forties, he generally wore a serious or curious expression. His messy mop of dark curls reminded me of Gavin's unruly hair. His pants and shirt appeared wrinkled from the drive, but I knew better. Aunt Anges had remarked more than once how Mr. Cole rarely came up for air once he started on a book, sometimes forgetting to eat and shower, never mind changing his clothes. Now that I'd found my passion with my own occupation, I could understand that.

"Welcome. I'll just run in and grab your keys and info sheet," I said. Moments later, Gavin and I returned, and I passed the items over to him.

"Thank you, Thea. I was sorry to hear about your aunt's passing. Wonderful woman." He patted my arm awkwardly.

"I appreciate that. If there's anything you need, please don't hesitate to ask."

He smiled tightly at Gavin, and I had no doubt his mind

was still deep in thought about his latest novel. "Thank you." Then he climbed into his car and was off.

"He's staying beside us?" Gavin commented, seeing the car park at the cabin next to Rory's.

"Yes. And you can see the car right out your bedroom window, I bet."

"Cool," he repeated.

The roadway appeared empty, so I figured our last guests were running a bit late or had stopped in town. Hopefully, they hadn't lost their way. It was easy to get turned around on the backroads here.

"Let's go inside and check on my friends. When the other guests arrive, we'll hear the doorbell."

"Okay," Gavin agreed.

Taking one last look around, I turned and headed inside, Gavin following close by. Alan and Jehrel's car was locked up, so I figured they'd unpacked everything. Come to think of it, though, they'd had a lot of luggage—even for Jehrel. I wondered if they planned to stay more than a few days. Not that it mattered to me. They'd be fine entertaining themselves while I got to work on my cabin reno.

Inside, I led Gavin into the library. His eyes traveled up the length of the two-story stone fireplace.

"Wow," he said, impressed. If he'd looked over the railing on our way upstairs earlier, he would have glimpsed the library. No doubt his gaze had been seeking the hissing cat-snake above instead.

Now was a good time to warn him about Lully. "Gavin, that cat the guys brought inside, it's not a very nice kitty, okay? It won't hurt you, but try not to approach it or startle it if you can help it."

"Why's it so mad? Is it cause the little carrier it was in?" he asked.

"I'm sure the carrier didn't help, or the long car ride, but Lully is generally pretty growly."

"Miss Martel at Waverley said I was a cranky pants," he admitted.

For some reason, my protective instinct reared up. Usually, it happened if someone was rude to Jehrel. One thing I especially couldn't stand was a bully.

"That's not a very nice thing to say," I commented.

He shrugged, his interest suddenly piqued by the rolling ladder. I'd have to nip that in the bud. "Sorry, buddy," I said, heading him off before he could begin climbing. "That goes way too high for you." Seeing his frown, I attempted to interest him in the view instead. "Look, you can see the lake from here."

We moved over to the window, which faced out over the deck.

"You got boats," he observed.

"Yes. Your dad does, too. He or I can take you out on the lake. But you must wear a life jacket, and you have to be with one of us. Even if you're just on the docks."

He sighed dramatically. It dawned on me that having him here was going to pose a bit of a challenge. We'd need to keep a constant eye on him, making sure he was safe around the lake and the forest.

I smiled in spite of the extra concern. Already, I was thinking of ways to entertain Gavin and all the places Rory and I could take him. He'd somehow become forefront in my mind, not the reno job I was contemplating. How had that happened so quickly? And really, I had to remind myself before my planning got too carried away that Gavin was not my responsibility. He was Rory's. Rory's son. Not mine.

Why did that thought make me feel sad?

Chapter 21

Alan, Jehrel, and I relaxed in the living room in front of the fire, eating popcorn later that evening. They shared the loveseat while I sat on one of the easy chairs. The hiss and pop of the flames reminded me of the cat.

"How was Lully when you last checked on her?" I asked Alan. Her name was short for Lullaby. When she was a kitten, Alan's mom used to sing to her, and she'd fall right to sleep. Whenever she got in a mood, Alan, or whichever one of us was nearest, would sing to her. Usually worked like a charm. Usually.

"Curled up on the bed. Tired out from the drive, most likely," he replied.

"We'll keep her closed up for a day or so until she gets used to the changes," Jehrel added. He'd been thoughtful ever since Rory had left with Gavin, and I think he missed the boy as well. Jehrel had been surprisingly civil when I'd made the formal introductions. I knew Alan wouldn't say anything to Rory about our four-year estrangement. I'd even suspected Jehrel knew better than to be snippy when a child was present. But I'd at least expected a few sideways glances or glares and maybe a few snorts or huffs. And yet, he'd kept his cool. I'd been quite impressed. Although, to be fair, we'd only really made small talk since we had been waiting for the last guests to arrive at any moment.

The young couple had rode in after five o'clock. There'd been no need for them to ring the doorbell since we'd heard the roar of their motorcycle. I had no idea how they packed for a weeklong vacation with what they could stuff into the small saddlebags and mini trunk on the bike. They hadn't seemed too concerned, however. Observing them, I wondered if Rory and I had ever looked that in love. Rory had handed out the keys and paperwork this time. He'd regretted missing the other guests, but I reminded him that with them being frequent flyers, they would know who he was. Plus, on the handout, I'd added Rory's position, contact information, and location. Promptly after the couple left to settle into their cabin, Rory had escorted Gavin home for dinner. It was their first night together, and watching them stroll down the road, I'd felt somewhat left out.

My friends had been a comfort to my melancholy. Alan loved to cook, and though I'd been getting low on supplies, he'd made an excellent dinner for us. We'd enjoyed a bottle of wine and easy conversation during the meal.

Throughout dinner, I'd endured the expected barrage of questions, mainly from Alan. Though not quick to forgive and forget, both of them had grudgingly allowed for the fact that Rory was doing a noble thing by stepping up and adopting Gavin. The lengths he'd gone to in order to qualify for the adoption had swayed matters greatly in his favor.

Jehrel yawned loudly. "Can't believe how sleepy I am."

"You forget every time you come here how the thick air affects you," I teased. It generally had the same effect on me, but when I'd arrived, I'd immediately been put through the wringer. By the time I had escaped, I'd adapted.

"It's only eight o'clock," Alan announced, looking at the grandfather clock.

"Well, it feels later," Jehrel insisted. "I'd swear we crossed a time zone. The drive took so long."

"It shouldn't be that bad on a Sunday afternoon. Although it is summer season, and a lot of rentals go from Sunday afternoon to Saturday morning like we do here. So you'll get that traffic."

"I'm glad you decided to stay and open the resort," Alan said. "And renovating one of your cabins is such a great idea."

"I want to check out that antique store in town. And the film crew if they're still shooting. We'd have been here yesterday, but Alan had to do work stuff," Jehrel said.

"Not everyone gets the summer off," Alan said in a sing-song voice.

By the look on Jehrel's face, he was going to go off, so I jumped in. "I have the summer off too. We've earned it, right?" My words had the desired effect despite the fact I didn't technically have the summer off.

"Ain't that a fact, darlin'." Jehrel appeared to deflate and slumped against the back of the couch. He was a kindergarten teacher, and having visited his class a few times, one of the best I'd ever seen. Kids appeared to hang on to his every word and followed him around in droves. He was fun and creative and made learning an exciting adventure. It was no wonder Gavin had taken to him so fast. Alan worked in a huge office building in downtown Toronto. He'd explained his job to me in the past, but it was complex, and I admit I may have zoned out when he went on about it. Whatever it was, he seemed immensely satisfied doing it. Some of the perks included an expense account, work-from-home options, and business trips. He and Jehrel were polar opposites in personalities and professions, but they fit together like two crazy puzzle pieces. The way Rory and I used to be. *Sigh.*

"I'm not sure if the movie crew has wrapped up shooting or not," I admitted, answering Jehrel's question. "They were in full swing yesterday, but I've no idea if they filmed in the park yet."

"It'll be hard for them with it being tourist season here," Alan predicted.

"Yes," I agreed. "Unless they've fit that into the movie somehow."

Jehrel got up and stretched, yawning loudly. "I've gotta go to bed." Alan agreed despite the early hour. While they both headed upstairs, I opted to sit by the fire awhile. My emotions needed examining, and I preferred to do that solo. Preferably, I liked to walk as I figured things out, but I wasn't about to head outside in the dark. One thing that made me relieved was I wouldn't be alone in the house tonight.

~

Rory congratulated himself on getting Gavin to bed and asleep only half an hour after schedule. Along with the other papers she'd left him, Erika had included a timeline Waverly had implemented. She'd stressed the summer months should be more lax and to use his own judgement and refer to the timeline as more of a guide. Rory had looked at it several times already. What did he know about schedules for kids anyway? He'd had to take deep breaths and control the urge to go barrelling down the road to Thea for help.

For dinner, he'd made spaghetti. He'd picked up a bag of frozen meatballs at the store and microwaved a handful for each of them. Red-faced, Gavin had told him dinner was great, which Rory took as a win before sending him off to wash. While Gavin was in the bathroom, Rory realized that for the next several years, he would not only have to plan but shop for and cook three meals a day. Again, he'd been tempted to run to Thea.

I can do this had become his new mantra.

He cracked a root beer and went outside to sit on the deck. The bullfrogs were croaking, and the gentle waves lapped against the shoreline. Mosquitoes buzzed, it being the season, but he'd never been overly bothered by them, much to Thea's annoyance. It was good she wasn't alone tonight; her friends having arrived from the city. He worried he may have to compete for her attention while they were here. Although Gavin may sway matters in his favor. But then he was annoyed with himself for thinking that way. It wouldn't do him or Gavin any good to become reliant on Thea for her time, considering she'd leave when summer passed. He couldn't put Gavin through that, never mind himself. They'd have to learn to get along on their own. It might be difficult since Gavin was so drawn to Thea already. Maybe Gavin had picked up on the way he felt about her? Rory finished his drink and headed to bed. The lights had all gone out at the main house, and he figured they'd opted for an early night. Knowing Gavin would probably be up bright and early, Rory thought it best he do the same.

The next morning, Rory was surprised to find he'd woken before Gavin. When he checked in on him, he was curled up sound asleep, holding tight to his stuffed bear. Rory took the opportunity to have a quick shower and then began breakfast. Gavin, rubbing his eyes, wandered into the kitchen soon after.

"Morning," Rory greeted him.

"Morning," Gavin replied, sliding into a seat at the table.

"Sleep well?" He put a plate of pancakes in front of him and then grabbed the syrup from the fridge.

Gavin's face lit up, seeing the stack, a slab of butter melting on the top. Rory poured syrup over it, and Gavin got busy with his fork. Before he sat down with his own stack of pancakes, Rory poured them each a tall glass of milk.

"So, what are you in the mood for today? Ride in the boat? Fishing? Hiking? Or we can go into town and do something?" He'd have to check in with Thea first and see if there were any resort issues that needed looking after first.

Gavin took a moment to gulp down some milk before he replied. "I want to play dress-up with Thea in the attic again."

"Um, Thea may be busy with her friends today, buddy," Rory said.

Gavin chewed a mouthful of food and swallowed. "Aren't we her friends too?"

"Yeah, sure we are. But Thea will be here all summer. Her friends are from out of town and won't be here long. She may want to be alone with them," he broke it to him gently.

Gavin smiled. "I like Ja-rel. He's funny and nice."

Rory nodded in agreement. "Yes, both of Thea's friends are nice."

"Can't we go and see them today? Please?"

How could he argue with that? "I'll tell you what. I need to talk to Thea about work stuff so we can go and say hello. If Thea and her friends are busy or they have plans, then we'll leave them alone, okay? But, if you think you might get upset, maybe we should go out in the boat instead."

Though Rory hadn't seen it himself, Erika had warned him Waverly had noted in Gavin's file how he tended to get upset and argumentative if he wasn't given his own way. Erika had explained that some children, when their lives had been upended, felt like they had no control over anything. Exerting their will to get their way helped them to feel they were taking back some of that control. She suggested it might be good to get into the habit of presenting Gavin with choices instead of expecting him to just go along with plans.

Gavin paused, fork partway to his mouth. His gaze narrowed as he appeared to ponder Rory's words.

"I won't get upset," he finally said.

Rory let loose a breath he didn't know he was holding. "Okay, great. We'll head over after breakfast."

Ten minutes later, they rang the doorbell at the main house.

Alan opened the door and smiled at them. "Hello."

"Hi. Is Thea here, and can we play, or do I have to do something else?" Gavin blurted out.

"Ah…" Alan began.

Rory shook his head. "Sorry. Gavin meant to ask if Thea

has plans this morning. Right, sport?"

Gavin nodded. "Yeah. Right."

"Okay, how about you come in and we'll...?"

Before Alan could finish his sentence, Gavin darted around him, kicked off his shoes, and took off for the kitchen.

"Thea!" they heard him call.

"Oh boy. Sorry about that. We need to work on decorum, I'm afraid," Rory said to Alan.

Alan laughed. "It's okay. He's excited."

They caught up to Gavin in the kitchen. He'd already seated himself at the table beside Jehrel across from Thea.

"Good morning," Thea said, including Rory in her greeting to Gavin.

"Can we play today?" Gavin asked her.

"Gavin, remember what I said?" Rory asked.

Gavin huffed and crossed his arms.

"How about you show me those trunks in the attic? We can let Thea and your dad talk about resort stuff, and Thea can come join us when she's ready?" Jehrel said to Gavin.

Rory saw Thea convey her thanks to Jehrel with her gaze.

"Okay!" Gavin yelled, jumping to his feet.

"Thank you," Rory said to Jehrel as he got up and put his coffee cup in the sink.

"No, thank *you*! I've been dying to get into those trunks," Jehrel assured him.

"Coffee, Rory?" Alan offered.

"Sure, thanks," Rory replied, taking a seat at the table. "I wanted to come by and see if you had any resort issues this morning? I haven't received any calls, but I haven't logged onto the website to check for emails yet." Thea had given him the password, and he had his own laptop back at his cabin he could use for business, along with his phone if he was out and about.

"No. I haven't heard anything. It's been pretty quiet,"

Thea said. "Gavin mentioned us doing something together?"

Alan passed Rory his coffee and sat down with them. "I have a feeling Jehrel will be keeping Gavin busy in the attic for some time. Especially if it involves fashion."

They all laughed.

"If you're not busy this morning, Gavin wanted to do something together. But no pressure. I know you have company and a cabin to renovate," Rory said. "I think I'll have to look into camp for Gavin to keep him busy this summer."

"That's a good idea. It'll be fun for him. In the meantime, I'm sure between us we'll be able to keep him occupied," Thea said.

"I feel bad. I didn't know I'd have him so soon. I mean, I'd hoped. But I'd not made plans just in case things didn't work out," Rory said.

Alan's phone rang, and when he looked at the screen, he excused himself and headed for the library.

"I'm really glad things worked out for you and Gavin," Thea said. "You'll make a great dad."

"Thanks, that means a lot," Rory replied. He sipped his coffee, feeling the sudden scrutiny in Thea's gaze.

"I wish you'd told me about Gavin," she said.

Rory put his mug down and fiddled with the handle. "I know. I'm sorry. Especially when you offered me the job of running this place. I should have told you, but I was worried it wouldn't work out. Not many places want to hand a child over to a single man without a steady job."

Thea smiled. "I'm glad I could help out in that department. But you also have a job doing upgrades."

Rory shook his head. "True, but it's mainly seasonal. And since I'd really just started up, I don't have a lot of clients. Having the resort job year-round really swayed things in my favor."

"I bet once word gets around about the upgrades you put

in here, along with the other cabins you've done, things will get busy for you."

"Hopefully, not too busy. I can get started on this place as soon as you're ready."

Thea got up to put her mug in the sink and leaned against the counter. "Let's wait a week. After the guys are gone and Gavin's had a chance to settle in."

"Sure. Sounds good."

They exchanged a smile, and Rory felt the warmth of it flow over him. He looked down to cover the rush of emotions he felt. That familiar feeling, that they could accomplish anything when they were together, had awakened.

It was the best feeling in the world.

Chapter 22

Wednesday afternoon Rory and Gavin, and I stood before Charlotte Lake. The last time I'd been here held bittersweet memories, it being the first place Rory and I had kissed. Then we'd returned home late and got in so much trouble I'd vowed never to come here again. And yet, here I was.

Rory said he'd been thinking about this place when he was in line at the store the other day, and as soon as he said *Island*, Gavin was all about hiking here.

"See the island out there, buddy?" Rory asked. He had a backpack slung over one shoulder, as did I. His held a small inflatable raft complete with plastic oars and a little pump. Mine held drinks and food and our towels.

"It's just like the picture Granny showed me!" Gavin exclaimed. The way he danced around led me to believe it was more than excitement that had him so jumpy.

"Why don't you take him for a little walk in the forest while I pull out the boat?" I said to Rory, indicating his son needed a washroom break.

"Oh…Oh! Yeah, sure," Rory said, giving me a wink and slinging off his pack. "Come on, let's go for a little stroll," he said to Gavin.

By the time they returned, I had the boat unrolled and the pump attached. Now, I was working on putting the oars together. Earlier, we'd stopped by the supply goods store in town to grab the boat, knowing Gavin would insist on seeing the island.

They'd had only one dingy left in stock, considering the horde of summer vacationers. We'd also swung by Genie's coffee shop and grabbed some caffeine to go, along with a hot chocolate for Gavin and a bag with giant chocolate chip cookies — those resting in my pack as well.

While Genie had rung us up, I'd asked how the movie shoot went. She'd filled me in on some of the details, and I vowed I'd be in either later in the afternoon or the next day with my friends to introduce them and hear more. I knew Jehrel would appreciate a first-hand accounting of the experience since the crew appeared to have wrapped up already.

On Monday, we'd played dress-up with Jehrel in the attic for a while. It'd given Rory a chance to wander around and see how our guests were doing. I'd been able to run into town and shop for groceries later in the day when Jehrel and Alan took out the paddle boat. On Tuesday, I'd taken the guys out for lunch at the one fancy restaurant in town, and we'd gone to see some sights. Rory had spent the day with Gavin, and later, we'd all gotten together for dinner at the main house, which Alan had graciously cooked.

"Gavin, you said something about your Granny showing you a picture of an island?" I said as he worked the pump, standing on the foot pedals, his arms moving up and down.

He nodded his head, keeping time with his pumps. "Yeah, looks just the same."

"You mean the island? Or the lake?" Rory asked.

"Both," Gavin clarified. "It had some girl's name."

He must have heard us talking about that as well, I assumed. "Charlotte Lake?" I asked.

Again, his head bobbed. "Yeah. That's it. Like the story with the pig and the spider."

"Charlotte's Web," Rory supplied. He knelt on the rockface, making sure the air Gavin pumped moved freely around the interior of the raft.

"That's the one. Granny always read it to me. She said the name Charlotte was also the name of a lake in the woods. She said there was an island. And gold. And she showed me a picture. A painting, I think."

"She had a painting of the lake?" I clarified.

"Yeah," Gavin confirmed. "But she kept it hidden in the back of her closet. Maybe she didn't think it was very good."

"Did she say who painted it?" Rory asked, obviously as intrigued as I was about this story.

Gavin shrugged. "I dunno. Can you pump now? My arms are tired."

He changed places with Rory, who took up the task for him. Over Gavin's head, Rory and I exchanged a glance.

"Did your Granny tell you the story about Charlotte and the gold?" I asked Gavin.

He appeared to ponder my question. "Lemme think. I remember her telling me some mushy love stuff. I didn't really listen to that part. But then she talked about an old mine filled with gold and how Charlotte stole some. She said she ran away to an island and hid the gold, and I guess that's why they named the lake after her."

"That about sums up the legend," Rory said. "Everyone who grew up in this town like your Granny has probably heard it. Did you know, years ago, when Thea and I found this lake, we swam across to the island and searched for the gold all day? We got home so late that we got into trouble."

Gavin smirked over that. "That's funny. You got in trouble for nothing."

Rory wiggled his eyebrows, earning him more giggles. "Oh, I dunno. What makes you think Thea and I didn't find the gold?"

Gavin snorted. "That's easy. Cause my Gran has it. At

least she did. Stashed somewhere in the basement of where we used to live."

"What?" Rory and I both said and froze.

"If you don't pump, the air's gonna run out," Gavin scolded him. Rory started pumping again.

Eyes on me, Rory asked, "Gavin, are you sure your Granny said she had gold in the basement? You mean of the hardware store your apartment was overtop of?"

What? I stood there, no doubt, with my mouth hanging open while I put it together.

Gavin's grandmother was the woman who'd lived in the apartment above Cassidy's store.

Until she'd been murdered.

I'd asked Rory about it, and he'd been cagey and evasive. Now I knew why. Maybe he'd been worried he would let something slip if he talked about the murder? He'd already revealed he hadn't wanted to tell me about Gavin and how he'd hoped to adopt him. That was all water under the bridge now.

Rory begged me with his gaze not to say anything. I gave him a curt nod, letting him know I would keep quiet. Though I really hoped my hard look conveyed the fact that he and I were not done talking about this.

Gavin nodded dramatically as though bored with the conversation. "Yeah. Can we go to the island now?"

Rory finished pumping up the raft and replaced the plug. We put the backpack I'd worn into the boat along with the oars and lifted the boat to the water's edge.

"Okay, we'll go across in our bathing suits," I said, distractedly. We'd put our suits on under our clothes. In the back of my mind, all I could think about was talking to Cassidy.

Soon, we stood ready, our clothes in piles set back from the shoreline. Rory helped Gavin climb into the dinghy and then helped me get in and passed over the oars. There was a thin rope lead on the front that Rory could use to guide the boat along as well. He was going to swim across since it wasn't that far, and all three of us couldn't fit in the boat.

Staring at the island, Rory and I exchanged another glance. I had a feeling he was thinking the same thing as me. About that poor old woman being pushed down the stairs. And now we might know the reason why. Poor Gavin. No wonder he'd wound up a ward of Waverly home.

Hours later, when we got back to the resort, we parted ways.

On the walk home, Rory and I had the opportunity to talk. He'd explained that Elaina had been about to move into a retirement home when she was killed. I'd already heard about that from Cassidy. I was relieved, however, when he told me Gavin hadn't been living with her at the time of the murder. He'd been sent to live at Waverly due to Elaina's declining health. That's when Rory had started the adoption process, he said. Rory admitted he didn't know any details of the investigation. Only that it remained unsolved, and there were no leads. I felt so bad for Gavin. All alone in the world due to a senseless act. I didn't ask Rory how he became aware of Gavin's circumstances. This being a small town, I had a feeling most people knew each other's business. He'd left the force so he would have a stable home life to offer Gavin. That was exactly the kind of thing the Rory I'd known and loved would do. That Rory didn't reconcile in my mind with the Rory who'd broken my heart four years ago. I still couldn't bring myself to ask him what had happened. Part of me hoped he'd tell me on his own. Until he did, I knew I'd never be able to fully trust him again. Or completely forgive him.

Before we parted, Rory told me he would make a call to his old partner on Hadleigh's police force and tell him what Gavin had said. Gavin, busy inspecting the last cookie I'd passed him, had rushed over and hugged me goodbye. Rory and I had exchanged another glance before he turned and walked away, Gavin following along. Another pang had risen up, but I'd pushed it down and forced my feet to turn and walk toward the main house.

If there was gold in the basement of Cassidy's store, I wondered if someone had found what they'd been willing to kill for. I rushed inside the house, anxious to talk things over with Jehrel. Inside, I could hear him call to me from the front deck.

"Oh, good," I said, finding him outside. "I wasn't sure you were here. Your car's gone."

He huffed. "Yes, it is. So is Alan. Work emergency. He'll be gone the rest of the week."

Judging by the look on his face, he wasn't happy about it. "I'm sorry. I know you were looking forward to spending some time together here."

He snorted, reminding me of Gavin. "Yes, here. There. Anywhere."

I patted his arm. "It can't be all that bad. I know he works a lot, but—"

"That's an understatement! It's all he does."

The only way to get Jehrel out of one of his sulks was with juicy gossip. And I had some. I led him inside and closed the door.

"You're never going to guess what happened."

His gaze narrowed. "Don't try to distract me with some made-up…"

I held up my hand. "Nope. Not made up. And this is juicy."

He huffed. "I'm not going to forget how upset I am."

"I know. But trust me, this is good." He sighed, and I knew I had him. We both took a seat before the cold hearth.

"Go on, then," he encouraged.

"Remember I was telling you about my friend Cassidy,

who owns the antique store? How she had to wait to take possession of the building because there was a murder?"

"Oh! Yes. And you thought Rory was—"

"I did not! You were the one—"

"Never mind that. Go on!"

I gave him the stink eye, almost tempted to let him sit and stew awhile. Except this was just so mind-boggling, I had to talk about it.

"So we hiked up to Charlotte Lake to take the dinghy boat Rory bought out to the island with Gavin."

"The lake where you and Rory first did the old sideways shuffle?"

"We did not! We kissed. Our first kiss!" I knew my face was flaming red.

"Whatever you say, darlin'." The look on his face conveyed he did not believe me.

"Anyway…" I told him the whole story, during which he shook his head sadly and muttered 'that poor child' more than once. By the look on his face when I finished, Rory and I weren't the only ones who thought the coincidence uncanny.

Jehrel processed my words a few moments before he spoke. "So, what do you think about Gavin's Granny having the gold? Is it possible?"

"That had me wondering as well. But also, why would she have a painting of the lake?"

Jehrel shrugged. "Could be she'd inherited it? Maybe Gavin's Granny was related to Charlotte?"

"Oh, wow. You're right. I never thought about that, but it makes perfect sense."

Jehrel preened over my praise. "Of course it does."

"Hey! Let's go into town. We could meet with Cassidy and see if she knows anything about the painting. Imagine if we found it in the apartment? Maybe it's signed, and we can figure out if there's a family connection."

"And see if that gold is still in the basement?"

A little shiver ran through me. "Do you think the murderer found the gold? Maybe Gavin's Granny heard them searching around and headed downstairs to investigate?"

"Seems possible," he agreed.

"But I wonder if she came upon the thief while they were still looking? Or, if they were on their way out."

"It could have been more than one person?"

I hadn't thought of that either. "Yes, it could have."

"Maybe Cassidy has more details?"

"Only one way to find out." I pulled out my phone and called Cassidy. When she answered, I gave her the bare minimum of details and asked if we could meet at her store. She agreed, and Jehrel and I headed out. When we got into the car, I hesitated.

"What's wrong?" he asked, anxious to leave.

"I wonder if I should let Rory know what we're doing?" He'd probably either try and talk me out of it or ask to come along. But if he wanted to come, he wouldn't want to bring Gavin, so that would leave me to watch him or maybe Jehrel.

"As much as I adore that child, I'm not staying behind to babysit while you two run off to play Cagney and Lacey."

Really? I couldn't blame him for not wanting to be left behind, either. "Let's just go. If we find out anything, I'll tell Rory later. Besides, he's probably elbow-deep in kraft dinner right now."

"Right on, sister."

Cassidy was waiting for us when we pulled up in the back parking lot of the store. She unlocked the door and let us in. "It's closing time, so we won't be disturbed." She ushered us in and secured the door.

"This is my friend Jehrel, visiting from Toronto. Jehrel, this is Cassidy."

"Hey," Cass greeted. Jehrel nodded once. "So, what's this about? You said something about a mystery painting?"

"That apartment upstairs, the one rented by the woman who died, did she leave anything behind?" I asked, gesturing to the stairwell.

"As far as I know, her stuff was packed up and donated."

"Everything?"

She shrugged. "I had help moving in here. If it was just me, I probably would remember seeing stuff left behind. We put my things here on the main floor and upstairs. The woman's apartment is where I put all my overflow stock. You've been in there. It's possible if any of her stuff was left behind that, some of her boxes got mixed in with mine. I'm not completely unpacked yet, so I couldn't tell you if all the boxes up there are mine."

"Do you mind if we head up while I fill you in?" I asked.

Cass shrugged. "Sure, okay."

"Buckle up, honey," Jehrel cautioned her.

On the way upstairs, I told Cassidy about the painting and what I hoped to find out. Jehrel kept inserting his theories and opinions, making the story twice as long. I finished the tale as we stood in the apartment.

"Gavin said she had the painting in a closet. Probably in her room."

"The master bedroom is here," Cassidy said, leading us over to the largest bedroom. Boxes were on the floor of the otherwise empty space.

I went over to the closet, which was shut tight. "Okay if I look?"

She nodded, and I turned the old glass doorknob. Inside, some old dresses hung from hangers, and the floor was packed with shoes and handbags, and other odds and ends.

"Whoever packed up her things missed all this." I knelt to get a better look inside the depths of the space. Moving aside the dangling gowns, I reached back against the wall. I touched what felt like a frame.

"I think I found something," I said. "I've got to move some of this stuff out though to get to it, if that's okay?"

"Sure," Cass said. She and Jehrel crammed in on either side of me and helped me move aside the contents. Then, slowly, gently, I slid the framed piece out. We all backed up to make room. It appeared to be a picture, but I couldn't see of what, it being turned to face the backside of the closet. I was surprised by how heavy and thick the frame was. I thought, from the way Gavin had described it, that the picture would be unimpressive. But it was grand.

Turning it around, I saw it was indeed Charlotte Lake.

In the bottom right corner of the painting was a name. "Mina Grey," I read aloud.

"That's the lake you were at? The one with the legend?" Cass asked.

"Yes, most definitely." Even though some of the details were slightly different, it could be because the painting was obviously done long ago. The shape of the lake and the island were spot on.

"Who is Mina?" Jehrel wondered aloud.

"No clue. There was no one by that name in the legend," I said.

Cassidy studied the frame, running her hands along the smooth, dark wood. "This is old." She turned the picture around to study the back, then turned it forward and studied the signature.

"What do you think?" I asked.

"I'd guess seventy years or so. The back isn't original. It's been replaced. Probably due to age. I'm sorry, paintings aren't really my area of expertise."

"Do you think we could take this?" I asked. "Rory has

custody of Gavin, and I think it should go to him."

"Sure," Cass said. "Anything here that belonged to his Granny is his now. I doubt he'll want a bunch of old clothes, but maybe you could go through the stuff and see what you think he'd like? You're welcome to bring him and Rory here as well if they'd like to go through it themselves."

"Thanks," I said. "That's really nice of you."

She shrugged. "No problem. I just wish I could get the previous owner to come get his stuff out of the basement. I don't know when I'm gonna find the time to go through it all."

"Oh!" Jehrel said. "Let's go look for the gold."

Cassidy's face lit up, and she laughed. "Totally!"

The painting, firmly in my grasp, we headed back through the apartment to the stairs. Reaching the main floor, I said, "I'm going to put this in my car. I'll tell Rory about it, and he can give it to Gavin when he feels the time is right. I'll also mention what you said about coming back and going through the rest of the stuff."

"Of course," Cass said. "Tell him there's no rush. Whenever they're ready, it'll be here."

They waited while I put the painting in my car. Just when we were about to journey into the basement, a loud knocking from the front of the shop got our attention. All three of us jumped about two feet in the air.

"I wonder who that is?" Cass said. "The closed sign is up."

"We'll come with you," I offered, and together we all headed into the shop.

Through the front door, we could see a man in a uniform.

"That's got to be Rory's friend," I said. "He mentioned he'd call him and tell him what Gavin told us."

"Well, there goes our search," Jehrel huffed. "I hope if anyone finds gold downstairs, the police don't confiscate it."

Cassidy opened the door, and the man introduced

himself. "Hi, I'm Officer Reynolds. I got a call regarding some new information about the death that occurred here a while back." He looked a bit embarrassed and unsure. I knew he must be questioning the legitimacy of the source, considering the information came from a six-year-old. The only reason he was here, no doubt, was as a favor to Rory.

"You mean the murder?" Jehrel said. I gave him a look, and he shrugged.

"Mind if I come in?" Officer Reynolds asked.

Cass opened the door and gestured him inside. "Not at all."

"Are you going to search for the gold?" Jehrel asked him.

He smirked. "No. Not yet, anyway. I just wanted to ask a few questions, if that's all right?"

"Sure, no problem." Cass wandered over to the checkout desk and sat down on a chair behind the counter. The rest of us followed. Jehrel and I leaned against the counter, and the officer took out his notebook.

"Okay, who can tell me the whole story?" he asked.

"That'd be me," I volunteered. "Though, if Rory filled you in, I doubt I'll have much to add."

"I'd like to hear it all again," he said. "Just in case he missed anything."

"Sure." I told him everything I knew, hoping I wouldn't have to hand over the painting for evidence.

Chapter 23

"You don't need the painting, do you?" I asked, finished with my version of events.

Officer Reynolds laughed, seeing the obvious distress on my face. I hurried to explain. "I'm not trying to withhold evidence. I just want to make sure Gavin gets the picture since it belonged to his Granny." His pen was poised over his notebook, and I had the feeling he was waiting for something. "I'm Thea James, by the way." He jotted that down and tucked his book back into his pocket. "My aunt and uncle ran the resort at Talon Lake," I added.

Recognition lit his face, and then he shook his head sadly. "I was sorry to hear about your aunt's passing. We attended the same church in town. I knew your uncle as well. Wonderful people."

"Thank you. Yes, I inherited the resort from them. Well, most of it," I added with a laugh.

He chuckled also, which led me to believe he knew Rory wound up with a pair of cabins.

"Anyway, I'll let Rory know I have the painting, and he can give it to Gavin when the time's right."

"Yeah, Rory said he'd been granted custody. I'm happy for them."

"I can show you the basement if you like, Officer Reynolds," Cassidy offered.

"Call me Glen, please. And sure, I'd like to take another

look around if you don't mind." He'd mentioned being part of the initial investigation, so he had probably seen the basement several times.

"Not at all," Cassidy said. She was blushing, and I wondered if maybe she was not used to talking to men in uniform or maybe she had a little crush on Glen. He was cute. Tall, dark, and handsome. Slightly more buff than Rory but not quite as tall. His eyes twinkled when he smiled, which I found endearing. He appeared to be in his early thirties, so not too old for my new friend. I also noticed Jehrel was checking him out. I gave him another look, and he mouthed *what?* to me while attempting to appear innocent.

"The painting is in my car if you want to see that first. I'm parked in the back lot," I said.

"Sure. I'm parked out there as well."

We went into the back hall again, and Glen and I headed outside. I unlocked my car and pulled out the painting. He put it on the trunk of his cruiser and took several pictures with his cell phone.

"If I need to see it again, I'll just call Rory," he told me. "He's staying at the resort?"

"Yes, in his cabin. He'll probably want me to hang onto the painting until he feels Gavin is ready to see it. Just in case it stirs up any sad memories."

Glen nodded. "Yeah, that poor kid's been through the wringer. First his dad, then his grandmother. I'm so glad Rory got custody. He's been such a big part of Gavin's life for so long."

"Has he?" That was curious. I thought he'd only become aware of Gavin after he was moved into Waverly.

"Yeah, around four years now," he said. He lifted the painting and returned it to the backseat of my car.

"That long?" I remarked, hoping he'd reveal more.

Glen frowned, his expression thoughtful. "It was really

hard on Rory after the shooting. We both went to break the news to the family. I'd offered to do it, he was still so shaken up. But he insisted. That poor old woman. She didn't even cry. We could see how upset she was, but she just shook her head like she knew it was only a matter of time before she got a visit from the police. Gavin didn't know what had happened. He was only two at the time. But Rory really stepped up for them. He didn't have to, but he felt responsible."

"How so?"

"Gavin's dad held up a gas station. I was inside, toward the back of the store, and he came in, not realizing I was there. Rory saw everything from the outside. He rushed in — he was just a rookie, didn't know any better — and the guy took a shot at him. He missed, but when he went to fire again, Rory shot him — fatally. It was self-defense, but still, it's hard knowing you've taken a life. And then the guy's family was left behind. Granted, he hadn't been much more to his mother than an ongoing concern, but he'd helped out, I guess."

Oh my God. Rory killed Gavin's father. I felt a pain grip my stomach as it flipped and flopped around.

"So, Rory helped them out," I finally said.

Glen probably suspected I knew the basic outline of the story. That I was aware of the shooting, just not the finer details. It would make sense him having been Rory's partner years ago when Rory and I had been a couple. He would think that Rory had shared the information with me. Maybe he also knew about our breakup, and this was his way of explaining Rory's side of things.

Glen nodded. "At first, it was probably out of duty and maybe guilt. But over time, they became like a family to him. It just seemed natural that Rory would adopt Gavin once Elaina couldn't care for him. And then she was killed. I'm really hoping it wasn't on account of a handful of fool's gold."

So Rory had begun the adoption process after Elaina became infirm and Gavin was moved into Waverly. "Fool's gold? You believe it's fake?"

He shrugged. "No. The gold mine was very real. As to the legend, I don't know how much of it is truth or fiction. And as for Elaina saying she had the gold? Who knows. She may have said that in jest to Gavin, or he could have taken what she said out of context or misremembered her words. Anything is possible. Although, I highly doubt someone is going to kill an old woman over a rumor of gold nuggets hidden in a basement."

"Right," I agreed, barely registering what he said.

He indicated we should return inside. In a daze, I followed him, and all of us went into the basement. Jehrel, oblivious to my shock, hurried off to look around the vast, dim space, searching for gold. Cassidy was busy talking with Glen, so in the pretext of looking for gold, I wandered toward a crammed area of shelves and boxes, my thoughts swirling.

Everything made sense now.

The timing fit. The sudden change in Rory when I'd come into town to talk about our wedding. It must have been just after he'd shot that man. Gavin's father. And he'd not said a word to me about it.

Why?

Why would he instead treat me coldly and send me away broken-hearted and disillusioned?

It didn't take me long to figure it out.

For years, we'd talked about leaving everything behind and moving to Toronto. Especially me. I'd wanted it so bad and had assumed Rory wanted the same thing. Maybe he had. Until everything had changed for him. The shock of taking a life was compounded by the guilt he felt seeing Gavin and his Granny being left to deal with the aftermath. Of course, Rory had taken on the responsibility of helping them. It was in his nature. For years, he'd made sure his mom ate and went to sleep in her own bed, not wherever she'd happened to pass out. He'd cared for her as she should have cared for him. He'd always been that kind of guy. One who wanted to help people. It's what had drawn me to him. It's why he'd wanted to be like the policemen he'd encountered so often.

Yet, at the same time, there'd been me. Standing in the wings, waiting for us to begin our new life.

He'd weighed the two options, and duty had won out. He'd broken my heart, not out of callousness or indifference. He'd done it to free me to get on with my life in the city.

He'd done it for love.

Cassidy found me. I'm not sure how long I'd been standing in the same spot, staring at the same shelf. "Hey, Glen found something."

I attempted to shift my focus to the present.

Then I heard Jehrel screech. We all rushed to find him.

We rounded a row of shelves and saw him standing before a stack of boxes, staring into the one on the top that lay open.

"Is it a mouse?" I asked.

"No, it's not a mouse!" Jehrel hissed.

We crowded around and peered at the contents of the box. It was full of purses.

"Really?" Cassidy said.

"Um, he loves fashion," I explained.

Jehrel actually stomped his foot in irritation. "Look a little closer, geniuses." He reached into the box and pulled the top purse out, and handed it to Cassidy.

It was very nice, but handbags and accessories weren't really my thing.

Cass was turning the purse this way and that, looking inside and outside, and then she turned her gaze to the box, appearing shocked. "I think these are Marc Jacobs," she finally said.

Jehrel snorted. Then, he chuckled in the condescending way he usually saved for moments when I'd said or done something dim-witted. "Now, the untrained eye may believe as much. But I, however, have a brilliant eye and exquisite taste. These," he eyed the box and waved his hand in a dismissive gesture, "are fakes."

"What?" Glen said.

Jehrel nodded. "They're good. I'll give you that. The lesser trained eye may be fooled…" he looked at Cassidy.

"He's right," she said.

"Of course, I'm right," Jehrel agreed.

"He's always right," I informed her. "It gets annoying after a while."

Glen lifted a few of the purses, then replaced them. He put the box aside and turned his attention to the one beneath it.

"I haven't gone through those yet," Jehrel said, indicating the row of boxes along the shelf.

"But I bet we can guess what's in them," Cassidy said.

"You may have just uncovered the motive behind the murder," Glen said to Jehrel, causing him to preen.

"Oh!" he exclaimed. "Is there a reward?" he added daintily, as though he wasn't invested in the reply,

Glen frowned. "For motive, no, I'm afraid not. If you found the murderer, however, there's a reward for that."

"If he found the murderer, he'd take two days to revive," I informed Glen. "He faints. A lot."

We all laughed except Jehrel.

"Cass said you found something too?" I said to Glen.

"Was it the gold?" Jehrel questioned.

Glen smiled. "No, not quite as exciting as contraband handbags or gold. I found a bin of baggies stuffed with pot."

"Oh," Jehrel said, deflated.

Glen pulled out his phone. "I'll make a call to the station

for backup. It's gonna be a long night, I'm afraid."

When he moved off to make the call, I looked at Cass. Despite my own shocking news this evening, I could see my friend appeared stunned.

"This is a lot to take in," I said.

"You got that right, sister," Jehrel chimed in. I gave him a look, and he huffed at me.

"If you want us to stay here with you, we can."

She appeared to ponder my offer. "No. It's okay. It's late. Well, not really, but it will probably be a late night."

"Alan didn't make us any dinner," Jehrel informed me.

"I can cook, you know," I said.

He shook his head and mumbled. "Not like Alan."

"I'll take you out for dinner. How's that?" I offered.

He nodded once and went back to looking through the next box Glen had started on. It, too, was filled with fake designer purses. Even for knockoffs, I had to admit they looked fabulous, even to me.

"Why didn't they notice this stuff when they investigated the murder?" I wondered aloud.

"That's what I'm wondering. Although, from what I've just seen, the stuff toward the front of the basement is tool and hardware supplies inventory. The contraband and drugs are in the back."

"I wonder how long this has been here. Do you think the previous owner knew about it?"

Cass shrugged. "Honestly, I have no idea. You would think with it being his store, he'd be aware of what was down here."

"He wasn't the only one with access to the basement," Jehrel chimed in.

"Oh. Wait. You mean the old tenants here?" Cass surmised.

"Glen was telling me outside that the murdered woman's

son had been involved in a crime," I admitted, without giving away too many details. I wasn't ready to share what I'd learned about Rory.

"Oh, wow. I didn't know she had a son living with her. As far as I knew, it'd just been her. I didn't even know she was Gavin's Granny until you told me."

"Gavin's dad passed away a few years ago," I said. "When Elaina—the Granny—became too infirm to take care of Gavin, he was sent to Waverly."

Jehrel tutted. "Poor little guy. At least he wasn't here when... you know."

"Well, he has Rory now," Cass said brightly.

Jehrel and I nodded in agreement.

Glen joined us, having finished with his call. "They're assembling a team and sending them over tonight."

Cass sighed.

"Hey, it'll take an hour or so," Glen said to her. "We could grab a bite and come back after?"

Cass appeared to turn a bright shade of red. "Ah, yeah, sure. We could do that."

"The Heron has an excellent menu. The fish and chips there are amazing." That was the fancy restaurant in town where the guys and I ate the other day. I wanted to head over and maybe grab a sub at the small nearby café and then go to Genie's for coffee and dessert.

"Yes, I agree," Glen said. "The fish and chips are excellent there. Shall we?" he said to Cass.

"Sure," she said.

They made a cute couple, I thought.

Before Jehrel could invite us along, I said, "We're just gonna grab a bite at the café and then head over to Genie's for coffee. She wants to fill us in on all the movie gossip." That quelled any arguments Jehrel might have. He squealed in excitement.

"Oh," Glen said, before we parted ways. "Let's keep all this on the downlow, kapeesh?" He nodded at the purses, and we all knew what he meant.

Jehrel ran his finger over his mouth. "These lips are sealed, officer." Then he winked at him.

I gave him another look, and he again mouthed *what?*

Chapter 24

That evening, Rory got a call from Glen. He'd just got Gavin off to bed after reading him the same story four times. He took the call outside so he wouldn't wake him.

"Hey, what's up?"

"I have some information," Glen said. Rory could hear background noise and surmised he was outside. "I followed up on what you told me about the painting."

"Oh, great. I wasn't sure if you would, considering the source." He chuckled.

"I don't have a lot of time. My team's arriving, some are already here, but I wanted to let you know what we found. Just keep it under wraps, okay?"

"Sure." Rory was intrigued. What had Glen found that would trigger an investigation?

"The owner's inside. She'll show you where to begin. I'll be in shortly," Glen called out. Then, to Rory, in a quieter voice, he said, "I'm at Cassidy's store. When I arrived, Thea and her friend were here. They'd already found the painting."

"Oh, wow, that's great." He was surprised it really existed. "I'd no idea she was heading over there tonight. She didn't say anything." It wasn't like she was doing something reckless. She was only following up on what Gavin had mentioned. And after hearing the information he'd withheld today about Elaina, he wasn't surprised she hadn't confided in him.

"She showed me the painting. It was in her car. She's going

to give it to you to give to Gavin when you feel the time is right. I took a bunch of pictures for our records, just in case. I can send you some now. It's not all we found," Glen revealed.

Rory's phone pinged, letting him know he'd received the pictures. He only glanced at them, more interested in what Glen was telling him.

"Thea and her friend went looking around in the basement for the elusive gold. I was down there speaking with Cassidy at the time, and we started poking around a bit as well. But then Thea's friend found a box of very expensive designer purses — all fakes. There were at least two boxes of them, possibly more. I also found a large amount of pot. I believe the counterfeit purses are the big-ticket items."

"I can't believe it," Rory said. "You think this is the motive for Elaina's murder?"

"Yes. I bet since she was moving and the building was being sold, whoever had that stuff stashed down there was trying to get everything out. She must have heard them and went to investigate."

"Maybe she thought they were trying to find the gold," Rory said. "Poor Elaina. She probably really believed she had it hidden in the basement."

"Well, we didn't find any gold. But the night's young. We'll have to go through everything now. Cassidy's store will need to remain closed for several days while the team combs through the basement."

"Oh, that's a tough break," Rory said.

"Yeah, I broke it to her over dinner to soften the blow. I know she had to initially wait to take possession because of the murder. At least she's not a suspect."

Rory heard a certain lilt to his friend's voice when he mentioned Cassidy. He wondered if he may be attracted to her. It would be good for him to find someone, he thought.

"I'm glad you figured out a motive. Do you think the previous owner—Jerry, Jerry Adams, that's his name—knew what was down there? Maybe Darren had some sort of deal with him? Remember me mentioning I suspected Darren of having gang ties? Maybe after he died, Jerry kept up the deal with them or whoever else it was?"

"It's possible. Or he was too afraid to back out? It could be he'd had enough and decided to sell and skip town? It seems he left town in a hurry."

"Yeah."

"It's another thing we're looking into. I've already got someone on it. Since it's now an active investigation again, I'm not going to be able to tell you much more."

"I understand," Rory said. "I appreciate what you've already shared."

"I'll be right there," Glen called out. "Look, I've got to go," he said to Rory. "But before I do, I have to warn you."

"About what?"

"I was talking to Thea alone when she was showing me the painting. Your name came up, and Gavin's adoption… I'm afraid I shared some things with her I felt she should know."

Rory felt a chill come over him. "Such as?"

"I'm really sorry. I thought she knew you'd shot Darren."

Rory's head dropped, and he sighed.

"Are you there?" Glen asked. "I'm sorry, man. But you guys were supposed to get married. And then you suddenly broke up. I figured you'd told her what happened. How you decided to stay and help look after Gavin and Elaina. I wanted her to know what you'd gone through, the guilt and the weight of responsibility. I thought she'd left you. And now that she's returned, you could put things back together if she knew your side of it. But when I told her, she acted like she'd never known. I feel bad. That wasn't my story to tell. I'm sorry."

It took Rory a moment to answer. "It's not your fault. I know you're only looking out for me. I should have told her the truth when it happened, but I couldn't. I didn't want to mess up her life and her future. I couldn't ask her to give up her dreams and stay here with me."

"She seemed pretty shaken up," Glen admitted. "I didn't want to dwell on it, especially since we were suddenly in the thick of things."

"No, I get it. Thanks for the heads-up. And let me know what you can when you find out anything else."

"Sure thing," Glen promised. "I better go."

Glen hung up the phone, and Rory sat down on one of the deck chairs. He didn't know what to do. Today, Thea had learned he'd kept a secret about Elaina, and she hadn't been happy about it. But then she hears from someone else how he shot Gavin's father. It wouldn't be hard for her to figure out it had been the reason why he'd broken things off between them. How would she respond? He stared up the roadway, half expecting her to arrive any moment. It would serve him right if she was furious.

The only thing he could do now was wait. If Thea wanted to let him have it, it was her right. Even after all he'd done to keep this from her, part of him was relieved. No longer did he have to keep her in the dark. For years, he'd carried this burden around with him, and now it was out in the open. If she was angry and never wanted to lay eyes on him again, he thought she'd probably leave. Rush to the city like she had before. She'd only just started renovating the cabin, and that was really the only thing keeping her here. If she decided to sell the resort like she'd originally planned, then he'd be out of a job, but he'd figure it out. The worst part would be losing her again. These past couple of weeks, they'd been rebuilding their friendship. He'd missed having her in his life. He hadn't realized how much. And now she may never forgive him.

Hours later, when Thea failed to arrive, he finally went to bed.

The next morning, he was relieved to get an urgent call from the Tallmon's needing his help. He sent Thea a message asking if he could drop off Gavin with her, and she responded right away. When she didn't say anything when he saw her, he was relieved momentarily. He knew it was only because of Gavin that she didn't berate him.

Afterward, when he picked up Gavin and told her they would be gone the rest of the day, she looked a little put out but waved them goodbye. He hurried away like a coward.

In town, they went to the library, and while Gavin sat with a few books, Rory got busy with the archives. What he found was intriguing.

The name Mina Grey on the painting was what had spurred his search. It took some digging, but with the librarian's help, together they uncovered a timeline. Charlotte Ellis (nee Ashley), born 1910, died 1949, had returned to England. There, she married and had a daughter, Mina Grey (nee Ellis) — the artist. Born 1932, died 1981. Mina, probably hearing the tale from her mother, came to Hadleigh not long after her mother's death and remained. She'd married and had a daughter — Elaina Caddel (nee Grey) — born 1953, died 2023.

Rory called Glen and gave him the information.

He kept away from Cassidy's store, not wanting Gavin to witness the police presence and ask questions. As they returned to the resort, he wondered when a good time would be to tell Gavin about the painting.

The rest of the day, he was able to entertain Gavin, keeping them busy going out in the boat and doing some work around the cabin. Mr. Cole was out on a stroll and waved at them before he journeyed down the roadway.

"When can we play with Thea?" Gavin asked for the tenth

time.

"Soon, buddy," Rory promised.

That night, when he sat out on the deck after putting Gavin to bed, he almost wished Thea would appear. The suspense was killing him, wondering when she would face him. After she failed to arrive, he felt a deeper fear. What if she didn't care? What if she had decided he wasn't worth the effort?

And that was worse than anything he'd felt before.

Chapter 25

As much as I'd wanted to stomp down the road, drag Rory out of his cabin by the ear, and demand an explanation, I'd refrained. It had been hard waiting to confront him about what Glen had told me. But after he'd swung by Thursday morning and asked me to watch Gavin while he dealt with a problem for the Tallmon's, he'd returned shortly only to say they had plans for the rest of the day. Barely making eye contact, he told me I could reach him by phone if there was something else needing looking after at the resort. Then he'd rushed off. So, I'd waited. And stewed. A million times, I'd gone over in my head the conversation I wanted to have.

I had to be honest with myself about what I hoped to gain by having it out with Rory. Would confronting him change things between us? Probably not. Did I want things between us to be different? I wasn't sure. My life had gone on without him, and despite the gaping hole in my heart, I'd prevailed. But I felt he owed me an explanation. I knew the truth now, and I didn't want to just throw my hands in the air and say, 'Oh well.' I wanted closure. He'd denied me the life we were supposed to have together. Even if his reasoning had been loving me enough to let me go, he'd not given me the chance to hear the truth and decide for myself what I wanted. He'd taken that choice from me. He'd obviously been overwhelmed by the events that had occurred, but that would only get him so much leeway. He'd had four years to come clean. Four years to get things right in his head and tell me what had happened.

So why hadn't he?

The excuses had been many in my mind, and I'd tossed and turned another night hashing things out. The only way to put this behind me was to hear his reasoning.

The doorbell rang, and Jehrel and I exchanged a look.

I'd invited Rory and Gavin over for dinner. Afterward, the plan was to have Jehrel offer to entertain Gavin so I could speak to Rory privately. I'd told Jehrel, who still was in the dark about my conversation with Glen, that I wanted to tell Rory about the painting. It was in my closet, facing the wall.

"Hey, you two," I said, opening the door.

"Hi, Thea," Gavin said. "Is Ja-rel here? His car's still gone." Jehrel had still been in bed when Gavin had come by the other morning. I'd assured Gavin that Jehrel was here, but he'd appeared unconvinced.

"I'm here, darlin'," Jehrel said, joining us at the door.

Rory smiled at us and came inside with Gavin. We all moved into the kitchen.

"Alan had to go home for work, but he'll be back this weekend to pick me up," Jehrel explained. He'd kept his voice bright, but I knew he was still annoyed.

"Cool. What's to eat?" Gavin asked.

"Gavin," Rory said, "Remember we talked about using our manners."

Gavin sighed. "Please, what's to eat?"

We all chuckled but did our best to hide it.

"Jehrel helped me to make tacos," I said.

"Awesome!"

"It's ready, so we can eat now if you like?" I offered.

"Sure, thanks for inviting us," Rory said.

I noticed he appeared distracted and still couldn't hold my gaze, but maybe I was imagining things. He could just be preoccupied by what he'd learned about the contraband contents of Cassidy's basement. I was sure Glen had informed him.

As we ate and made small talk, I wondered if Glen may have also told him about our conversation. I hoped not. Part of me wanted the unrehearsed version of what he had to say for himself. Another part of me hoped he'd had a chance to refine his answers.

Either way, hurt feelings were going to abound.

After dinner, I brought out a lemon pie I'd picked up in town earlier. On our hike, Gavin had told me how Waverly never served it and how much he missed it. His face lit up when I put it on the table.

"We were invited to the Tallmon's tonight for a fire," Rory said.

"Yeah, we're gonna make smores," Gavin added, his tone void of excitement.

"Oh, yum," Jehrel said. "Sticky, but fun."

"They'd probably not mind if you join us," Rory invited.

"Please come," Gavin encouraged.

I had the feeling the Tallmon's hoped to have a fun evening with the kids. I wasn't sure how Gavin felt about it and guessed he wanted some backup, just in case.

"We'll see," I said, noncommittedly.

Right on cue, after dessert, Jahrel said to Gavin, "I was thinking it might be fun to play in the attic again." He looked at Rory. "If it's okay with your dad?"

"Yes!" Gavin said.

Rory glanced at me, and I got the feeling he knew this was a set-up. "Sure, why not?" What else could he say?

As Gavin and Jehrel headed up to the attic, Rory started filling the sink with dishes and running the water.

"Leave that for now," I said. "I'll get to it later."

"All right," he agreed.

"Mind if we go outside and talk?"

He sighed, as though defeated. "Okay."

We went down to the shoreline and traveled the length of the dock. Knowing how the lake had a tendency to carry words, we kept our voices low.

"I have the painting from Gavin's Granny. It's in my bedroom closet. I'm sure Glen told you about it?" I began.

He nodded once.

"It's Gavin's, along with all the stuff left behind that we found in the apartment. Cassidy said you're more than welcome to go through it and take whatever you like for Gavin. You being Gavin's dad now, it's up to you when you feel Gavin's ready."

Another nod.

"I meant to tell you all this when we got back from town Wednesday night. But it was late, and then I had to wait until we could be alone."

"I appreciate that."

Now, it was my turn to sigh. "Glen and I talked."

He looked out across the water as though searching for something on the other side.

"I understand why you didn't want to talk about Elaina's murder. I know she was Gavin's Granny."

When he refrained from comment, I continued my voice almost a whisper. "I also know what happened to Gavin's father."

Rory stuffed his hands in his pockets and studied his feet.

"I can imagine how hard and terrible that was for you. And I get how you felt responsible for them. Seeing you with Gavin, I know he's much more than an obligation to you. Anyone can see how much you love him."

"I do," he said.

I took a deep breath. "What I don't understand is how you decided to sabotage things between us in the misguided belief you were doing me a favor. Yes, I wanted a life in Toronto. But was it everything to me? No, it wasn't. Did I want to stay in Hadleigh so you could put things right? I don't know. But you didn't give me a choice. You decided. And maybe, at the time, you felt it was the right thing to do. Perhaps it was. But it's been years. Years that you could have told me what happened. Instead, you let me think it was my fault. That I wasn't enough. That you didn't love me anymore. And that's what hurt me the most. Not knowing."

Rory remained silent for a long while. Then, he finally spoke. "You're right." He looked at me finally, holding my gaze. "I know I handled it badly. Right from the beginning, I should have told you everything. I was overwhelmed with guilt, and regret, and duty. But that's not an excuse. I should have let you decide. It was wrong of me to assume you wanted the life we talked about having more than the option of giving you a choice. I knew my fate was sealed. And I took that on willingly. But at the time, I didn't want my mistakes and decisions to hinder your life going forward."

"You should have told me."

"I know. I'm sorry, T. You have no idea how much."

Tears welling up, I turned my gaze away. "You hurt me so much." The feel of his hand on my shoulder startled me, and I shook him off.

"Watching you walk away from me, knowing I'd hurt you, just about killed me."

Forcing myself to be strong, I looked at him. "I'm glad I know the truth now. I just wish you had been the one to tell me."

He shook his head. "I know. But look at the life you have. You run a successful business and have friends and a home in Toronto. Just like you always wanted. I was afraid if I told you what happened, you would—"

"What? That I would give it all up and rush back into your arms?"

"No. I don't know." He sighed again. "I guess I was afraid

you'd feel sorry for me. That you'd realize why I did what I did, and you'd forgive me and want to give us another chance. And it would be for the wrong reasons. It was always going to be there, my mistake, between us. I didn't want you to wind up hating me for it."

"What? It was easier on you having me hate you for breaking my heart?"

"Yes. Then, you wouldn't be sacrificing your happiness for my actions. I couldn't let you do that."

"Again, you are making decisions for me," I charged.

"How can you make the right decision if you're doing it out of pity?"

"You don't know that I would be. I am capable of being rational."

He held up his hands. "I know. But the weight of what I did was hard enough for me to carry. I couldn't ask you to carry it, too."

We were going around in circles. I understood his reasoning, misguided or not. We could talk about it till the cows came home and still be no closer to a solution. "What does Gavin know?" I finally asked.

"One day, I'm going to have to tell him the truth. He may wind up hating me for it, but it would be worse if he found out some other way."

"Yes, it would," I agreed. "I can state that for a fact."

He cringed at my double innuendo.

"Hopefully, Gavin will understand," I said.

He stared down at his feet again. "I never want him to think I did all this out of duty or to assuage my guilt. That was the tiniest part of it."

"I know why you did it," I said. "It was because you saw yourself in Gavin. You had the opportunity to give him the life you always wanted. That's not being selfish or guilty. That's being a parent. Every parent wants their child to have that."

The acknowledgment of what I said lit up his face. "You're right. I've never been able to put it into words like that, but it's true. I want Gavin to have the best chance at happiness."

I smiled at him. "With you at his side, he'll have it."

Gently, as though waiting for my permission, he pulled me into his arms and then hugged me tight. I let him hold me, and for the first time in a very long time, I felt at peace.

When we returned to the house, we found Gavin and Jehrel in the attic. To my surprise, Gavin was sitting on the trunk beneath the window, Lully curled up in his lap. By the look on Jehrel's face, he was surprised as well.

"Awe," Rory said. "I love cats. I always wanted one when I was little, but my mom was allergic."

Gavin gently stroked Lully's fur.

"Um, how did that happen?" I said to Jehrel.

He shrugged. "She just came wandering up here and went right to him." Now that she had settled in, we'd let Lully have the run of the house. Mainly, she kept to the second floor, preferring to sleep on the guys' bed.

"Hey, I have an idea. Why not see if Alan will let Lully stay here over the summer? I could use a mouser, just in case. And if I'm not around, she can stay with Gavin and Rory—if that's all right with you guys?"

Jehrel beamed. "I like the idea. I'm sure Alan will, too. Lully loves you, and she seems so content with Gavin. And it's not like we won't come and visit."

"Can we, Dad? Can we?" Gavin begged.

"Before you agree, I have to warn you, Lully can be pretty unpredictable. At the moment, she's calm, but boy, when she dislikes someone, you'll know it," I said.

Rory chuckled. "She looks pretty tame right now." He went over and squatted down by Gavin so he could scratch Lully behind the ears. Jehrel and I both held our breath. Amazingly, she began to purr.

"Awe," we all chorused.

Chapter 26

The month of July passed all too quickly. Guests arrived and departed from the resort each week, except for the elusive writer, Mr. Cole. After about a week, things wrapped up with the investigation at Cassidy's store, and she was able to get back to business. Between Cassidy's discoveries and some town auctions I attended, several retro items now furnished my cabin. I had completed the tear-out, and it was full steam ahead on the renovation. Rory had been busy at the main house installing upgrades, taking full advantage of the days Gavin spent enrolled in a summer camp in Hadleigh. Both of us were busy but found many moments to share together while the summer marched on. In the back of my mind, I knew, soon, another month would pass. Once I completed the work on the cabin, it would be time to return to my life in Toronto. The moments shared with Rory, each day bringing us closer and closer together, were bittersweet. As much as I knew I should guard my heart, I couldn't deny our rekindled attraction and deep friendship after too many years apart.

The film guys I'd used to tape my first whole house reveal were due to arrive at the resort. I'd extended the offer to them to take one of the cabins for a week when one of my renters unexpectedly backed out. My offer was made in exchange for them taping a few segments of me working on the '50s reno. They also agreed to return for a weekend at summer's end to tape the reveal. I hoped this would lead to some excitement for themed rentals for my other cabins, which I hoped to work on the following summers. Thinking about the end of summer was hard, giving me a strange ache in my chest every time I thought about leaving Rory and Gavin. In such a short amount of time, the three of us had bonded so dramatically that it began to feel like we were a family.

The honk of a horn gained my attention, and I hurried outside, seeing the Caught on Camera van pull up. Jake waved, and I returned the gesture, happy to see that Joe and Cory were also with him.

"Hi," I said, as Jake parked and climbed out of the van. The others got out and stretched their legs, and glanced around. "I hope the drive wasn't too bad." It was still before noon on a Friday.

"We left early to miss the traffic," Jake said.

"Good idea. You may want to unpack and head into town for supplies if you need them before it gets busy." I handed over the keys to their cabin, which was presently vacant.

"Your cabin's over there." I pointed to the one beside my reno. "I left an information sheet and map on the kitchen table. Hopefully, you'll get a chance to get out in the boats and explore the area and check out town."

"Great. We're really looking forward to it," Joe said.

"Yeah," Cory agreed.

Purposely, I'd delayed some parts of the reno for them to be filmed as I completed them. And though I wanted to be meticulous about detail, I also had to admit, if only to myself, that I was in no hurry to complete the job. Rory had come around regularly while I worked. After the tear-out, he'd upgraded the cabin with backup battery power, which we cleverly hid from view.

"Hello," Rory said, joining us. He shook hands with all three guys as they introduced themselves.

"I saw the reveal video you guys made with Thea. Great work," Rory said.

"Thanks," Jake responded. "It's such a unique idea doing retro renovations."

"Yeah, it's been gaining momentum, though, all those streaming shows coming out with flashbacks or being set in earlier decades. The popularity is increasing. You'll probably have more business than you can handle soon," Joe said.

"And more competition, no doubt," I predicted. That was the most I'd ever heard Joe say.

"Okay, we'll get settled in and then probably head into town. We can meet up in a few hours, and you can give us a tour?" Joe proposed.

"Sounds good."

The guys loaded back up into the van and rolled down the road toward their cabin.

"They seem all right," Rory said.

"Yeah, Joe was sick when they taped the reveal, and it still went well. With all three of them here, it'll probably go even better. Cory is Jake's little brother."

"I always wanted a brother," Rory admitted. It wasn't news to me. In the past, we'd both said having a sibling might have made things easier on us growing up.

"Maybe one day Gavin will have a little brother or sister," he said, wiggling his eyebrows at me.

I laughed. His hand caught mine, and he pulled me in close for a hug. My head rested against his chest for a moment, the sound of his heartbeat and breath filling his lungs familiar to me.

"Oh, hey, I heard from Genie when I was in town this morning that the movie crew is returning."

I moved to look up at him, our hands remaining clasped. "Great. I'll have to call Jehrel. He missed them last time, so hopefully, he can make it here before they wrap up."

Rory made a face.

"What?"

"Nothing." He let loose a dramatic sigh. "He just hogs you when he's here."

I chuckled. "He's still my best friend."

Rory leaned over and nuzzled my neck. "Really? I thought I was gaining ground on reclaiming my title."

My heart thumped faster, and my skin tingled with delight. "Oh, no. You still have some way to go."

Though we both teased each other playfully, I sensed an underlying question in every touch, glance, and word. I'd forgiven him for breaking my heart, and he knew I had. Yet, I was afraid to surrender myself. Vulnerability meant allowing for the chance of love and a life together, but I was afraid. I'd felt that soul-tearing pain of loss, and it terrified me. Alone at night, I'd lay in bed wondering how us being together again would look. Things were so different now. We couldn't talk about running off to the city and exploring our careers. There was Gavin to think of. And Rory's commitments here in Hadleigh. Whereas I had commitments in Toronto. There was my business to think of. My friends, my apartment. My life there. Although, if I were being honest, nothing was stopping me from uprooting and starting over here. I could travel for business and have visits with my friends back and forth. So, what held me back? Fear that Rory would just casually toss me aside again? I knew that wasn't being fair to him and what he'd faced. There had been extenuating circumstances. But the first time our relationship had been put to the test, we'd failed. I didn't think I could handle it again.

"Want to have a fire tonight?" Rory asked, oblivious to my chaotic thoughts.

I shook free from the worries that plagued me. "Sure." There'd be time enough to figure things out later. Right now, I had another month before I had to make any decisions. I was determined to make every moment count.

~

Jehrel and Alan arrived late afternoon the following day. I was thrilled they'd been able to clear their schedules and come up at the last moment. Lully purred and did figure eights around their legs, gaining her a scolding from Alan, who almost tripped carrying a suitcase.

"How long can you stay?" I asked Jehrel.

He bent down to pick up Lully and stroked her long, multi-colored fur. She nestled against him so docilely anyone would think she was gentle and sweet. Not the termagant we knew she could be.

"A week, unless, of course, Alan decides to rush off again."

"He can always come back for you," I soothed.

Jehrel set Lully down. "I better help with the bags." Knowing him, there would be plenty to carry in.

The guys headed off to have dinner in town, and Rory came by later with Gavin for a fire inside.

We sat together on the couch while Gavin sat on the floor with a bowl of popcorn, Lully curled up beside him. Gavin's face illuminated as the flames reflected, dancing against the walls of the dark room,

"She's going to miss sleeping with Gavin," Rory said, meaning the cat.

The first night after Jehrel left for home from his last visit, I hadn't slept in the main house. My reason being I wanted to be close to the reno. In truth, I was unnerved. I wouldn't go so far as to admit I was afraid. But that night I'd been alone, I could have sworn I'd seen shapes moving around my room, as though someone was there. I'd even smelled a faint scent of perfume. Part of me feared I'd brought home Charlotte's or Mina's ghost along with that painting. So, I'd asked Rory to take Lully so I could spend my nights in the cabin. I couldn't abandon the poor kitty to sleep alone, no matter how fearless she was.

With the guys arriving, I'd moved back into the main house and brought Lully home. Rory had raised an eyebrow but not questioned my decision. He knew better than to tease me about my fears in front of Gavin, and I took full advantage of it.

"Oh," I said, having an idea. "Why not move in here for a bit? It'll give Gavin a chance to get used to the main house, and he won't be separated from Lully."

He looked at me a moment, and I think my choice of words might have shaken him.

"You still want us to take the main house when you leave, don't you?" he asked, his voice low and hurt, confirming my suspicion, not to mention that tell-tale squinty eye of his.

My gaze turned to Gavin. Lully was staring at him and squeezing her eyes. I'd told him it meant she loved him. I'd melted when Gavin had then turned to look at me and squeezed his eyes.

Ignoring his question, I said, "You could put Gavin in your old room, and you can take the master bedroom." I never wanted to sleep in there, considering it'd been my aunt and uncle's room. Though it'd been unused for several years, I still felt weird about it.

"Okay, we can talk about it later," Rory said, taking the hint.

Seeing the hurt on his face, I reached over to give his hand a squeeze.

"Hey, Gavin. What do you think about having a sleepover here? You can sleep in my old room?" Rory said.

Gavin hooped in joy, and Lully sprang to her feet, eyes casting around for the reason. Her fur stood on end, and she was battle-ready.

"Lully, it's okay," I soothed, preparing to sing if necessary.

Gavin bent to scoop her up in his arms and spun in a circle. "Can Lully sleep with me?"

Amazingly, Lully snuggled into him. Cat crisis averted.

"Sure, I don't see why not." I didn't think the guys would mind.

"Dad, I need my stuff," Gavin said. "How long can we stay? Should I bring all my toys? I need my pillow."

Rory and I exchanged a glance. Gavin was reading more into the invitation than we both thought he would. Perhaps I'd made a mistake? I didn't want to give him false hope something else was happening here. I'd seen him casting glances between Rory and me many times. Plus, he'd made references to us being a family. Once, he even came out and asked me if I wanted to be his mom.

That had gutted me.

Guilt abounded, and I could see Rory struggled with it, too, during those moments. But neither of us knew what to say. We'd quickly changed the subject, and I admit I may have offered the idea of getting ice cream in town once too often. All delaying tactics to avoid the inevitable conversation Rory and I needed to have.

"Let's see how things go tonight," Rory suggested. "And we'll take it from there."

"Your room here is bigger than my room. And it has a fireplace. But I really love my room at our house, too," Gavin added, old enough to understand his casual observations could inadvertently hurt feelings.

"Well, thanks, buddy. That means a lot to me," Rory said.

Gavin set Lully down. "Wait here, and I'll come back," he said to her. She sat down and began licking her fur as though biding her time.

At the door, they got their shoes on and headed out. Jehrel and Alan pulled up just as I was about to move away from the door. I waited for them to come inside. The evening stars were just making an appearance in the dimming sky. There were few, I noted, and I saw the dark clouds moving in. *Great.*

"How was dinner?" I asked.

"Nice. We went to Genie's afterward so we could get the movie gossip," Alan told me.

Jehrel squeezed my hand and led me into the kitchen with them. "It's so exciting! They'll be here on and off the rest of the summer. She doesn't know all the locations since they keep things so hush-hush. But she did say they'd rented her place out again for a couple of nights through next week."

"Wow, that is exciting. When we have more details, we can head down there and watch. Cassidy's place is close by. We can see if she wants to join us."

"Oh! We saw her and Glen out tonight at the restaurant," Jehrel informed me.

"Lovely couple," Alan said.

"They were sharing a sundae. It was so romantic!"

Cassidy had told me things were going slow but steady between them. I was happy for her and for Glen. She'd even suggested we get together for a double date one night. I'd been able to put her off, saying we didn't have a sitter for Gavin. No doubt she saw Jehrel and Alan tonight. And knowing Jehrel and Cassidy, they'd already made plans for us. Not that I minded the idea of a night out. But being seen as a couple was more than I was ready for right now.

"Hey, Rory and Gavin are going to sleep over here tonight, possibly more," I said. "Depending on how it goes. And Gavin wants Lully to sleep with him."

Alan had coffee on and leaned against the counter while it brewed. He got out two mugs and looked at me. I shook my head, knowing the caffeine would keep me awake. I didn't want trouble falling asleep, especially if a storm was brewing.

"Oh yes, you said you'd been sleeping in the cabin 'cause you were afraid to sleep here alone?" Jehrel said.

Alan looked at me, and I blushed. "I did not. I said I wanted to sleep in the cabin cause I was working long hours there—"

Jehrel waved his hand around. "And blah blah blah, I can read between the lines."

"What are you scared of?" Alan asked me.

"I'm not—" I began.

"It's that painting! It's haunted. Now, there's a ghost here. Maybe we should sleep in Rory's cabin if he's not using it," Jehrel said.

"I don't think that's—" Alan started.

"It's true!" Jehrel insisted.

"Shhhh!" I hissed, hearing the front door. "I will not have Gavin frightened to be here." The look I gave Jehrel made him zip his lips.

"Hey, guys," Rory said, entering the room. He had a backpack in one hand and a duffle bag in the other.

"Ja-rel!" Gavin cried, rushing over to hug him. He reached out and shook Alan's hand next. "We're having a sleepover party!"

"Us too!" Jehrel said.

"It's getting late. Do you mind if I run a quick bath for Gavin?" Rory asked. "I figured it'd be easier to do it here."

"No, not at all," I said. "I can get the rooms ready while you do that. Would you like to stay in the master?" I knew I shouldn't call it that. It was an outdated title, but it was hard to break the habit of saying it. *Primary is the proper name. Why can I never remember that?*

"If you don't think it'll be weird?" His gaze included me and the guys. "Unless you guys want it?"

"No, thanks. We're fine where we are. Honestly, the view of the lake suits us," Alan assured him.

The 'primary' bedroom was like mine, facing out back or the driveway. Rory's old room and the guest room faced out front or lakeside.

Rory bathed Gavin and got him ready for bed while I worked at readying his room. As I draped an extra blanket at the foot of the bed, he tore in wearing his jammies and dove under the covers. Rory wasn't far behind.

"We brought a few books so I can read some stories," Rory said, grabbing Gavin's backpack and pulling out some books and toys. He went over to sit on the edge of the bed with a book and passed Gavin a stuffed bunny. Lully waltzed into the room, honed in on Gavin, and leapt onto the bed. Settling in beside him, she glared at Rory as though saying, 'Proceed with the story, sir.'

Before I left the room, I kissed Gavin goodnight. "Don't forget Daddy," he said, so I kissed Rory on the top of the head as well. I remained by the door a moment. Rory began to read, and Gavin listened intently while he snuggled his bunny under one arm, his other hand smoothing Lully's fur. Watching them, I felt a funny pang in my belly. The word *family* popped into my head, and instead of pushing it aside like I usually did, I let it linger there for a while.

Chapter 27

"You didn't have to do that," Rory said. Thea was finishing making up the bed for him.

"I don't mind. No one's slept in here in a long time." He noticed she'd opened the window, most likely to air the room out. "I haven't checked the fireplace over, but all the sheets are fresh. I washed everything the first week I was here."

She stood staring at him a moment as though unsure of what else to say, and then she went over and closed the window again.

"There's a chilly breeze coming in, I think we're in for a storm. I'll have to go around and check all the windows. I'm glad you installed backup power, so we don't have to worry about the lights going off again."

Remembering, he smiled. "That wasn't so bad."

She shivered, and he thought it didn't have anything to do with the cool night air.

Rory made his way over to her slowly. The way her eyes darted everywhere and how she wrung her hands made him think she was ready to bolt. Reaching out, he brushed a stray hair from her cheek.

"I should—"

She was about to leave, but he took her into his arms. Feeling her tremble, he held her gently. When she looked up at him, his head dipped so he could kiss her lips. Just a single kiss, but as he went to pull away, her fingers crept to the back of his neck, her fingers playing with his curls. A warmth spread over him, and the room suddenly felt hot.

Then his phone rang.

Reluctantly, they pulled apart, and he yanked the cell from his back pocket.

"Hey, Glen," he said, seeing his name on the screen.

"Hi. I have an update I can share with you. We've made an arrest."

Rory went over and sat on the bed. He motioned to Thea to close the door. She did and then came over to sit beside him. He put the phone on speaker so she could hear as well.

"Glen, Thea's here with me. I've got you on speaker."

"Okay, no problem. It'll be public knowledge soon enough. We questioned Jerry Adams—the previous owner of the store—and made a deal for immunity and protection. He was an unwilling partner with a gang from Toronto. Darren's old buddies, just like you suspected. Darren had been keeping the contraband purses and drugs in the basement for them, and when Jerry found out, Darren threatened him. When Darren was killed, Jerry was visited by a gang member before he could contact the police. He was scared, and rightly so. He kept up with the deal, storing stuff for them until he couldn't take it anymore. When they got wind of him selling the place and couldn't reach him—he'd gone into hiding—one of them came to clear out the stuff. Jerry gave us his name. It was the guy he'd been dealing with. We've apprehended him, and he's been charged with the death of Elaina. He said it was an accident, but that's for the courts to decide now."

Rory shook his head and exchanged a look with Thea.

"I guess it's over," Rory said.

"Yes. Finally. Anyway, I thought you'd want to know."

"Thanks, I appreciate the call."

"Good night," Glen said. "To both of you."

"Good night," Rory and Thea said. Rory hung up the phone. "I can't believe it's over." He took Thea into his arms again, and they just held each other for a while.

On their way downstairs, they peeked in on Gavin, who was fast asleep. Lully was curled up beside him. Alan and Jehrel greeted them when they walked into the library. Jehrel was seated by the fire, finishing Gavin's popcorn, while Alan stood before the tall windows staring outside.

A big flash of lightning lit up the sky over the lake.

"Wow, see that?" Alan asked. "I love storms."

"Thea doesn't," Jehrel said. "Especially if a ghost is wandering around."

"Jehrel!" Thea hissed.

Rory looked between them, not sure if it was a joke. "A ghost?"

"Yes, Thea brought it here when she brought the painting," Jehrel informed him. "Oh, Gavin's asleep?" he asked in afterthought.

"Yes, he's asleep," Thea confirmed, making a face at him.

"It's on the move," Alan informed them, seeing another flash. "Coming closer."

"Great." Thea hurried to check the windows and left the room to check the rest of the house.

"What's this about a ghost?" Rory asked Jehrel.

"Right after Thea brought the painting here, I heard some banging around. And there were shadowy shapes. I had to leave for home a few days later. I told Alan about it."

"And I said you have an active imagination. But you just had to go and tell Thea, and you scared her. You know she was already uneasy about being here alone," Alan scolded him.

Rory already knew that. "Ah, is that why she started sleeping in the cabin after you left?"

"Yes," Jehrel confirmed.

Rain began to fall on the roof and splash against the windows. Alan backed away from the glass suddenly and whipped his head around. "Did you see that?"

"See what? Oh, you're just trying to scare me!" Jehrel accused.

Alan looked over toward the fireplace and then the doorway. "No, I'm not. The reflection—I would have sworn I saw someone rush from the room."

Thea entered the room, her face white as a ghost. "I saw it too. It rushed past me up the stairs."

The look on her face concerned Rory. "I'm gonna check on Gavin."

All of them hurried from the room after Rory. At the top of the stairs, the lights suddenly went off.

"Don't you dare scream." Rory heard Thea's threatening tone and assumed she was talking to Jehrel.

"The backup power will come on any second now," Rory assured them.

A flash of lightning lit up the area, and Rory saw a white blur rush down the hall. He barreled after it, and everyone barreled after him.

The lights came back on just as he rushed into Thea's room. Seeing a young woman standing at the foot of the bed, he froze. She was dressed in an old-fashioned gown, her long brown hair hung to her waist. She stared at the closet, pointing. He could see right through her.

The others came up behind him. Rory could feel them at his back. Thea ducked under his arm, which braced against the doorframe.

The ghost stared at them, appearing frozen in fear as well.

"Oh my—" Jehrel started.

"Shhhh!" They all hissed.

"I, I can't," Jehrel cried, and then he was gone, rushing

back down the hall. Alan tore after him.

Thea stared transfixed at the apparition, a curious look on her face. "Charlotte?"

The ghost's eyes widened in acknowledgement. She nodded her head once.

Rory felt lightheaded suddenly, and a blur of white appeared before him as though something or someone had passed right through him.

"My love," came a deep voice, causing them all to stare at the figure taking shape before them.

"Renald," gasped Charlotte. "Is it truly you?"

Renald glided over to take Charlotte into his arms. "It is I, my love."

"But how? I've looked for you, waited endlessly."

"I've been lost, searching the forest," Renald explained.

Charlotte reached up to touch his cheek. "I was in town, but then I came here."

"The painting," Thea said. "You must have come with the painting."

Charlotte nodded. "Yes. Mina, my daughter, painted it. I told her stories of the lake. Of us." She stared at Renald, her face animated in joy.

"Your daughter?" Renald said.

Charlotte nodded. "After my father made us return home, he forced me to marry. I did not much care for my husband, but he was kind. And we had a daughter, Mina. I loved her very much. I remember dying when she was but a young woman. I did not move on to the afterlife. I stayed with Mina. And then she moved here, and I journeyed with her. She married and had a daughter, and I was there, watching from the shadows. I felt..."

"I felt it too," Renald said. "I never married nor had any children." His tone did not chastise, neither did his glance. He did not begrudge Charlotte the life she'd led without him. "After

I died, I stayed. I felt I must wait for you."

"And now, we are together at last," Charlotte said.

Rory reached out and took hold of Thea's hand. Though it seemed impossible, he felt caught up in the long-lost love story playing out before them. He couldn't help but think about his and Thea's estrangement and how they, too, were now together again. Thea squeezed his hand, and they glanced at each other.

"We can go," Renald said. "Now that we are finally together, no one shall part us." When he took Charlotte's hand and went to guide her away, she paused and looked at Rory and Thea.

"Wait," her gentle voice was determined. "There is something I must show you." She directed those words at them.

Again, she pointed at the closet.

"The painting is in there," Thea said. She let go of Rory's hand and went over to open the door. Moments later, she pulled out the painting. Rory came closer, having only seen it in the pictures Glen had sent him.

"It's a great likeness," he said.

"My Mina was gifted," Charlotte spoke with a mother's pride. "But look," she glided closer.

"The back?" Thea asked. When Charlotte nodded, Thea began to fiddle with the frame. After a bit of maneuvering, it came open.

Two slips of paper floated to the floor.

Gently, Thea lifted them.

"A map," she said, looking at Charlotte curiously. "And a deed."

"Yes, to my father's mine. Long abandoned, but it passed to me upon his death. And in turn, it passed to Mina, then Elaina." She looked at Rory. "And now, Gavin. My great-great-grandson. Mina had no use for an old mine. My father had emptied it of all the gold he found. It is probably not worth much, but the surrounding land may be valuable today. Elaina, fearing her son Darren had lost his way, hid the map and deed, hoping to one day pass it on to Gavin when he came of age. If Darren, my great-grandson, had got his hands on it, he likely would have squandered any opportunity it presented. But I have such great hope for Gavin."

Rory took the map Thea passed to him and looked at it. He recognized the location. It was near the settlement by Charlotte Lake, which made sense. Charlotte's father would want the workers near the mine.

"I cannot say for all certainty every trace of gold is gone. But if you discover any, it belongs to Gavin. You will see he gets it?" Charlotte asked him, determined.

Rory nodded his head. "I will. And I promise you, I will love and care for Gavin all my life."

Charlotte smiled. "I know you will. You are a good and honorable man."

She went back over and took Renald's hand. "Let us go, my love."

They gave us one last smile and then wandered off into a haze, hands clasped tight.

Thea put her hand in Rory's, and they shared a smile.

"I can't believe this," she said.

"Love will always find a way," Rory said. "No matter how long it takes."

The next morning at breakfast, Gavin wandered downstairs to where the four adults sat at the table, not having gotten much sleep. Last night, Rory and Thea had gone downstairs and found Jehrel and Alan. They'd filled them in on what had happened and showed them the map and deed. Alan had looked at the deed and declared it still valid to the best of his knowledge. Jehrel had almost screamed in excitement, and Thea had to keep shushing him.

"Sleep okay, buddy?" Rory asked, tussling Gavin's curls. Gavin sat down at the table, and Lully wandered in and yawned.

"Looks like you had a rough night," Jehrel said to her, scooping her up in his arms.

"Yeah, the woman came in and said goodbye to me. Lully never hisses at her, but she had a man with her this time, and Lully was mad."

Rory noticed he wasn't the only one standing there with his mouth hanging open.

"Usually, she just says goodnight, but this time it was different. She said goodbye." He shrugged. "Can I have French toast?"

"Sure," Alan said and got busy making breakfast for everyone.

"What are we gonna do today?" Gavin asked, staring at Rory and Thea.

Rory smiled. "How about we all go on a little adventure?" He shared a smile with Thea.

"Okay!" Gavin and Jehrel chorused.

Chapter 28

Rory sat across from me on a picnic blanket on the island at Charlotte Lake. We were alone, Jehrel and Alan having insisted on taking Gavin shopping in town. I couldn't say I wasn't enjoying the quiet. It was the last week of August, and time felt like it'd gone by in a blur.

"I can't help but think about Charlotte and Renald whenever we come here."

"Me too," Rory agreed.

The day after seeing the ghosts, all of us had headed out on an excursion to find the lost mine. Hours later, hot, sweaty, and bug-bitten, we'd uncovered an entrance practically obscured by nearly a century of brush. If not for the map, it would have remained unfound for probably another century or more. Flashlights shining, we cautiously entered within and wandered the long-abandoned mine as far as we dared. The walls shone in some places, and Rory, thinking ahead, had brought along a hammer pick and hacked chunks of it off to stash in our backpacks. When we'd taken it to be checked in town, we'd discovered a wealth of iron pyrite containing trace amounts of gold. Gavin wouldn't be filthy rich, but it would pay for college one day and maybe a downpayment on a house.

Cassidy never found the missing gold in the basement of the store, but she'd been given a reward for information leading to the arrest of a criminal, which she had shared with Jehrel. She'd offered to split it three ways to include me, but I'd declined.

Jehrel was over the moon, deciding to splurge on the honeymoon of his and Alan's dreams. To my surprise, he and Alan chose to get married at the chapel in Hadleigh. Rory and I hosted their reception at the resort. It was our wedding gift to them. That had been mere days ago, and the newlyweds had decided to remain at the resort a while before taking a cruise later in the year.

Speaking of cruises, my father and his new bride — they got married while on vacation — made an appearance at the wedding, and Rory had graciously offered them the use of his cabin since he and Gavin remained in the main house with me. My new stepmother was lovely, despite the fact she was less than a decade older than me.

The most exciting thing that happened besides the wedding (I was Jehrel's best woman, and Rory was Alan's best man) was the appearance of a producer at my door. He'd seen my card in Cassidy's store and, intrigued, watched my video reveal of my newly completed '50s reno cabin. The guys from Caught on Camera had come up when I'd completed it earlier than expected and made the video with me. The producer, saying he'd been impressed, asked to see the cabin in person. He'd also wanted to hear my plans for the other cabins. Then he'd offered me a job as a set designer and consultant on a series he was planning. It was due to begin filming in a few months, and he admitted to me that he planned to have it run for a minimum of five or six seasons. The retro flashbacks required my area of expertise, he assured me, and after I had Mr. Bailey go over the contract, I'd signed it. The best part was a lot of the scenes were going to be filmed right in Hadleigh since they'd enjoyed working here so much. And the other parts would be filmed in Toronto and the surrounding areas.

Rory had been thrilled for me when I told him about it. Jehrel had screamed so loud I thought my eardrums exploded.

"I hope you don't mind that I've decided to stick around

for a while," I said to Rory, teasing him. We'd already discussed my plans to stay. He'd agreed to continue running the resort since I'd be too busy. I planned to keep running my company, but I'd have to schedule renos around my film work schedule. I'd also opted to keep my small apartment in Toronto for the times I'd be there for work. It was strange, I thought. I'd arrived in Hadleigh two months ago, anxious to sell and leave, to get on with my life in the big city. But coming here, I'd found so much more than I'd bargained for. Every corner of the resort, and every inch of lake and forest, and even in town, were whispers of my past. And promises of my future.

Rory opened the picnic basket. We'd floated it, along with our backpacks, across the water in the dinghy boat we'd brought as we swam over.

When he pulled out two plastic wine glasses and a bottle of sparkling cider, I laughed.

"Ah, so that's why you insisted on carrying it," I said.

"You got it." He popped the cork and poured us each a glass, and passed me one. "Cheers to you and your new job."

We clinked glasses and sipped.

"And here's to you and your new son," I said. We clinked glasses again and sipped.

He set his glass aside and dug into the basket once more, looking at me intently.

"T. I want to say something to you."

He looked so serious. I hoped he wasn't going to tell me he and Gavin were moving back into their cabin.

"I want to thank you for coming back here. For giving me another chance at being your friend. For learning the truth about what happened years ago and not resenting me for it. For taking Gavin and me into your home and into your heart. For being there for us. I want to thank you for being my friend growing up. I wouldn't have made it without you by my side. I can't think of my life without you. That time we were apart is something I never want to experience again. What I'm saying is… Please," he removed a ring box from the picnic basket and got up on one knee. "Will you do me the absolute honor of becoming my wife?"

He opened the ring box, and I could see it was the engagement ring he'd given me years ago. The one I'd tossed back at him when I'd walked out. The ring had been the one his father had given his mother. The setting was slightly different than I remembered. He'd added a tiny blue sapphire. Representing Gavin, I realized.

"I…" I didn't know what to say. This was so unexpected. Yes, we'd put our past behind us. We'd held hands and kissed and laughed like we used to. But it'd been so different this time between us, maybe because of Gavin. This time, we were a family.

Rory was frozen, and his eyes were closed. I think he held his breath.

Looking at him, I could see us as kids, playing, laughing, crying. And then as adolescents, then young adults falling in love. Always together, always the best of friends. Except for one dark time which no longer affected my life. We'd moved past it together. And now, I couldn't imagine my life without Rory. Or Gavin. I loved them both with all my heart.

When I reached out and touched Rory's hand with mine, his eyes sprang open. His gaze asked a million questions, but only one that really mattered. *Do you still love me?*

I looked at him and smiled, nodding once. "Yes, I will marry you."

He slipped the ring on my finger and held me tight. I knew I wasn't the only one crying. A heron swooped in close and circled us, making us exclaim in delight. We took it as an omen that Charlotte and Renald approved.

"Are you happy?" Rory asked.

"I am." If I had written down my perfect life on paper, I

don't think I would have changed a thing.

It'd been a hard road traveled, but I had finally found my way home again.

This time, I intended to stay.

Julie is a long-time resident of Hamilton, Ontario, where she lives with her husband of 25 years. She has two grown sons who recently left the nest. Working in a library for several years inspired her to pursue her long-time love of writing. Please check out her website julieparker.net